For Richer,
For Poorer

Also by Faith Baldwin
in Thorndike Large Print

And New Stars Burn
Beauty

For Richer, For Poorer

Faith Baldwin

Thorndike Press • Thorndike, Maine

Library of Congress Cataloging in Publication Data:

Baldwin, Faith, 1893-
  For richer, for poorer / Faith Baldwin. -- Large print ed.
    p. cm.
  ISBN 1-56054-019-2 (alk. paper : lg. print)
  1. Large type books. I. Title.
[PS3505.U97F67   1990]   90-10936
813'.52--dc20   CIP

Thorndike Press Large Print edition published in 1990 by
arrangement with Henry Holt and Company.

Cover design by James B. Murray.

The tree indicum is a trademark of Thorndike Press.

This book is printed on acid-free, high opacity paper. ∞

List of Chapters

Chapter One

BEAUTIFUL BUT BROKE

Time and again the plane was delayed; time and again the pilot set her down for an unscheduled landing on an emergency field. They waited out a brief, blinding April snowstorm over mountains, a thunderous, torrential rain farther on. All day the passengers had been restless, questioning the pretty stewardess every time she passed up or down the aisle, every time she said, "Fasten your safety belts, please; we are going to land."

There were men who looked at their watches and swore in several languages; men hurrying to complete a business deal, to meet a woman, to ask for a loan or a job or merely going home. There was a woman flying east to be with her daughter, who was having a baby; she had had it by now, very likely. There was a little boy who had left his mother in California after a six months' visit and was on his way to visit his father in Connecticut for six months. A governess was with him, a haggard creature, weary of her well-paid position and of the innumerable questions a five-year-old mind could promulgate.

Some were impatient, some were frightened, none was resigned except possibly the girl halfway down the aisle, at the window. She was outstanding, not alone because of her appearance, which was unusual, but because of her serenity, relaxed, unbroken, undisturbed.

Each of her fellow passengers had looked at her a number of times. The women concentrated upon the sable coat across the back of the seat, upon the suit, soft gray tweed flecked with red, upon the string of pearls doubled and looped at the neck of the cashmere sweater. And they looked at her shoes, alligator and matching her handbag, and were curious or envious according to their temperaments. But the men looked at her face and whistled in their minds.

She kept herself to herself. The man next to her had spoken to her early in the flight and she had answered him courteously with just the faintest possible accent coloring her low voice. What accent? He was not a man with an ear for accents, and this had been so slight. He had not much opportunity to pursue his investigations for she was definitely not encouraging, and after three trials he gave up, but was quick to look at her hands when she took off her gloves in order to eat her luncheon. They were ringless except for what might have been a very fine emerald — he was no judge of jewels.

The man across the aisle, who was a painter, was not interested in emeralds nor in accents. But he was interested in faces, and this face was peculiarly memorable. It was not beautiful in the accepted sense, the eyes were too large and of a most indefinable color, neither gray nor green, and the mouth was too wide. But the girl's coloring was extraordinary, the light eyes, an olive skin with rosy undertones, and the densest, blackest hair he had ever seen, not blue-black nor jet-black, but black as soot, unshining, heavy, seemingly soft as smoke. She wore it parted in the middle and coiled at the nape of her neck. It was perfectly straight and, though she wore no hat, as undisheveled as if she had just risen from before her mirror.

He judged her to be about twenty-three or -four. It was hard to tell. He thought, *No one could be as placid as she looks.* He longed for something to distress, anger, or irritate her so that he could watch her face flash into life. But nothing, neither the delays nor the landings, neither the crying of a baby near by nor the almost uninterrupted airsickness of the man with a hangover four seats away.

9

Twice when they landed, she sent a wire. At all landings, scheduled or not, the passengers clustered in small groups, in waiting-rooms or outside, briefly drawn together, but this girl walked alone, and discouraged without word or gesture, the normal friendly approach.

The painter asked himself, *I wonder what she's thinking?*

She was not thinking so much as planning, or rather looking over her already formulated plans much as one might regard a list of household shopping. After her visit to Helen Lannis, she was promised to the Cotters in Asheville. That would bring her into the beginning of summer, which offered the Davidsons on Cape Cod or the Griswolds in Newport. There were various things to consider; she liked the Davidsons and tolerated the Griswolds. But Newport had its advantages.

She thought, *One step at a time.* And wondered, *How many steps? Three months, six, a year?* She might manage for a year; beyond that she did not know. And was suddenly, and savagely, homesick for hot sunlight and brilliant flowers, for brown faces and quick speech, for the smell of oils and spices, the chatter of bright birds, the splashing water in fountains, and for the smoking mountains and the thin pure air, for the heat and rain on a coast washed by a blue sea.

Forget that; it's gone; it will never come again. Besides, it was never yours for long.

Long before they reached LaGuardia the April sky was a pale, capricious blue, with low woolly clouds; toward twilight it darkened, streaked with a clear, wintry green, and then the misty dusk came swooping in like a dark bird, and far beneath them were the lights of many towns.

It was night when they landed, and the woman who was expecting her first grandchild went distractedly into the arms of her son-in-law, crying, "Not yet?" and he answered, "No, but everything's all right, and you're in good time, Mother." And the five-year-old boy yawned and stumbled sleepily into the embrace of his father, who always dreaded their first meeting because the child so much resembled a woman they both loved. And the other passengers went away, met or unmet as the case might be, but the stewardess, too late to keep her date, decided she would call a number she had never called before, and did so later, with disastrous results.

Only the painter looked for the girl with the sable coat slung over her shoulders. He had been curious about who would meet her — surely a young man, a man in love, or perhaps an older woman with white hair and elegance?

11

But, he told himself, *I should write fiction instead of painting portraits,* for the woman who met her was under thirty, small and voluble, a good friend of his, as it happened. He had painted her portrait some years ago.

It amused him to step forward and interrupt the greeting. He said, smiling, "Helen?"

Helen Lannis looked at him as if for a moment she did not see him and then cried, "You were on the plane, too? I wish I had known."

She made the introductions. "Miss Austin, Mr. Southard." And added, "Why didn't you pick her up, Jim? It would have relieved the tedium for both of you."

"I didn't dare," he answered gravely. "I watched her seatmate make the attempt and fail. Besides, sometimes Katie meets my plane. She couldn't tonight."

"May we take you home?" Helen asked, and Southard answered, "It would be very kind, if you have the time — and room?"

"All the time and room in the world. Frank couldn't come, he's in Cleveland. Terry, what's happened to your luggage?"

Teresa Austin was carrying her handbag and a little jewel or cosmetic case. James Southard carried his own small battered bag. And Terry said, "It will be along. Just two pieces, but overweight, of course. I've sent

12

the rest by express to your address, Helen, I'm afraid it's mountainous."

Helen was unperturbed. "You can sleep in the scullery," she suggested, "and put the trunks in your room. You must be starved, both of you."

"They fed us at intervals," Terry said, smiling. As she walked beside Southard he noticed that she was not so tall as he had thought but she carried herself as if she were. And now she asked, "You're the painter, aren't you, Mr. Southard? I've read so much about you."

He was inordinately pleased, though, a very successful and even truly gifted man, he was, at fifty, accustomed to having people know his name. He asked, "If I admit it, may I paint you one day?"

"Not tonight," said Helen. "Terry and I are going to sit up until dawn and talk. We were at a convent together in Paris a good many years ago. I was the big girl, very homesick, and she was the little one, who consoled me. The last time we saw each other was in England — how long ago, Terry?"

"In the summer of 'thirty-nine," Terry answered.

"I was nineteen," said Helen Lannis, "and had just met Frank." She was silent for a moment, remembering. Then she said briskly,

13

"Well, here we are, let's do something about it!"

The luggage was put in the car, and they drove off, Helen at the wheel. She drove very well in the heavy traffic. The car had a wide front seat, and Terry sat between Helen and Southard. She was physically tired and somewhat keyed up, so she deliberately relaxed her muscles as she had been taught to do. She was glad Frank was not at home, much as she had liked him. She wanted a good, solid talk with Helen, with whom she could be entirely candid. She did not know how much Helen or anyone knew. The North American and European papers had printed only the bare facts of her father's death. A little about that death, a great deal about his life. Of course, there might have been some reports which she had not seen.

She heard Southard ask Helen, "Why have you been keeping Miss Austin from us?" and Helen answered, "I haven't. She's been buried alive in Central America, and I couldn't get her to budge. I tried."

Terry roused herself and said lazily, "I did budge. I budged all over the place, but naturally after the war began I didn't go abroad. Except to come here; we were here briefly in 'forty-one and again in 'forty-three. You knew that, Helen."

"I was in England," said Helen, "so you didn't budge in the right direction. Not that it *was* the right direction."

She had remained there all through the blitz; now she and Frank were established in the States, and safe once more.

And happy, thought Terry, *the happiest people I've ever known, I suppose.* Yet not altogether. Helen had lost her first baby during the war years and she would not have another child.

Southard asked, startled, "Is it possible that you are Mark Austin's daughter, Miss Austin?"

"Of course she's Mark Austin's daughter," said Helen, as if it were unthinkable that she could be anyone else's, as, indeed, it was.

And Terry asked, not too quickly, "Did you ever know him, Mr. Southard?"

She listened for the note in his voice with which she was familiar; practically everyone who had heard of Mark Austin, rich or poor, successful or a failure, sounded that note when confronted with the daughter, who embodied all that his name stood for — storybook adventure, fabulous wealth.

The note was sounded as Southard said regretfully, "No, I am sorry to say I never met him. He would have been a man to know. I read of his tragic death with dismay. He was

15

truly a great man, a pioneer in the American tradition."

Horatio Alger with trimmings; poor lad with a dream, a dream come true.

"An airplane accident," said Helen, sighing. "I wonder how you bring yourself to fly, Terry."

Terry said quietly, "But he was piloting his own plane, and he was a very good pilot, not at all reckless. The doctors think he may have had a stroke and lost control. His blood pressure had been high. We'll never know, of course." She knew.

Southard said, directing the conversation into less unhappy channels, "I can account for your accent now, Miss Austin."

"My accent?" she repeated, amazed. "But I haven't any!"

Helen chuckled. "My poor darling, indeed you have. That's what comes of going to school in France and Switzerland, of holidays in England, and of being born in a Spanish-speaking country and returning to it."

"But I was born here," said Terry, laughing. "Didn't you know that? I was born in New York City."

"And I thought I knew everything about you!" said Helen.

You don't, thought Terry. *Not now.*

She said aloud, "And I haven't an accent!"

16

Southard disagreed. "It's very charming," he said, "don't lose it."

They reached his house, an old brownstone in the Fifties with a big studio on the top floor, and he took his leave of them, asking Helen, "Can't Katie and I coax you to bring Miss Austin to dinner? I know Frank is allergic to dining out, but — "

"Tell Katie to call me," said Helen, "and give her my love. We'll come, of course, and it's been nice seeing you, Jim."

Driving away, she remarked, "He wants to clinch a portrait deal. But you have the flattering consolation of knowing he wanted to paint you before he realized who you are. Now that he does, he might make a special price of, say, ten thousand. He did me for free, incidentally. He likes us, we couldn't afford his prices — why should I be immortalized in oils, anyway? — and it's all or nothing with him. I lend the portrait to exhibitions. Go and look at it and listen to people saying, 'What a plain woman — but quite interesting.' "

"You aren't plain."

"He won't have much difficulty in making you glamorous," said Helen.

"I hate being painted," Terry said.

She had been several times, and the portraits were in storage now. She wondered if she would ever see them again.

"I could have killed him," said Helen, "for being on the plane, but I had to ask him to come with us. He's a nice old thing, really, and retains a sharp eye for the ladies. But Katie keeps him in line. She's quite wonderful, really. Anyway, we couldn't have talked much even if we'd been alone. I mean, about things that mattered. I'd rip through a red light, and Frank would murder me."

"How is he?" Terry asked. Her head ached slightly and she felt a deep, bone-aching fatigue.

"Fine. I wrote you he was pretty battered up when I got him back. And of course it took more time and energy than you'd believe to persuade him to leave England. The selling of the place was a nightmare. After all, it was his home. But you remember that his mother died, soon after we were married, and his father — "

"I know," said Terry. And could feel again the horror with which she had read Helen's letter telling her that Frank's father had been killed in the blitz.

"He hasn't gotten over it, naturally," said Helen. "Frank adored his father. Well, there's no one left but his sister — you remember her, don't you, Terry? and they never got on very well — and stray cousins and such. He likes it here, and is in the process of becoming

18

a citizen. His job interests him — Here we are," she said, and the car slid to a stop.

The apartment house was on a side street in the upper Sixties. The doorman came out to carry the bags and to say that he would take the car around to the garage for Mrs. Lannis. And in the elevator Helen explained, "You have no idea of the parking problem — it's incredible. We were awfully lucky to get space in a garage not too far away."

A pleasant maid opened the door for them when they reached the apartment on the tenth floor, and Helen took Terry to the guest room, which was on a corner, spacious and graciously furnished. She said, "Get out of your suit into something comfortably sloppy, and we'll have a celebration supper on a tray — the way we used to, remember, at the Embassy when no one was looking? When your wires came and I had checked with the airport, Margaret gave me my dinner — not too much of it. Haul something out of a bag, we'll do the real unpacking later." She was not a demonstrative woman but now she put her arms around Terry and hugged her. "I'm so happy to see you, dear."

Terry's heart turned over with gratitude, for this long, rare friendship. She looked at the small face lovingly, a face distinguished only by its expression, the lively brown eyes, and curly red hair.

"You don't know how glad I am to be here," she said truthfully.

"Well, get washed or whatever, and make it snappy. We have only the rest of the night to do our scratch-the-surface talking." She eyed the matching bags wistfully. "Alligator," she murmured, "such lavishness. I'll be back for you in ten minutes. If you want anything, yell. I'm next door."

Terry got out her keys, opened one of the bags, and took out a soft wool robe and slippers. She took off her suit and blouse, hung them in the closet, and went into the bathroom and looked with longing at the tub and shower. But that could wait. She washed, brushed her hair, and reddened her lips. Dusting powder over her face, she looked at herself in the mirror. No one would dream that she was frightened, she thought. Perhaps all the many years of safety had set an imperishable seal upon her — the way she looked and moved and spoke. But once the seal was broken —

Her dressing-case was open. She took from it the small, silver-framed picture of her father and set it on the bedside table just as Helen knocked on the door.

"Ready?" she asked. "What a lovely robe." She walked over to the bed and looked at the picture and added, sighing, "He was the *best-looking* man — "

She linked her arm through Terry's, and they went out of the room, down the hall to the living-room, a square, attractive room, with old polished pieces of furniture, a particularly wonderful desk, and over the fireplace, Helen's portrait. Terry stood looking at it. She said slowly, "It's pretty good, I think. He's caught something of you."

Something of the candor and kindness, something of the warmth.

"Oh," said Helen, laughing, "when he paints for love — don't misunderstand me, Terry, love of his art, I mean — he does a good job. Sometimes the ten-thousand-dollar jobs aren't so good, I think; too slick, too smug. Here, sit down on the couch beside me."

Margaret came in, smiling, with the tray and put it on a low coffee table. It was laden with sandwiches and hot rolls, with cheese and fruit, and a coffee service. "Also," said Helen triumphantly, "there's champagne, to toast our reunion. Margaret's going to bring it in a minute."

After the maid had gone, Terry found herself eating with more appetite than she had believed she possessed. And they talked or were silent, as they wished, reminiscing for

21

the most part, speaking of the convent days in Paris, of the Embassy in London, of meetings in Switzerland, in Munich, in Cannes.

"The good old days," said Helen, "or so I suppose. And gone forever."

When Margaret had cleared away the tray and the wine bottle, leaving only fresh coffee, Helen asked, "Have you any plans?"

"Nebulous," said Terry, smiling faintly.

"I suppose you'll take a flat here," said Helen, "that is, if you can find one, or perhaps a hotel suite — not that they aren't scarcer than ten family doctors — but I dare say you'll manage. I'd love to help you look. What have you done with the houses and all the properties — or are people managing them for you? There's so *much* I want to know. I still dream of the holiday I spent with you — the mountains and the horses and the wonderful way of living. I have never known anything like it before or since."

That was when she was a young girl and Terry younger, and Helen had gone to the hacienda in Guatemala with her friend. A long, wearisome, exciting trip before the day of airplane travel. She remembered sunlight and flowers, she remembered the friendly Indian faces, the bright colors, the long siestas during the day's heat, the nights —

She asked, before Terry could speak, "You

aren't planning to go back there and live, are you, Terry, alone? It isn't as if you'd lived there all your life; most of it you've spent in Europe, after all."

And there was more than one hacienda. Mark Austin's interests had been varied, coffee, sugar, cattle, gold mining. He had been brought up in South and Central America, the son of an American mining engineer, and had returned there from his education in the States, an ambitious, hard-driving young man. Before he died he owned properties in Nicaragua, Guatemala, Honduras, El Salvador.

Terry put down her coffee cup. She said, "I shan't go back, Helen. I'm staying here."

"That's wonderful." Helen leaned back against the couch and said thoughtfully, "You might get a place in the country. Connecticut?" she asked herself. "The Johnsons want to sell theirs, it's small and quite perfect. They'd sell furnished, unless, of course, you want to ship your furniture out — not that I can see it in a Connecticut farmhouse, but — "

Terry said, "I haven't any furniture, Helen. I haven't anything" — her hand went to the string of pearls at her throat — "except these, my clothes and furs, and some jewelry of my mother's. And an income of about two hundred dollars a month."

Helen's eyes widened, and her mouth was

jarred open. She stared at her friend in bewilderment. After a moment she said, "I don't believe it, I *can't*."

"It's true," said Terry steadily.

"But what *happened?* I mean, why? That is — " She gave up, shaking her red head. She asked, after a moment, "Can you tell me, Terry? From the beginning?"

"The beginning was long ago, and I don't know much about it. My father, I suppose, overextended himself and was steeped in the sort of intrigue that is common enough, has always been. After my mother died, when I was eight years old, after he had decided to send me to Paris, he immersed himself in business, as a substitute for everything, for wife and child, for happiness, perhaps, and love. He liked pulling strings. He grew rich pulling them, and it wasn't the money that interested him, I'm sure. It was the power. The war curtailed some of his activities, stepped up others. And there were always border disputes and revolutions. He backed the wrong man last time — and lost everything. I don't know how. It was explained to me by the lawyers, but I still don't know how. He wasn't alone in his interests, of course. He couldn't be. When he realized — he took the plane out and crashed it."

"Terry!"

"Yes," said Terry somberly. "There were a few things that couldn't be touched legally. One was the insurance he had taken out years ago when I was born and had almost forgotten, though the premiums were kept up. I turned in the jewelry he'd given me, there was a good deal of it, and kept only my mother's, the pearls, her engagement ring, and some old pieces. He gave the pearls to her just before she died. My furs — " Her voice trailed off, and she looked at Helen blindly for a moment. "That's how it is."

"But there was nothing in the papers," Helen began.

"Not here or in Europe," said Terry, "nor in Central America. So many people were mixed up in the failure, important people. The — the man he didn't back, the man who came into power, had been under obligation to him once. Perhaps that's why they let me off lightly. It wasn't a money obligation. My father had gotten him out of a bad scrape once, something to do with a woman — Well, it doesn't matter now."

Helen asked, on a deep breath, "But what are you going to *do?*"

"It's what I'm not going to do," said Terry. Her heart hammered in her breast, she felt sick with insecurity. This was a sensation which up until a year or so ago had been

25

utterly unknown to her and she could not accustom herself to it.

"What do you mean, not going to do?"

She said, "Sometimes one can coast along on credit. I don't mean," she said quickly, "that I'm about to run up bills. I mean social credit. No one knows the situation here, apparently, except yourself."

"Someone must," said Helen. "What about our consuls, the official people?"

"They do, of course, if not everything. I told you it was all kept under wraps. The people involved didn't want public investigations and all that. And the officials, as you say, are there and not here. So for a while I'm reasonably safe. It's logical to assume that everyone not knowing would figure that it would take a long time to clear up the estate, that the other partners would buy father's interest, and that I'd" — she smiled a very little — "be amply taken care of, Helen."

Helen said blankly, "I can't get it through my head."

"Don't try." Terry reached for a cigarette and lit it. She leaned her dark head back and half closed her eyes. She said, "I haven't many tangible assets, nor intangible. I can't do anything useful. Oh, I speak a number of languages, which would be fine in a secretary, if I knew *how* to be a secretary; or a governess, if

26

I knew how to be a governess. I sew very well, we both do; that's convent training. But I would make a poor seamstress, Helen. I can make over my own clothes because it amuses me, but I am not interested in anyone else's. The things I do best have no market value. I swim, for instance, and play excellent tennis and fair golf. I ride, I drive a car. I dance, with a good partner, superlatively, but not superlatively enough for professional purposes. I play intelligent contract. I am a marvelous amateur guest — I can become a professional."

"You can't mean that!" Helen said.

"I do. All this past winter in Palm Beach I managed to use my talents in the only possible way. I had enough money for personal needs, which were few — my food and lodging, my transportation, even my laundry was supplied. I could tip, if not lavishly; and everyone knows that people of great means, if not new to money, aren't lavish tippers! I could send my hostess flowers, or fish for a little gift from my luggage, something I'd managed to bring with me. When I was taken somewhere to dine, I couldn't of course repay in kind as I was staying elsewhere but I could always send flowers. Helen, I can go on like this just as long as people don't know. When they do, it will be different. They do not think of me as Teresa Austin but as Mark Austin's daughter.

I'd still be asked, to fill in, to amuse dull men, to give my hostess a hand — on a different basis. 'Poor Terry,' they'll say, 'let's ask her down,' or 'Let's ask her to stay with the children while we're in Bermuda,' or 'We need another woman for dinner, how about Terry? She's always willing, and so decorative.' "

"Decorative," repeated Helen, wanting to put her hands over her ears. "You're beautiful!"

"Beautiful but broke. *That's* what they'll say."

"Two hundred a month isn't broke," said Helen, "except by comparison. Dear, you're mixed up. There are other ways. A job, with which you could supplement your income. You could model — "

"I don't want to," Terry said passionately. "I'm spoiled, I tell you, rotten spoiled. I've had over twenty years of spoiling. This last year and over, living from day to day on sufferance, being permitted to stay in my own house, the one I most loved — " Her voice broke, she was silent, thinking of it, with the mountains in the back yard, thinking of dim high-ceilinged rooms, of tiled floors, of the pillared corridors on the patio, of wooden grilles and thick doors, of distant voices, singing, laughing.

"Don't look like that," cried Helen

sharply. "Don't!"

She leaned closer to Terry, touched her shoulder. "So you don't want to model. All right. But there must be something you can do. All the things that make you, as you say, a marvelous guest, they are assets."

"Socially, yes; professionally, no. It took months before things were settled as they could be. One of my father's partners looked after me, he managed to see that I lived. I stayed in the house in Honduras, with old Maria — you remember her — who had been with my mother. I was in mourning. Mourning is respected in the Latin countries. I was not expected to go out, to entertain. People came to see me with their condolences. Others came, too — men who sat in the library and went over the papers, who opened safes, read correspondence, making up their minds what to do with this and that. Everything was confiscated, everything possible."

"But he had interests other than in Honduras."

"They were all linked. When I was free to leave I went to Florida and stayed with the Pearsons. They had visited us several times. They were very kind to me."

"You should have come here to me, at once. I begged you to, I cabled as soon as I knew about your father."

29

"I know, but I couldn't. I had to tell you, of course, and couldn't bring myself to it. I had to live in the illusion — at least so far as other people were concerned."

"Terry, isn't there anyone — close to you? There must be someone — "

"Close?" Terry looked at her for a moment. Then she smiled. "Oh, I see. You mean a man? Being married, and happily, you think that's the solution. It is, but unfortunately there's no one. I was always too wary. Who among them could see and love me without the aura? None, I thought. There were a few I couldn't accuse of being blinded by the Austin dazzle — older men, for the most part — and I wasn't interested."

Helen asked, "What did you mean when you said 'it is the solution'?"

"There must be, as you put it, someone in these United States," Terry answered, "and how am I to meet him unless I continue to do as I have begun to do? Go places, visit people, the charming guest in search of a solution — an eligible one."

"Must he be eligible?" asked Helen sorrowfully.

Terry nodded. "I'll not make a success as the wife of a poor man. I haven't the education for it, and it is too late to learn now."

Helen looked incredulous. "I don't under-

stand you any more, Terry. And I thought I
did."

"I don't understand myself," said Terry,
somewhat wildly. She thought, *I was insane to
tell her. But you can't go on carrying a burden
like this and not sharing it, you* can't. *But I wish
I hadn't, it is too much of a risk.*

She said, "Helen, I've never had any close
friends but you. You know how I felt about
my father. There were long periods when I
did not see him but he always stood for something out of a fairy tale — big and laughing
and with a perpetual Aladdin's lamp in his
pocket. I had only to wish — I remember my
mother, of course, she was loving and kind,
but her interest was not in me, but in him.
You can understand that. She had left everything for him, her family, who never became
reconciled, even her church. She was eighteen
and very beautiful."

Helen said, "I know very little about her.
She was a Brazilian, wasn't she?"

"Yes. There's a huge family there — I've
never known them. After she died, I was sent
to Paris, and to Switzerland — you know all
that. But I lived for the holidays at home or
for the times Father came to meet me in
Europe."

"I know," said Helen softly.

"I had everything — and nothing. Now I

31

have just nothing."

"Terry —"

"Don't say it," said Terry. "Don't say, 'You have looks and youth and good health and an education, more equipment than most women.' But I am not equipped. I'm soft, I'm lazy, I'm spoiled, I tell you. You're talking as a one hundred percent American, Helen. I'm not, except by birth. I haven't the viewpoint, I haven't the drive, I haven't the stamina."

"You can acquire them."

"Can I?"

Helen said, "Terry, I've a little money of my own. Take it and equip yourself to do something you will find yourself liking to do — dress designing, modeling, anything."

Terry's eyes filled slowly. She put her hand over Helen's for a moment. "You sit there and look at me and think, 'I've never known her really; she's mercenary, and rebellious and a born parasite,' and yet you offer me your money — the backlog, the legacy. I remember when you wrote me about it. No. And that's one thing I won't do, I won't borrow, not from my nearest and dearest; not from friend or stranger."

"All right, but it's there if you want it, and you can sell the pearls and the emerald."

"I shan't sell them," said Terry, "until I have to, until I am starving. And I shan't starve."

Her chin went up, and her beautiful skin was suffused with color. "They're all I have; they are, in a way, my luck. Besides — " and she smiled with a sudden childlike mischieviousness — "they'll serve to preserve the legend. The pearls, the emerald, the sable coat, the alligator luggage — all necessary accessories before the crime, as it were."

"You appall me," said Helen simply.

"I know, yet I love you very much. You are the only close friend I have ever had, of my own age. I soon lost track of the girls at the convent and those in Switzerland. When I was home, we entertained continuously, but generally older people. I was never more than mildly friendly with their daughters — not being Latin nor yet American, I didn't fit in. Nor did I have intimates in the American colonies. When my father died — " She paused. "When he killed himself," she corrected firmly, "there was no one. People were very kind — until the truth began seeping out, whispered in patios, on dance floors, over dinner tables. Then they were less kind."

"My poor Terry."

"He wanted it his way," said Terry, "dying quickly of his own resolve. He left a letter for me. I burned it. He was a gambler, of course, a little drunk because he held the good hands for so long, because the right number came up. He was," she added, with a white line around her mouth, "dishonest. Big larcenies, Helen, not little ones. Staking men's lives and their reputations on a palmed card. Playing one man against another — "

"Dear, don't talk about it."

"I have to, now. I shan't again."

She had been frozen with shock, with incredulity. The long slow thawing out was more painful than she could have believed possible. It was still painful, her very mind was sore, wincing away from facts.

Helen said helplessly, "You can't get away with it, Terry. You can't go on making round after round of visits — "

Terry said with sudden lightness, "There'll be someone. In Palm Beach there were two — one is old and rather pleasant and the other is young, twice divorced, and rather nasty. Both are as rich as taxes permit."

"Well?" asked Helen.

"I can't imagine anything more absurd," admitted Terry, "but I've also made the final, probably impossible condition. I have to fall in love, *too*."

Helen burst out laughing, with a lunatic relief. She cried, "But that doesn't make sense! Either, as you said, you are mercenary, willing to go to any lengths, *or* you're romantic — you can't be both."

"Why not?" asked Terry. "There must be some attractive as well as eligible men."

"And you won't settle for less?"

"No. I won't settle for your money and a dark little flat or a club for women, and being pushed around in subways and busses and doing my own cooking, except when someone buys a meal for me, and my own laundry. And I won't settle for a bank account attached to a man who makes my flesh crawl and my stomach curl into a knot. Or for one attached to a gentleman I can only respect and admire. Nor will I settle for the Prince Charming who can offer me a little house in the suburbs with a cleaning woman in twice a week. I'm a gambler, too, Helen."

"And if it's impossible?"

"There are the pearls. I could live on them for a time. But in the meantime, as I said, they'll help preserve the illusion."

Helen rose. "You look wretched, Terry. Get to bed and to sleep. We'll talk more tomorrow."

Terry got to her feet. "You can help me, you know."

"How?"

"You know people — "

"Darling, we do not move in the gilded circles."

"But you know people," Terry said stubbornly, "you're bound to. Your father was a diplomat; Frank's family is as well known here as in England."

"The only eligible young man I know is twenty and an alcoholic," said Helen. "He's a cousin of the Johnsons, whose house I wanted you to buy." She heard herself, and then Terry laugh, with inner astonishment. But it was funny, in a way. "He has a trust fund which would amaze even you. And he's no good. You'll meet him. The Johnsons have asked us up next week-end, and you, of course, are included. They are dying to know you. If you want to preserve the illusion you'll have to pretend to look at the house, at least with a view to its future possibilities."

She took Terry to her room and looked in. The bags were unpacked, the bed turned down, and a wisp of a nightgown laid across it.

Terry said, "How wonderful! Perhaps I'll sleep. I haven't, very well, in a long time. Helen, you won't stop being fond of me, because you — Well, you just wouldn't. But how much difference does all this make?"

"I was pretty impressed," said Helen, "by — the legend. Who wouldn't be? But now that it's gone, no difference. Because I wasn't fond of the legend. Just — impressed. And I still don't see why it's necessary to keep it up."

Terry sat down on the edge of her bed. She

36

said, "Has it ever occurred to you how many fortunes are united by marriage? I've seen pictures of brides and grooms, looking just as happy and quite as much in love as if there were no fortunes. But it has been my experience that very rich young men are wary of poor but beautiful girls. They fear, as I once feared, that they will be married, or at best loved, for their solvency. But they are never afraid of girls with comparable backgrounds — *and* solvency."

"Terry," said Helen, on a long breath, "I'm scared of you because it is just within the bounds of probability that you'll get what you want."

"You'll help me?" asked Terry softly.

"May heaven have mercy on me," said Helen, not at all facetiously, "I am also afraid that to the best of my ability I will."

Chapter Two

A GILT-EDGED PROSPECT

During her first few days in New York, Terry was occupied with surface things. Helen saw to that. She took her sight-seeing — "You haven't been in New York for a long time, it's appalling, where all the people come from, heaven alone knows" — gave a small luncheon for her, had people for dinner and for tea. Frank came home, and Terry renewed her acquaintance with him. She had met him at the time Helen had, in London, and remembered him as a tall, quiet young man with a slow, charming smile and enormous poise. He had changed; he had remained quiet, his smile was the same, and his poise, but he had matured, and what had once seemed shyness was now reserve. That he and Helen were deeply in love was apparent, and Terry envied them passionately.

At night too often she dreamed. Sleeping fitfully. However tired, she dreamed of a plane falling, a lost star spinning idly in space, without direction but with lethal purpose, and crashing with sound and fury and the upward roaring of flame, and with the crash her own star was demolished.

Because it eased her, she talked of her dreams to Helen when they were alone, speaking of her father and the events that had brought about his spiritual and physical destruction with a desperate detachment. Helen listened, alarmed and deeply concerned. There was so little one could say, there was no possible condolence, no comfort. Her initial bewilderment at Terry's attitude began to pass, and she realized, if dimly, that it was not the loss of a way of life that had so altered her friend — for surely she was altered — as the loss of a rooted belief in a human being. She offered this explanation hesitatingly, on the night before they were to go to the country. Frank was out to dinner, and the two women sat long over their coffee after Margaret had cleared the table.

"I can't believe that what you had means so much to you," said Helen, "had, in the sense of possessions, I mean. If your father had lost his money in an ordinary way; if he had died — "

"In the ordinary way? Is there an ordinary way?" Terry interrupted.

"Yes, of course. But it was the shock," said Helen, "that made the alteration, the turning upside down of everything. Yet I believe you have forgiven him."

"It isn't a question of forgiveness. He asked me, in the letter, could I forgive him. If you love someone, I don't believe you think in that term. What remains is grief, I suppose. Not the sorrow because he's gone and I'll not see him again, though that's something from which I can't easily recover. I suppose I idealized him, as a child would, and never quite grew up where he was concerned. No, not that, but the sorrow for what he did to himself and to other people."

"To you? Then you do resent it."

"Not to me. I'll make out. No, the others — the many who also trusted him. For heaven's sake, don't be sorry for me, it's the one thing I couldn't stand."

And one reason, thought Helen, with a flash of insight, *why you don't want people to know.*

"It's funny," Terry went on, "but all my life people have envied me — for things which had nothing to do with me, really, which I hadn't brought about, which I hadn't created — but because of my father, because of the things he had created, also because I was young, reasonably attractive, and had, as the phrase goes, everything. Like most people I can accept envy but not pity. And most of them would pity me now with a touch of smugness." She paused. "Not people like Frank," she amended. "He'd just be sorry. But he and others like him would stop being sorry if they really knew me; they'd be impatient and repelled by the way in which I propose to work things out. You are now, though you don't say so."

"I do say so," Helen contradicted stoutly. "Yet impatient isn't exactly the word, nor repelled. And I am so fond of you, Terry. I'm just sad about it and incredulous."

"Oh," said Terry, "it would all be so very different if I were the noble, romantic, fine American girl, bravely putting her past life behind her and embarking upon a crusade of high thinking and plain living. Taking up a career singlehanded — office or shop, it doesn't matter what, because it always turns out for the best, and has a happy ending. Smiling through and an uncomplaining acceptance of struggle and privation, a cheery smile and the knowledge that all that glitters isn't Fort Knox nor can money buy happiness. If you're a good girl, such a course leads to marriage to the boss or to the gentleman who comes in to buy lilac toilet water for his dear old mom on Mother's Day."

"Terry, stop it!"

"Well, it's true. Only I've finished with fairy tales. I lived one far too long. And I am

41

not an admirable person. I suppose I might not have known or acknowledged it if the fairy tale hadn't ended — in the middle. No, not admirable at all and honest only with myself and you."

But who is myself? she wondered miserably, feeling disintegrated and insecure, as if she were half waking from a dream.

Helen said, "Let's go finish your unpacking."

She thought as she went into Terry's bedroom, *This is just a phase, bitterness born of shock; and it will pass.*

Terry's trunks had come, so she was unpacking the things she would need for spring and summer, and repacking for storage. Helen had said there was storage space in the trunk rooms downstairs where she might leave her things.

There were many clothes, enough to last a long time. "I can always alter them," said Terry, looking at the frocks laid on the bed, "and they'll do." There were heaps of lingerie, handmade in French convents, delicate and lovely; traveling things and the other furs, a short mink jacket, a stole of baum marten, an ermine cape. "Good window dressing," said Terry, "if I can afford to store them this summer!"

She had brought gifts with her. "They were

mine," she said. "I had so much. These are things I have never used. Please take them, Helen." And for Frank, a cigarette case, handkerchiefs, scarfs. She added, "There are still plenty for the gracious hostess, such as your Mrs. Johnson."

Helen said, "You've enough to stock a shop!"

"But I'm not going to," said Terry warningly. "Initial stock isn't the whole story."

"There's my money," Helen began.

"Which will stay where it is. Can you imagine me in a gift shop," Terry inquired, "on the wrong side of the counter?"

Helen couldn't, no matter how she tried.

"Grand opening," suggested Terry, "in the suburbs. Cheaper rent, or isn't it? And everyone flocking — the first week or so; and everyone saying, 'Poor girl, reduced to running a gift shop, and selling her own things.' No, thanks!"

Helen said, "All right, Terry. It's just that I've racked my brains and can't come up with an adequate answer."

"All you have to do is trot out amiable people who will in turn trot out the unattached and eligible men. After that I'll do my own shopping."

"Don't you still mean selling?"

"No, because I'll fall in love, and since

when has that constituted a business transaction?"

Helen rose. "Here, let me fold those things. You had a maid too long, and you're still living in the fairy tale, darling."

They drove to the Johnsons' on Saturday morning, a forty-mile drive up the Parkway and off on back roads. The day was fine, with a clear pale-blue sky, sunlight gilding the bare boughs, and a soft wind. The Johnson house was in a valley, but from its upper windows you could look to the hills. A little river ran through the property, beyond an old orchard, and the house itself was very old and had been lovingly restored and furnished.

Their hostess, Gwen Johnson, was a small, voluble woman in her late thirties; her husband, somewhat her junior, was lean and astringently pleasant. There were two sons, both away at school.

"We've just one guest room," Gwen said, "and Helen and Frank rate that. I'm going to put you in Sam's room," she told Terry. "I hope you don't mind, it's all over with souvenirs friends brought him from the war, as well as banners and half-assembled radio sets. Also, it has bunks, not beds, for the boys are always bringing someone home." She laughed. "It will be like camping."

"It's a good room," said Terry, regarding it. A normal sort of boy's room. The floors were uneven, the wide boards sagging, covered by a hooked rug. Evidently Sam liked the sea, for the walls were crowded with photographs of shore lines, stretches of ocean, ships under sail.

Gwen said, "I was a little worried when Helen told me you were visiting her. We run this madhouse on one so-called maid, a cleaning woman-laundress, and me. During the war, just me. We bought this place so we wouldn't be tempted to do a great deal of entertaining but, of course, we did. We sleep people practically anywhere." She sighed and added, "I hate to give it up and move back to town, but Paul refuses to commute any longer, and last year his mother died and left us, actually, a house in New York. It's rented, of course. But when we sell here we'll move in, I hope."

"You should have no difficulty selling," said Terry sincerely. She remembered what Helen had said and made the necessary effort. "How many acres have you?" she inquired.

"Thirty, mostly woods and fields. There isn't too much lawn or garden," said Gwen earnestly. "Paul's allergic to lawn mowers and weeding. It would be perfect for a couple without children — which we were when we bought it — or for a single occupant."

45

"But surely," said Terry, at the window, looking out at the treetops and the hills beyond, "with the housing shortage you must have had innumerable offers?"

"At the height of the boom, yes, but then we had no intention of selling. There aren't as many now and, frankly, not at our asking price. We've put a lot into it, not just money."

Before luncheon she took Terry through the house, and talked, not too much in the real-estate manner, of the heating system, the brass pipes, the good cellar and attic. Storm doors, storm windows, insulation. "The works," she said, and smiled at her guest. "Perhaps I should let you discover the good points for yourself and also come clean. When Helen told me that you were coming to New York, she suggested that she might persuade you to stay on, and I thought, 'How about the country?' And that naturally led to mercenary speculation on my part, although frankly," she added, surveying her guest, "I can't imagine that a girl your age would want to coop herself up away from town. You look much more like an apartment in Sutton Place to me."

Terry laughed, liking her hostess. She said, "Well, to tell you the truth I haven't made up my mind where I'll go or if I'll stay. I suppose eventually I'll have to have a place of my own,

46

but for a time I'm going to visit."

"Oh, dear," said Gwen, "then I may as well drop the sales talk. For someone's bound to sell you on Florida in winter and Long Island in summer, or a shooting-lodge in the Carolinas or *something*."

But the house was lovely, complete with Dutch oven and corner cupboards, old furniture, faded chintzes, and reproduction wallpapers. It was a friendly house, and Terry thought that, if things had been different, she would have loved living in it from spring to late autumn, staffing it adequately, filling it with pleasant people.

At lunch, "Paul's uncle and aunt live up the road," said Gwen, "they're grand neighbors, although as a rule here only in summer. But their younger son is here now for the weekend, I believe, though we haven't seen him. I dare say he'll be over."

Paul, contemplating with dismay a company soufflé, which seemed frothy fare to him, said, "Frank and Helen know all about my dear young cousin, and Miss Austin will as soon as she lays eyes on him. She might as well be warned."

"But he may be all right," said his wife swiftly; "after all, we haven't seen him in months."

"Which is all right by me," her husband

remarked and turned to Terry. "Unlike my branch of the family, my uncle has pots of money. He has, as well, three sons. Two are good, sober, hard-working fellows with nice, suitable wives. The youngest, just turned twenty, is a pain in the neck. He has been kicked out of every school he's attended since he was thirteen. He didn't get into college. Doctors and so-called sanitariums haven't helped him. But when he's not drinking he's a likable boy."

"But that's dreadful," said Terry. "Surely something could be done?"

"They've tried. But I believe the passport to a cure is the patient's consent. He doesn't want to be cured, evidently. He may turn up sober or he may not. If not, I apologize in advance. He's not violent or terrifying when he's drunk, Miss Austin, just mildly idiotic. Unfortunately he has an income, a legacy from his maternal grandfather, and when he's twenty-one he inherits the principal."

Gwen spoke. "Don't bore Miss Austin, Paul. And besides, Aunt Elizabeth wrote that he — Dick — was fine. You know what that means. Ever since Chris Russell took him in hand — "

"Chris Russell?" repeated Terry slowly. The name was familiar to her and suddenly remembering, she asked, "One of the sugar

48

people from Hawaii?"

"I haven't met him," Gwen said, "but it seems to me that Aunt Elizabeth did say something — "

Helen was scowling slightly in an effort at concentration. She said, "I've seen that name lately in the columns."

Frank spoke for the first time. "Of course you have. Parties, entertainments, night clubs. The Russells have a place or places on the West Coast, San Francisco, San Mateo, or wherever. *And* an island in the Pacific. Fabulous people by all accounts. Apparently they don't come East often, for there was quite a hoopla when this particular one arrived here."

Helen carefully avoided Terry's eyes. She asked, "And you say he's with Dick now? Are they the same age?"

Terry almost laughed aloud. She thought, against her will, *She's in there pitching.*

"No, he's older, twenty-eight or -nine," said Gwen. "He ran into Dick somewhere — "

"Saw him shining in the gutter, I suppose," said her husband dourly, "and fished him out."

"And took an interest in him," Gwen went on blandly. "It seems that he had a brother who died in the war, who also was a problem child."

"Euphonious way of putting it," said Paul,

49

and attacked his salad, which he loathed.

After luncheon, Paul took Frank out to tramp through the orchard, and the women sat talking in the living-room. Then Gwen excused herself to consult the maid. "She knows what we're having for dinner," she explained, "but I always have to check; sometimes I think she can't read." Terry smiled at Helen. She said, "I've heard about the Russells. Sugar, pineapples, and ten fingers in other pies."

"Not so fast," warned Helen, "nor so soon."

"It's a big family," Terry said, "we entertained some of them once. I was about fourteen, my first trip home in some time. Helen, you must remember, you were there!"

"There were so many people — "

"I know, but they talked about the Islands. They said we must return the visit" — Terry looked more animated than Helen had seen her since her arrival — "and Father promised that one day we would. We spoke of it in later years. We always intended to, but we didn't. Then the war came. I wish we had while there was time."

Helen said quietly, "Don't forget your impossible condition."

"I haven't. He'll be short, fat, and dull," sighed Terry. "Well, we'll see."

At four o'clock Dick Johnson appeared with his guest. He walked in without knocking and inquired, "May I, or am I in disgrace? And is it teatime? And who is this completely glamorous — Oh, hello, Mrs. Lannis."

"You can't mean me," said Helen, as Gwen made the introductions. They were all talking at once. "This is Chris Russell," Dick said, a little proudly.

Russell was tall, with thick fair hair. His eyes were blue as the Pacific. He had a little scar on his temple, the finest hands Terry had ever seen, and the most beautiful teeth. Evidently the silver spoon had not injured them.

Gwen nudged Helen aside. She said, awed, "Dick's *sober*. He says he wants *tea!*"

So they had tea, and Russell refused a highball, as did Frank. "Don't mind me," said Dick, grinning. "You can take it, *I* can leave it alone."

He was a thin boy, looking much older than twenty, with a sharp, precocious face and tired eyes. He was intensely restless, and Terry noticed that Russell kept an eye on him, not at all ostentatiously. Chris himself was the most relaxed person she had ever seen.

He came to sit by her presently, and said, putting his cup on the table in front of the couch, "So you're Terry Austin. I used to hear about you."

51

She said, "Years ago some of your family visited us — it was in Guatemala. Your father and mother, perhaps?"

"No, my father's cousin and his wife," he said. "I heard about it the following summer when I returned from college on the mainland."

"Are you here for long, or are you going back?"

He shrugged. "I don't know for how long. There's a job waiting but I've been home only once since the war ended. I've been knocking around South America, Cuba — and all over the mainland. I find it hard to settle down."

She asked, "Didn't I read about you during the war?"

He said hastily, "If you did, forget it. It's over now."

But she had read something. He'd been in the navy, the ship had been torpedoed. She looked at the little scar again. He had flushed slightly, and the scar stood out white. She thought, *Even if he weren't Chris Russell —* But he was; and you couldn't separate him from his background.

They stayed for dinner, though Gwen cried distractedly, "There isn't enough to go round, Dick."

But Dick insisted over Chris's protests. He said, "I'll go light, Gwen. Chris deserves a break, he's been nursemaiding me for three months in the apartment, while the family was south. And tutoring me as well."

"You were in town," asked Gwen, "and didn't let us know, or come out?"

"Chris kept me under cover. But I let him out now and again."

Paul asked, "What do you mean, tutoring?"

Chris grinned. "I had nothing to do," he explained, "and all Dick needs is to learn to concentrate and to brush up on math, where he's weakest. He can get into college now if he wants, if, during the summer, he's willing to try again."

After dinner, Chris took Terry aside. He said, "Put on a coat and come on out. There may not have been enough to go around for Gargantua but there was more than enough for me. Let's walk it off," he suggested.

Terry went upstairs to get the mink jacket, and Helen tore up after her. Watching her friend redden her lips before the mirror on the high chest of drawers, watching her bright, reflected eyes, Helen warned uneasily, "Really, Terry, not the first man you meet!"

Terry swung around. "Why not the first instead of the twenty-first?" she demanded. "Sometimes things happen like that. Don't you think he's attractive, Helen?"

"Yes. Also he's Chris Russell, not that I

need remind you. I had no idea, of course, at first what that meant. If he wasn't Chris Russell, would you find him so interesting?"

"How can I tell? How do you detach anyone from the things that are part of him?"

"I wouldn't know," Helen admitted.

Terry smiled at her. "Don't fuss, darling." She caught up the jacket and moved toward the door, adding, "He'll be off guard with me, you know."

Helen understood. She said grimly, "I wish you luck," rose, and put her arm through Terry's. "Come along, then. And I meant it when I said — good luck."

In the corridor Terry said, "A toast, if we had anything to toast in, to the Austins and the Russells."

"A plague on both your houses," Helen said, and was sorry at once when Terry's eyes clouded. She added swiftly, "I didn't mean that — it was stupid of me, Terry."

There was a sliver of a moon, like a silver shaving, and the wind had dropped. Chris and Terry walked on the terrace and then stopped to lean on the low wall that ran around it. And he said, "I like this place — not only the house but the setting, all the country around it. I have never before been in New England. I went to college on the West

54

Coast, where I didn't, I may add, graduate. I was too anxious to get in from the beginning, so, in 'forty-one, I left."

She asked, "Shall you be here long?"

"I don't know. I can't seem to settle down. I've never had much heart for the sugar business. And less now. I suppose that eventually I'll go back. And you?"

They talked easily, almost as old friends do. She said, "There's no incentive for me to return to Central America, Mr. Russell. And as Helen Lannis is my closest friend, I'd like to be near her. I expect to make some visits during the summer. But perhaps I'll return to New York to stay."

He said, "Our paths might not cross again unless we plan that they shall. May I call you at the Lannises' next week?"

"I wish you would." She added after a moment, "I admire you for what you are doing for Dick Johnson."

He said, "It may not stick, but I hope so. He's not the hopeless case his parents believe. There's nothing wrong with him but no interests and too much money. And the fact that ever since he was a kid his sterling-citizen brothers have been held up to him as examples, in sports, deportment, and scholarship. Dick's never liked sports, his deportment has always been an outward expression of rebellion, and his scholarship scanty. But I think he'll pull out of it. I became interested in him mainly because my brother, who was killed in Italy, was much the same type. And then I had time on my hands." He added, "Next week Dick is going south to be with his parents. I think it will be all right. If it isn't, I'll join them. Meantime I'll call you."

He stood quite close to her, and she was very conscious of it. She looked through the bare boughs delicately branched against the dark sky and thought that soon they would be misty green and later laden with bloom. She felt a longing for spring that was almost physical pain. And a lightness, a lifting of her heart. She thought, *He may not be drawn to me particularly, perhaps he is just being courteous. It would be too good to be true.*

Then to her astonishment he said just that, breaking their silence. "This is too good to be true," he said.

"What is?" she asked faintly.

"Meeting you," he answered.

Driving back to town, "Looks as if you've made quite a conquest, Terry," said Frank, at the wheel.

Helen, sitting between her husband and her friend, sensed the quick tenseness in Terry's body. But Terry answered lightly. "I dare say he was only being courteous, and perhaps he's so used to making conquests himself — "

"Not more accustomed than you," said Frank cheerfully. "You're an extremely good-looking couple, by the way. And how suitable an alliance it would be — sugar from Hawaii to Central America, practically a monopoly."

Helen warned, "Don't tease her, Frank."

"Why not?" he asked, astonished. He turned and looked across his little wife at Terry, and added, "The girl's actually blushing."

"It's the wind." Terry defended herself.

"Russell's a personable chap," Frank commented, "which is fairly unusual, when it comes gilt-edged. I like him, and he's doing a good job with young Dick. Most men of great means, particularly those who haven't earned their way, have, no matter how amiable, the taint of arrogance. It's discernible, no matter how hard they try; it has something of royalty about it. You can't help being conscious of this. When rich men run around embracing, so to speak, the taxi driver, the bartender, the average Tom, Dick, and Harry, I am always suspicious. 'Look at me, how democratic I am' is written all over them. Nor have I much patience with this pity-me-because-I'm-richer-than-mud attitude. I suppose they can't help it. Nevertheless, Mr. Average man, though generally dazzled and as snobbish as the next fellow, grows a little suspicious of the back slapping. All saving your pretty presence," he added, smiling.

Helen was amazed. "Longest speech I've heard him make since that night in London when he came home fried to the eyes, having met up with several old comrades in arms," she said.

Frank grinned. "Maybe it's envy. Who knows his own motives? But I generally take a dim view of the idle rich. Except Terry. And she, too, is rather unique, as the taint is not an exclusively masculine trait."

"*Mucho en el suelo, poco en el cielo,*" said Terry solemnly.

"Come again?" suggested Helen. "My knowledge of Spanish is confined to the few phrases you once taught me, a couple of which, I regret to say, were not wholly conventional."

"This is," Terry assured her. "It's one of those quote-unquote things. Old Maria was fond of saying it when I was especially trying. It means, 'Much on earth, little in heaven.' A Spanish version of the rich man, the camel, and the needle's eye, I suppose."

"You," said Frank generously, "are going to make a very handsome angel in about ninety years." He added, "But to return to our discussion — "

"Monologue," Helen corrected.

"You like Russell?" asked Frank.

That he addressed Terry there was no doubt. She answered, "I like him a great deal." She was obviously disturbed. The slight accent was more pronounced than usual, Helen thought.

"Good," said Frank genially. "And if I'm any judge, it is, as Miss Duffy is wont to say, mutual, I'm sure. Which will be wonderful for Helen and me. Look at the choice vacation spots we'd have, lolling in the sun by sea or on mountaintop."

"One if by land, two if by sea, or is it the other way round?" his wife inquired.

"Silence, woman," said Frank dreamily. "A glass of coconut milk, ice cold and laced with rum, a couple of beautiful gals to fan me — Hawaiian, Indian, it wouldn't matter — guitars playing, my choice of samba or hula — Truely, Terry, great vistas open up before me."

"Surely," inquired Helen, "you haven't been drinking at this horrid hour?"

It was very early in the morning, the Johnsons having persuaded their guests to remain until Monday. The air was cold and fresh, and the Parkway almost deserted.

Frank said, "I did my moderate tippling last night. I was interested to note that Russell

59

doesn't appear to need the genie in the bottle, or was that because of Dick?" He added, "I'll make an inquiry or two — you needn't dig your nasty little elbow into my side, Helen, we stand *in loco parentis* to Terry here, if my Latin is as correct as Terry's Spanish."

"Loco is right, at any rate," Helen murmured.

"Anyway, I feel somewhat responsible for her."

"How too fearfully British," said his wife, "man of the house, master of all the females in it."

"Not a bad custom," Frank suggested.

"Where," asked Terry blandly, "will you inquire?"

"Here and there. I know some people," he said obscurely.

"Christopher Russell is hardly a fortune hunter," said Helen, "if that's what you mean."

"That aspect hadn't occurred to me," said Frank, "in the circumstances. What I'm after is a character reference. How many discarded wives, if any, what vices, what virtues?"

Terry spoke with calculated laziness. She said, "Darling Frank, for an Englishman you are singularly quick on the trigger."

"I'm an American now," said Frank. "I

60

love to jump to conclusions."

Helen yawned, "You'll break a leg someday," she said.

Chapter Three

FOR MONEY — AND LOVE

Chris did not telephone for several days. Helen, Frank, and Terry went to dine with James Southard and his plain, delightful wife, and Terry spent the evening admiring the house, enjoying the dinner, exclaiming over the studio and the portraits, and parrying Southard's insistence that she sit for him. "How soon?" he demanded.

She slid out deftly enough. She wasn't at all sure of her plans; she was booked for a number of visits; she would just be in and out of New York for a considerable time.

Helen applauded with her eyes.

On Friday, at breakfast, Frank, who had come home late the night before, announced that his various spies and agents had made a complete dossier on Christopher Russell.

Terry said, "Interesting but unnecessary, as I haven't heard from him. For all I know he may be back in Honolulu by now."

"Of course," said Frank, ignoring that, "his war record is well known; when he first came to town it was in all the columns. That, and the heavy sugar." He beamed at the pun. "All I've learned bears it out, and is, I hasten to add, favorable. No wives at any time whatsoever; only child, parents deceased. Great lashings of relatives. Houses in Honolulu, also offices, also places on the other Islands plus an island all their own, invitations to visit which being scarcer than to Moscow."

"All this," said Helen, "is common knowledge."

"Newspaper knowledge. But I talked to chaps who have investments in Island properties," said Frank.

He was on the verge of departure for the brokerage office in which he labored when the telephone rang and Margaret reported that it was for Miss Austin. "A Mr. Russell."

"How fortuitous," said Frank, grinning. He kissed his wife, smote Terry on her shoulder, and went out whistling.

Helen followed Margaret into the kitchen, to discuss dinner. She closed the door firmly against the temptation to listen to Terry's side of the conversation. She sat perched on the high stool, her reading-glasses sliding down her short nose, a pad and pencil in her hand. She was greatly troubled. She thought, *If she really likes him?* She thought, *If she's in love with him? But that's nonsense*, she assured herself, and then she shook her red head, conscious of disloyalty. Had she not fallen in love with Frank the moment she laid eyes on him? Falling in love at first sight was far from impossible. Loving came later, and it was different; and not guaranteed, either. She and Frank were two of the lucky ones.

If, she thought, *Terry has fallen in love, and if Chris has, or does, she'll have to tell him, of course, but in this case it won't make any difference.*

Cheered, she returned presently to the living-room, which was empty of humanity, and then knocked at Terry's door. She found her scrabbling in the clothes closet, the door half open.

"Well?" demanded Helen.

"I'm lunching out," said Terry, her voice muffled. She emerged with a suit over her arm. She asked, "Isn't it wonderful that I still have clothes and can let down hems?" Her eyes were very bright, and a faint flush stained her high cheekbones.

"Where are you lunching?"

"I don't know. He's coming here to get me." She put the suit on a bed and asked distractedly, "What blouse? I wonder." She added, "Some place quiet, not a lot of people, no music. Just good food and conversation."

"Good grief," said Helen, "it must be serious!"

She sat down on the edge of the bed and added gently, "Terry, don't go rushing into things."

"I'm not. And if I am — " Terry paused. Then she said slowly, "I told you that my father was a gambler. I am, too."

Terry postponed her visit to the Cotters in Asheville. Dick Johnson had gone south to be with his parents, and no distress signal reached Chris. He stayed on in the Johnson apartment, having been, as he told Terry, courteously evicted from the hotel in which he had quarters when he first reached New York. "They permitted me to stay far longer than the allotted time," he told her, "and I don't like the idea of moving every seven days. The Johnsons were very kind, offering me the apartment until, at least, their return. There's a restaurant downstairs."

She had asked at the time, as casually as possible, "How long are you remaining in New York?" and he had smiled and answered, "That depends on a great many things, principally you."

"Me?"

"How long are *you* staying?" he'd countered, and after a moment they had both begun to laugh.

She saw him almost every day. Now and then they went to one of the publicized places, but not often. For if they did, it was sure to be in one of the columns the next morning. After an excursion to the Stork, Winchell wrote: *Terry Austin, beautiful heiress from Central America, and Chris Russell, Hawaiian sugar planter, are a very sweet twosome.*

"Suppose," she had suggested after that, "we really see New York — not just the other visiting firemen?"

If the columns, which were widely read, should reach anyone who was aware of her altered situation — and they were bound to, she thought wretchedly — then the explanations must be forthcoming before she was ready for them. Helen had asked her when. She had asked, "When are you going to tell Chris the truth?"

"Not now, and don't make it sound as if I had an insane husband or a maniac grandfather or had committed murder."

"Why not?" Helen had inexorably inquired.

"Because then he'll think — "

She broke off, and Helen asked, "What will he think? And won't it be true?"

It was then that Terry had said, her eyes grave and direct, "I suppose so, in one way; but not in another. Because I'm in love with him, Helen."

Achingly, wonderfully, frighteningly in love. He had not kissed her as yet; he had touched her only casually, conventionally, taking her hand when they met or parted, holding her in his arms when they danced. But she was continually aware of him when they were together, it was as if her breath were smothered, as if her flesh were informed with a terrifying languor.

For the rest of April and during early May they were tourists. "No stone unturned," he announced hardily, "not even Grant's Tomb." They explored the Village, walked in the Cloisters, rode on the Staten Island ferry. "It's done," he informed her, "in fact and fiction." They borrowed Frank's car and drove across the George Washington Bridge, and again across the Manhattan to Brooklyn, out the Shore Drive, and finally had lobster at Lundy's in Sheepshead Bay. They rode on busses and ate hamburgers in odd places; they went to the movies, looked out over the soaring towers from the top of the highest of them, by sunlight and again by night. And Mrs. Cotter wrote plaintively that if Terry didn't come at once, they would soon be leaving Asheville for Chicago — did Terry prefer to come to them there or wait until they went, for the summer, to Michigan?

She told Christopher that one night during

the second week in May when he came to dine with her, Frank and Helen having gone out.

"Business," said Helen. "Ask Chris to dinner. Margaret will cook you a honey and then retire to wash dishes. The perfect chaperon. Also, we won't be late."

"My duenna days are behind me."

"Even so," said Helen firmly, "Frank has very old-fashioned notions, and I don't mean the kind with orange peel!"

So Chris came to dinner, and afterward, when Margaret had taken the coffee service away, they sat in the living-room, and he sighed. He said, "This is better than the Staten Island ferry. I like this apartment. I like it better every time I come. I like your friends, too, Terry. There's something about them that is special."

She said quietly, "They love each other very much. And for such a long time they thought they would never be together again. I expect that has something to do with it."

He said, "It's nice being alone with you, which, to coin a phrase, is a masterpiece of understatement. We are never alone really, as unfortunately other people ride on busses, haunt museums, travel to the top of the Empire State."

She said, "I like it, too."

"You do?" He put out his hand and took

hers. That he felt humble, devoutly hopeful, and bemused by a miraculous enchantment, she had no way of knowing; nor he that her mood was as his own.

She did not take her hand away. She was as conscious of it as if it had been flayed or burned; conscious of it apart from the rest of her body, if not in pain.

She said, "The Cotters — I spoke of them to you — are leaving Asheville the end of the month. If I'm to go at all, it must be now. They are a little upset as I promised to go the first of May."

"Must you go at all?"

He was an essentially gay and casual young man. He had fallen in and out of love a dozen times, never from the initial moment believing that it would endure. After this fashion he had fallen in love, during an April weekend, but it had endured and would. She was everything of which he had ever dreamed, this girl with the soot-black hair and eyes of no determined color.

"I suppose so. I can't stay here forever. It isn't fair to Helen and Frank, for one thing. For another, I've promised so many people."

Her voice sounded strange in her ears, as if it had been recorded and she, coming into a room, heard the record being played and wondered, for a split second, *Who is that speaking?*

69

He said, "I didn't mean to tell you so soon. But then, you don't have to be told. I love you, Terry. I've been in love with you since that day at the Johnsons' — that evening, perhaps, when we walked on the terrace. Is there any possible chance that you could love me, too?"

She said, "I do love you, Chris," on a great breath of utter thankfulness and put her arms around him and lifted her mouth to his. She thought, closing her eyes, *We will be lucky, too, as Frank and Helen are* — And then she ceased to think.

A little later he asked her, "When will you marry me? Must we wait, darling?"

She answered, hardly knowing that she spoke. "Of course we needn't wait. I'll marry you whenever you say, Chris."

She heard him shout as a boy shouts, with astonishment, with triumph. His eyes blazed blue, incredulous. He asked, his arm hard about her, "Do you know what you're saying?"

"I think so. I'm not awfully sure. Let me go," she insisted, "just for a moment, so I can think properly."

She sat away from him a little and put distracted hands to her hair. She said, "But how about you? Your family, I mean. They'll want to come on. We can be married here. I'm sure that Helen will want that."

"My parents are dead," he told her. "Surely I told you that? As for the rest," he shrugged, "they'll be annoyed, some of them, but I don't suppose it will really matter beyond family vanity. And they're scattered all over the Islands, anyway. But you," he asked, "there must be people — "

"I have no relatives," she told him, "except what is left of my mother's family and I've never known them. Couldn't we be married here?" Then she asked quietly, "Just Helen and Frank, and those of your friends you wish?"

"The Johnsons?" he asked. "We owe them a great deal. Are you sure you want it this way? Most girls wouldn't. They'd want the trimmings."

She said slowly, "I used to believe I did, too — white dress, long train and veil, and flowers and a church crowded with people. And myself going up the aisle with my father. But since he died I've never thought about it. I wouldn't want it that way now."

He said, "It shall be as you want, darling." He caught her to him and held her. "I'm so idiotically happy, I'm not sane."

"Me, too," she said unsteadily.

He released her long enough to fish in his pocket. "Just in case," he said, "I brought it

71

along. I hope you like it, Terry. It was my mother's."

It was a simple ring, with an old-fashioned setting and a very fine diamond. He put it on her finger, and it shone there like a star, like sunlight on water.

She said, "I'd rather have it than anything else in the world."

After a long time, she asked, "Will we be going to the Islands?"

"Of course, if you want to, Terry."

"I've always wanted to. Are they wonderful, are they magical?"

"All changed since the war," he said, "or so I hear. Of course the little island hasn't, very much. It's somewhat like Niihau, which has been in the possession of the Robinsons since about 1864, but not, of course, as well known nor as legendary, yet almost as hard to crash if you're an outsider — and, like Niihau, privately owned. Not that any of the family is there much. The older generations were, but now, as I said, we're scattered — Honolulu, Kauai, the Big Island — "

She asked, "We'll live there, Chris?"

He said again, "If you like. We'll fly out and see. It will be up to you, darling. I haven't thought of settling down, until now — I've been too damned restless."

She put out her hand and touched his

cheek. "Not now," she said confidently, "not any more."

"Not any more," he repeated, and took her in his arms.

When Helen and Frank came home they drew apart and rose, and Helen without a word put her arms around Terry, and Frank pounded Chris on the back, and everyone talked at once. And presently Helen disappeared into the pantry and came back with cheese, crackers, and a bottle of champagne. "Our last," she said, "sacrificed in a worthy cause."

"A meager feast," complained Frank, eyeing it. "How about going out? I'll shout."

"He means he'll treat," said his wife. "He picked up some very Down Under expressions in Africa."

"Let's stay home," said Terry. She flushed beautifully. "I'd feel so — so exposed," she murmured.

So they stayed home, made their plans, and drank the champagne, and it was all like the wine in the glass, golden, sparkling, and heady.

After Chris had gone and Frank had dutifully taken himself off to bed, "You women will want to gab," he deduced brilliantly, Terry and Helen sat in Terry's bedroom, and

Helen turned the ring around on Terry's finger, for it was a little too large. She said, "It's beautiful. Terry, you're sure, and you're happy?"

"Never more sure, never more happy."

"Did you — tell Chris?"

"No." She looked startled for a moment. "I didn't think of it. I forgot entirely."

"You must, you know."

"I suppose so." She looked troubled, briefly. She said, "But it will sound silly, won't it? I mean, saying, 'Look, my father died bankrupt.'"

"I suppose it will. And it's odd," said Helen, "usually by the time people come to marry they know all about each other."

"Which isn't so," Terry denied, "and you know it."

"I mean, the surface things. I believe you're still scared Chris will think that you are marrying him because of what he has and not what he is."

Terry turned her head aside. She said painfully, "Yes, of course. I *have* known what it is to wonder, to be in doubt and realize that there's no way of knowing, none at all. There were two, maybe three men, at home whom I might have — despite differences in background, nationality, everything — but I never got further than that. I couldn't. There was always the crazy barrier, like barbed wire bristling with questions, sharp with doubting — Is it I, myself, or is it Mark Austin's daughter? So I could feel attracted, even excited, but never fall in love. I thought perhaps I never would — unless — " Her voice trailed off and she was silent.

Helen said, "All right, have it your own way. Perhaps I see your point. But when the time comes, and it must, for explanations, won't Chris look back and feel some of that doubt in retrospect?"

"No," said Terry, and her voice rose a little, "because by then he will be sure of me and of my love, so sure that nothing could ever shake it. By that time we'll be married, Helen," she said and thought, *We will belong to each other, and he can have no doubts.*

Chapter Four
BRIDE'S CONFESSION

Terry was married in a white gabardine suit, and a white batiste blouse exquisite with embroidery. She did not possess a hat, so Helen marched her out and bought her one, also white, with the faintest pink blossoms and a swirl of veiling. Her flowers were gardenias.

The Johnsons came, Gwen and Paul, Dick and his parents, and the ceremony was performed by the Lannises' clergyman. Afterward Margaret, supplemented by an extra maid, served the simple breakfast, and Frank opened the wine. The wedding was his gift, that and some silver which had belonged to his mother. "From Helen and me," he told Terry, "and to blazes with Chris for not letting me give him a bachelor dinner, small but select, and complete with hangover."

From Helen, the blue garters, the beautiful handkerchief, the bottle of perfume, and a check. She gave the check to Terry privately. She said, "It isn't much, darling, just — mad money. And it will keep you in stockings for a while."

"I won't need stockings," said Terry, bemused. "I'll live on a beach and eat fish and whatever the other things Chris talks about. Poi." She began to cry at that juncture. "I'm so happy and so grateful," she explained.

They had not known where to go on the wedding journey. Hawaii eventually, but before that, where? they asked each other. Chris suggested a number of places. Sea Island? He had been there, she would like it. Pinehurst? Dick's parents urged Asheville, or Virginia at this time of the year. And the other Johnsons offered their house "until you make up your mind," they said. "Not that our Susan is much of a cook, but what do you care?"

Paul was going on a business trip to the West Coast and Gwen with him. The boys would not be home until the middle of June, Sam was staying in school to take some examinations, and Paul Jr. going to visit a friend before returning. So the house was theirs. And it was where they had met, so entirely fitting for a honeymoon.

You couldn't buy a car for love or under-the-counter money on such short notice. But Chris was able to rent one for the short time they were to be in Connecticut, through a friend of Frank's. After that they would stay in town for a while and then decide. Chris had managed to wangle reservations.

There was rice in the rented car and in Terry's hair when, driving out of town, she took off the absurd pretty hat and shook her head vigorously. "But," she said, "thank heaven for civilized friends. No signs on the car itself!"

"I'm sign enough. Fatuous," said Chris, "positively smug. Don't let me drive too fast. I won't want to spend a day in the pokey. Not this day."

"Pokey?"

"I forgot that you still have things to learn about our language," he told her. "Jail, darling."

The Parkway was beautiful, the trees in new leaf, the orchards along the road wild with white and rosy bloom. It was a flawless day, warm and wonderful.

She said suddenly, "We don't know very much about each other, Chris, which seems strange, because we've talked and talked."

"But we do know," he assured her, "the essential things. I know all about you. You are afraid of snakes and not of mice, you like hot weather and hate the cold, you like green and white and gray and wood-violet, you like gardenias, yellow roses, and most tropical flowers. You are a Bing Crosby addict and a

78

Disney fan. I know most of your dislikes, including your curious distaste for ballet. I know your taste in music and in books — fairy tales, happy endings, poetry, French for choice. You don't like mysteries, on the screen or in books. I'll have to re-educate you there."

She said, "Is it enough to know each other's likes and dislikes?"

"It is enough," he said quietly, "to know each other's love."

And so they came, by the Parkway and back roads, to the house in the valley where Susan, greatly excited, was waiting for them. There were flowers from the spring garden downstairs and in the big guest room and new candles on the dining-room table waiting to be lighted.

Chris went off to take, he said, a look around, and Terry changed into the frock she loved best, and which Chris had never seen. She thought, *I wish I had trunks and trunks of new clothes I'd never worn.* But her trunks, full of clothes she had worn, were still at Helen's until their course was decided, and her furs were in storage.

The dress was long, the violet color she loved, and very plain, a beautiful dress. It had been made for her shortly before her father's death. It would always be in fashion. She put the pearls about her neck, the gleaming, double rope, and went downstairs to find Chris. The light was long and golden on the trees and hills.

Chris made cocktails in the pantry with Susan's fluttering help and brought them to the terrace. He went upstairs and fetched Terry a white coat, against the possible chill of sunset, and they sat there for a long time, had their drinks, and watched the rosy light deepen to dusky blue. And then it was dinnertime and they went in and faced each other in the flickering candlelight and did not know what they ate or drank — which was perhaps fortunate, because Susan, although carefully instructed by her employer, had been liberal with the salt and generous with the flame. The meat was slightly scorched, the vegetables like brine. Who knew or cared? Not even Susan.

Gwen had left them some wine. She said, "We hate the stuff, we're strictly Scotch or beer. Drink it up, it came from one of Paul's clients. And you won't get the bill," she had added, laughing, as she and Terry had discussed the provisioning of the house.

Burgundy, therefore, with the steak, a good vintage, and Médoc. Chris lifted his glass. "To us," he said, "and to the happily ever after."

After a week they returned to New York and took up their reservations at the hotel, in a suite overlooking the Park and with a mammoth living-room, "We can give a dance," said Chris, surveying it after the bellboys had gone. "May I have the pleasure, Mrs. Russell?" He held out his arms, she went into them, and they danced gravely around the room laughing immoderately. There was considerable mail on one of the tables — a note from Helen, sent by hand — when would Terry and Chris dine? she inquired — mail from the Cotters and others who had read the inconspicuous item that announced the marriage, mail for Chris, and cables. He showed a sheaf of them to his wife. "All of the clan," he said, "very congratulatory and when are we coming out?"

It was wonderful, the suite was full of management flowers, the weather not yet too warm, although neither of them would mind that, and Chris said, "Let's celebrate."

"Again?"

"Always."

He telephoned downstairs for theater tickets, and cajoled the agency into producing them; he telephoned, later, for dinner, which came up on a table, with rosebuds in a silver vase, the entree in a portable oven, wine in an ice bucket. And Terry put on a long frock, and they went to the theater, and afterward to a dance.

During the following week, they dined with Helen and Frank, with the Southards, Jim Southard drawing Chris aside to say, "You simply must persuade your wife to sit for me. I thought her strikingly attractive before but now she is beautiful," and with all the Johnsons, at the home of young Dick's parents. Dick was all right, he was going to take his examinations, he would get into college this time, for sure, he promised.

Friends and parties and window-shopping, lazy mornings and late nights, and then Terry sitting up in bed and yawning, at the end of the week. "I must pull myself together and buy some clothes. Oh, not many — just town things for summer if we're staying any length of time."

The desk sent up the papers and mail, most of it for Chris. The breakfast table was wheeled into the living-room and Terry got out of a shower into some lingerie and a robe and went to pour the coffee. She was drinking hers when Chris asked amiably, "Can you let me have some money, darling?" He waved an envelope. "The bill," he said.

"Money?" She got up and went into the bedroom. She thought, *This is it*. She had a little in her purse, ten or twelve dollars. The insurance check was not due until July first. She had the check Helen had given her, not yet cashed. She brought the purse back in the room, her heartbeat accelerated, dumped the bills and coins on the table, and put Helen's check on top. "With all my worldly goods I thee endow," she said.

Chris turned over bills and coins with a fastidious finger and looked at the check. He said, "I didn't mean change, Mrs. Miser."

She sat down on the big couch, shut one hand hard in the other and heard him say, half absently, "If you'd write a check, perhaps — "

She said steadily, "I can't, Chris. I have no bank account. Just the little check each month from my father's insurance. I didn't tell you because — " She swallowed hard. "Helen knows," she began again, "she is the only one who does know. She wanted me to tell you before this but I thought it wouldn't matter, how could it? But I was afraid that if you knew you would think that I — "

"Knew what?" he asked, swinging around to look at her.

She said, "It's a long story, but my father died bankrupt, Chris. I haven't any money, none at all."

He was quite still for a moment, and then he began to laugh. He laughed and laughed, while she sat there shaking, watching him.

Then he rose, went over to her, and swept her up into his arms. "So you are Mark Austin's daughter," he said, "but you haven't any money. And neither, my darling, have I!"

Terry stood very still within the hard circle of his arms. Then she asked in the loud, un-inflected voice of shock, "What are we going to do?"

"Eat," replied Chris. "Even if we can't pay for it, it's available. We might as well fortify ourselves. Only a fool faces ruin on an empty stomach. In this case, two fools, two empty stomachs."

She shook her dark head. "I can't," she said faintly. She released herself, went to the couch, and sat down. She added, after a moment, "But I don't understand. You're Chris Russell." She looked at him, her eyes widening. "Or," she asked, low, *"aren't you?"*

Chris came and sat beside her. He laid his arm lightly over her shoulders, and answered, "I am Chris Russell, my darling, but not the right one."

Incredulously Terry asked, "Is there another?"

"Certainly. My estimable cousin, who is a couple of years older than me. We were both named for our mutual grandfather. Cousin Chris, who is sometimes called Stinky, comes complete with heavy sugar, not all of it in

84

cane, a set of doting parents, who have even more, plantations, stock, houses, islands — the works. A fine, upstanding lad, Stinky. Excellent scholar, conservative gentleman, hard-working, and intent upon the principle that them as has gits. Also, he is very agile. One of the most eligible men in the Islands, he has so far safely escaped the matrimonial halter. You bet on the wrong horse, Terry."

"But I still don't understand. Surely, if your father and your cousin's father were brothers — " she began in bewilderment.

"Mine," said Chris, "was a bad boy. He hated the sugar business and wouldn't play on the family team. Also the Russell wives were, in those days at least, hand-picked by elder members of the family. My mother did not come from missionary or pioneer stock. She worked for her living, quite respectably, in a shop on King Street. Her grandmother was Hawaiian. The family had no objection per se to the Polynesian blood — there is plenty of it in Island families and most of them are proud of it. But Mother was not, as it were, of chief or royal blood. Also, when very young she had been married and divorced. Divorce is not countenanced among the sacrosanct Russells. Marriage, however unhappy, is not held lightly; it is to be endured. So Pop had two strikes against him to begin with, and Grandfather cut him off with a small annual allowance. It was ample, however, to feed and clothe us and do what Pop liked most, which was travel. He, my mother, and I roamed the world over. Now and then he sat down and wrote, which resulted in one bad novel, some excellent journalism, and a book of minor verse. We were happy together."

"Chris — " She put her hand up and took his, and held it. "Go on."

"When my grandfather died," Chris went on, "he left my father a sum of money in trust. The income equaled the allowance. And when my parents died in a railroad accident — it was in Paris, I was twelve years old and had been left behind that day in the hotel — I inherited this. I returned to the Islands to live with my aunt and uncle. They sent me to college on the mainland when the time came. It was kind of them, as they often reminded me. The gimmick was that I must return to the Islands and go to work, in a lowly capacity, in order to learn the business. A life job, you see, and eventually under Cousin Christopher. It was all pointed out to me, my good fortune. If I married well, it would better matters. Numerous girls were trotted out for family inspection all of whom knew my status as a poor relation. But the name out-weighed that, or so my aunt Cordelia thought; while Uncle

Hugo was, he said, willing to make financial concessions if a proper alliance was established. And a more lucrative job if I worked hard and married correctly. Also, he might even consider leaving me some stock — "

"Why didn't you?"

"Work or marry?"

"Both."

"I must be a romanticist at heart. The girl didn't materialize. The only girl in the Islands who — " He paused, and she saw his eyes cloud. He shrugged. "Hell," he said, "she was married."

Terry felt a curious twinge like a stitch in her side. She said, "I see. What about work?"

"But I don't like to work," he said cheerfully. "I did during vacations — hard labor, dear, to prove myself both democratic and a Russell. But after I left college, in that brief interlude before war, I was promoted to *luna* — overseer to you. The whistle blew for work at four-thirty. Morning, not afternoon. By six, rain or shine, I was riding up and down a stretch of cane field. At first, saddle sores and screaming muscles. But it passed. By three-thirty I was through. And I'm telling you, *through*. The war was an escape. They were talking of having me serve a term in the office, another in the mill. I was to learn the business from the ground up, and I do mean the ground."

Terry asked, "Was your cousin in the service?"

"Natch."

She swallowed. Everything was unreal — herself, Chris, the room in which they were holding this incredible conversation.

"Which one of you was torpedoed?"

"I was. And I don't blame you for the crack. Mind you, my ship was not torpedoed because the enemy command realized I was aboard. Nor was the procedure anything but very uncomfortable. I was lucky. As many medals are given for luck as for valor." He grinned. "Besides, no one would have the gall to torpedo my cousin Christopher."

"Hasn't he another name? This is very confusing."

"Isn't it? But also, you must admit, fortuitous. Has it not brought me a beautiful wife?"

"Chris, please — "

He said, "Relax, Terry. Somehow we have to find a little humor in the situation. When we were kids I called the dear boy Stinky, a term he much resented, being as clean as the proverbial hound's tooth — how clean is that? You are bitten, you may get an infection, too. Pardon the digression. As my senior, he was entitled to be Chris the elder. But his middle name is John, and he prefers it. There is something so reliable about John. So everyone called him that to distinguish him from me. Not that it was hard to do, looking at us or our records. But I haven't a middle name. Okay, so we will settle for Jack, my esteemed cousin. I could call him names, and with pleasure, but he was born in exceptionally holy wedlock. Jack also went to war. He was in the army. He returned unscathed. No bullet would presume to have his name on it."

Terry asked, "But your brother, Chris? The one you spoke about when I first met you." She halted. It seemed a long time ago, a lifetime of excitement and happiness compressed into weeks.

"That was Bob," he said gravely. "He was younger than me, and not very strong. He was born about two weeks after my aunt Cordelia's second and stillborn child. My mother couldn't nurse Bob, so Aunt Cordelia did. He became the apple of her eye. And when my parents started their peregrinations and took me with them, Aunt Cordelia kept Bob. I think she was fonder of him than of her own child, and with reason. He was a gay little boy, and looked like the Russells. He did all they expected of him and more — went through school with honors, came back to work, hated it, and was too grateful to clear out. You see, they'd adopted him when our parents died. So Bob drank — and then he was killed, in Italy. Aunt Cordelia has not forgiven me. If one of us had to drink, why not me? If one of us had to be killed, why not me, the worthless Russell?"

He stubbed out his cigarette and went on. "That's the pitch, Terry. People on the mainland, at least in the East, confuse me with my cousin. I don't deny that I am Chris Russell of the Honolulu Russells. Why should I? I am. No one has ever asked, 'Of which branch of the family?' They don't know anything about branches. Unlike most Island families, the Russells don't frequent the mainland. Oh, we have cousins with a place in San Mateo, and elsewhere. But none of the lot ever comes East. Too cold, they say. As for Uncle Hugo, Aunt Cordelia, and Jack, they don't ever go to the West Coast except, in Uncle Hugo's case, on business."

She asked, her voice tight, "How do you live?"

"As I've always done. I travel light. The income from the trust fund takes care of the extras. I can wear casual, even shabby clothes — a rich man can get away with that, dear. After I was discharged from the navy I banged around Mexico a bit. It cost little and was entertaining. I like people and odd places and I don't care where I sleep nights. When I finally came East, I became a charming guest, an eligible bachelor. For, with board and roof gratis, I could afford the gracious gesture toward my hostesses and the calculated tip."

She started to say, "How can you?" She didn't. She laughed instead, and Chris asked anxiously, "You're not going hysterical on me, Terry?"

"No. It just sounds so idle, so worthless, so inexcusable and dishonest. Yet, how can I condemn you? It's what I'd begun to do, and what I planned to go on doing."

"So?" he asked steadily.

"You haven't asked me about my father, Chris."

"I was too busy giving you my dossier. I lost sight of the fact that with you, too, all is not gold that glitters." He grinned. "Tell me," he said.

She told him the whole story as she had told it to Helen, and more, as Helen knew so much of what had gone before. And after she had finished, he said gently, "Well, you poor kid."

"Literally, I suppose?"

"That, and otherwise, for you and your father were devoted. But, you see, although I was fond of my parents, Terry, they shut me out. Not that they weren't good to me. But

91

they were so devoted to each other that they had little to spare. Bob was cared for, and if Aunt Cordelia — who was also born a Russell and is a distant cousin of her husband's — had been as besotted over me as she was over Bob, they would have given me to her, too. But she didn't like me much, so they had to take me along, the third wheel." He added quickly, "Don't get the idea that I have acquired a neurosis or something fashionable and extenuating. I just acquired, I dare say, an allergy to work. I have never found anything I actually *want* to do. I don't like the sugar business. I don't like the passion for toil that motivates my uncle, my cousin, and the other relatives — there are many of them scattered around the Islands. And I did like the way my father lived, by his wits, perhaps, and hand to mouth, but he had a hell of a good time. So I was just easing along until something came up."

"A rich wife?"

"Well, that, too, if I could fall in love with her. A very difficult condition. I have met a number of pretty girls with money. They do exist. I dare say I could have managed gracefully. But I didn't want to. I wanted to fall in love — and did, with you."

"Thinking that the gilt was on the gingerbread?"

"Thinking just that; and how damned lucky I was."

She said, closing her eyes and leaning against him, "I had much the same idea. Helen was deeply distressed because I didn't want to do all the expected things, carve a career, work in a shop, or model clothes."

He said, "That's easy to understand. You were brought up with a checkbook in your hands. Its loss is recent. I haven't that excuse; either I took pot luck with my crazy, impoverished, delightful parents or I ate the bread — and sugar — of avuncular charity."

She said, "I suppose we aren't any good, either of us."

"Not, in any case, useful. Merely decorative."

She was silent for a long time. The telephone rang, and Chris answered. He picked up the instrument, spoke into it, made routine pleasant noises. "It's for you, dear," he said. "A Mrs. Cotter."

Audrey Cotter, with whom she was to have spent the spring in North Carolina. If she had done so —

She went to talk to Mrs. Cotter, and presently said, "I don't know, Mrs. Cotter, I'll have to ask Chris."

She put her hand over the mouthpiece. "They want us for dinner tonight.

93

St. Regis roof," she said.

"Natch," said Chris. "Have we a choice?"

She spoke into the transmitter. "We'd love to. Yes, at eight."

When she hung up, he asked, "Who are they?"

"Middle-aged," she said vaguely, "and nice. We entertained them a number of times — at home — " Her voice trailed off. "Chris," she asked, "what are we to do?"

"You asked that before. First, we pool our resources and pay our hotel bill. Then we get the hell out, if we can manage an invitation somewhere and keep on wangling invitations until we have built up a backlog — enough to get us back to the Islands, if necessary. We can always stay there awhile. Uncle Hugo will bend all his energies persuading me to go to work; Jack will bend his, persuading me not to — he doesn't even like minor competition. But it's a roof, while it lasts."

The room waiter knocked, and Terry called, "Come in." Chris went over to the breakfast table, picked up the loose money and check and put them on the desk. The waiter regarded the condition of the table and clucked sadly. So little eaten, such a waste. But these were honeymooners.

Chris sighed, fished in the pocket of his dressing-gown, and put the tip on the table.

The door shut behind the waiter, and Terry said, "Helen's check. We can cash it, but it won't cover the week here. I could ask her to lend me money — she offered to when I first came to New York. But then, she'd *know*."

"The trick," Chris warned her, "is not to let anyone know. Otherwise fewer, if any, invitations. Impecunious charming couples are a dime a dozen. At that, even well-heeled, and I use the word advisedly, we are not so valuable a property from the hostess's standpoint as when we were unmarried and apparently so eligible. Still, any good hostess can always use us."

Terry was very pale. Her voice shook when she spoke. She said, "I do feel very odd."

"Delayed shock." He came over to sit beside her. "Put your head down," he ordered.

"I'm not going to faint!"

"Down, on my shoulder. There."

She said, "Chris, I have some assets. The pearls, my emerald ring. My mother's antique jewelry is of little intrinsic value, I suppose, but there are my furs, and" — her voice began to go out of control — "my engagement ring."

"That," said Chris, "has been in hock, not for the first time. With an eye to the future, I always got it out when I could. I had my father's evening studs, so I sold them. Dick Johnson has showered me with gifts, a set of studs among them, and his parents gave me a watch. I still have those. I sold my cigarette case, too."

Terry spoke, low. "I don't *want* to sell my things. I can't bear to. You see, I've never cared much about jewelry. My father gave me other things instead, except the emerald and the pearls. And because he gave me those and I was permitted to keep them, I thought I'd starve before I'd ever sell them."

"Maybe you will, then. You mustn't sell them, Terry. The hell of this situation is, we have to keep up the façade, have to trim the Christmas tree, have to illuminate the legend. Therefore, we can't borrow, nor can one of our emeralds be suddenly missing."

Terry drew away from him. She said slowly, "I was very honest with Helen, and it appalled her. She said so. It didn't me. I had no talents, and no grim do-or-die character traits. It didn't seem very reprehensible to me to believe that someday, in the environment I was determined to keep, I would meet a man I could love and marry."

"Same here," said Chris; "substituting a girl I could love. Well, we have that."

Terry looked at him. She asked, "Just what have we, Chris?"

"Youth," he replied promptly, "good looks — beauty in your case, personality in mine."

96

He laughed, his eyes very blue. "And, if I may say so, a terrific amount of nerve. We can see it through. We can coast. I know all the angles, and you can learn. Then we'll go out to the Islands." He paused and added, "Uncle Hugo is quite a character. He is of another world and generation. But he's always had an eye, properly downcast, for the ladies. When he married he chose double security. Aunt Cordelia is no beauty. So, I have an idea you could charm dear Hugo. And if you do —"

"Suppose he insists that you go to work?" she interrupted.

"Why should I," he asked lazily, "with a rich wife?" He bent to kiss her cheek, just at the corner of her mouth. "Uncle Hugo prefers to dispose of his mortal holdings where there is already a holding, so to speak. He might not leave money to an improvident nephew, but his nephew's wife is another matter — Why do you draw away?"

"I have no patience with either of us," she said.

"Of course not. I should be out looking for a job and a cold-water flat; you should be out looking for a job, too. Terry, do you love me?"

"I'm in love with you, Chris. You don't get over that from one minute to the next," she said slowly.

"But you fell in love with a different man,

97

didn't you? He looked just like me, but wasn't."

"Perhaps so. And the same holds true of you. You fell in love with Mark Austin's daughter. You didn't know about Mark Austin then. We couldn't detach each other from our backgrounds, so we fell in love with the backgrounds, too. Chris, if you'd known, what would you have done?"

"Run like hell. One look at you, that day, and I would have smelled danger. I wouldn't even have stayed for dinner, darling, and you wouldn't have seen me again."

She said, "And if I had known I wouldn't have wanted to — that is, even if I had wanted to, I wouldn't have."

"What remains?" he asked, after a moment.

"We're married, Chris, and — we are in love." She waited. She added, in a small voice, "Aren't we?"

He caught her close and kissed her. "It's sad and absurd, and it serves us both damned well right, but we are, we are!"

She thought that, shorn of what she had termed background, love was something else again; it was no longer that of legend and the fairy tale, it was honest and sharp, it saw the flaws and the weaknesses, and admitted the strong, compelling pull of an almost frightening physical attraction.

He said, "Okay, so we'll make a bargain. Play it my way for a while, Terry, and see what happens. If another man comes into the picture, the sort of man you thought I was, I'll bow out gracefully."

"That goes for me, too," she said, her heart tight and sorrowful, imagining it. "If there's another woman — "

"Shake," said Chris, and held out his hand.

She put her own in it. It was very cold, and he held it hard. He said, "But there's the gimmick, remember. We have to be in love — again, you with the unknown gentleman, blast him, and me with the hypothetical heiress."

"Of course."

"Not of course. One rarely risks an illusion the second time. But we, we are different. Crazy, both of us." He released her, rose, went over to the desk, looked at the money, and turned out his own pockets. He asked thoughtfully, "When did you say your next check is due?"

"July first."

"Mine, also. Until then — " He shrugged. "I'll get rid of some of the trinkets. That Johnson watch is a nice little gadget; tells you what day it is, as if we cared. Also it's platinum. We can pay our bill. Terry, did you say you had once planned to visit the Cotters?"

"Yes. In Asheville. I don't know where they will go now. I was going to Newport or to the Cape — I had several invitations."

"We will latch on to the first and make our plans from then on out," Chris said.

She said dimly, "No one would think it odd if you wanted to work; many men in your supposed circumstances do. In fact, people hire them just because they don't need the money."

"In a broker's office, perhaps? I know nothing about Wall Street, care less. Has it occurred to you that I am your masculine counterpart, that perhaps the two halves of which we read as kids have really been reunited? I ride, I play polo, I swim, I play tennis and golf — all well, but not professionally. I play good contract, and rarely lose money. I do not play for high stakes. It's well known that men who have always had means, inherited means, rarely do. We leave that, and other forms of gambling, horses, dice, the wheel, to those who earn their money, to the gentlemen who become suddenly rich, and to the professionals — I could, of course, be a waiter or a valet," he said, and smiled at her. "I know how one should be served and dressed."

"Chris!"

She thought, *No, not now.* Later perhaps, something might turn up. There are always men who ask, Would you be interested in this job or that, for the fun that's in it? But not now. She thought, *He would go out, he would find something if I stormed, made scenes, if I said I was willing for everyone to know — but he'd hate me.*

She shrank from that, wincing as if his hate were already directed toward her, an arrow, poisoned and barbed, in her flesh. Furthermore, she realized with clarity, she did not want people to know about her father if it could possibly be avoided. Nor about Chris Russell, of the other branch of the family; nor how you set a thief to catch a thief.

Her head ached. She said desolately, "I can't go out tonight."

"Yes. And look your prettiest. But you will never do that. Each day you are prettier than yesterday. Tomorrow even more so. I'll dress, Terry, and go out to consult the uncle who drives as hard a bargain as dear Hugo, and we will pay our debts. Meanwhile you will lie down, take a bromide, and try to sleep. And in the afternoon, because neither of us wants lunch — "

"I think I'll be hungry by lunchtime," she said.

"Then we'll have lunch and go over to the Park and look at the animals in their cages. We may be broke, but we are free. Or are

101

we?" he asked her. "Are we?"

She did not speak, following him into their bedroom, listening to the roar of the shower, watching him come out, a towel belted around him, watching him dress. She lay down on her bed and closed her eyes, and he came presently to put his shaven cheek against hers. He said, "Terry, we'll make out. If you can bring yourself to believe it, it will be fun, because we have each other. It's often a lonesome business, otherwise. But at night, in the best guest rooms of all the best people, we can look at each other and laugh. After a while, you won't mind the ice being thin."

"Chris, someday, somehow, people are sure to learn about my father."

"We can keep on moving," he said; "they'll still have to catch up with us. I've been wondering if perhaps the word has reached the Islands — about your father, I mean. Which reminds me. It was Hugo and Aunt Cordelia who visited your father in Guatemala. They spoke of it in their cable. Do you remember them at all?"

"I wasn't there, Chris. Father wrote me about it."

Chris went over to the door mirror and looked at himself in it and at her lying on the bed. She saw him smile in reflection. He said, "Well, we'll risk it."

102

Terry felt drowsy, limp with fatigue, as if all her vitality had been drained from her. This had been going on within her for a long time, ever since Mark Austin's death; and she was sick of it. Only for a little while had she known respite and alleviation. Now it began all over again, the makeshifts, the mask, the self-control.

Chris turned. He said, "Here, only Helen Lannis realizes your situation, as far as we know; and she doesn't know about mine. You've had to have someone to confide in, and she's your closest friend. But from now on in you have me, and only me. For better or worse, remember?"

She moved her dark head on the pillow and answered in a remote voice, "I remember telling Helen that you needn't be on your guard with me; that you'd feel I, at least, wasn't fortune hunting. Perhaps you felt the same way about me?"

"Check," he said cheerfully. "Which reminds me, I'll bring you a pen, and you can endorse Helen's check." He did so, and she sat up to write her name across the back of the check, twice; *Teresa Austin*, as the check was drawn, and then *Teresa Austin Russell*.

Chris put the check in his pocket. "I'll be back soon. And as to how I feel about you, darling — "

He bent to kiss her, and said, straightening up, "Genuine, and without alloy. All the vanished Austin money plus the Russell interests can't buy that, Terry."

"It's mutual, I'm sure," she said primly, making an effort, watching the light and laughter in his eyes. When the living-room door closed behind him, she lifted her eyes and looked at the electric clock on the mantel of the bedroom fireplace. It was a fraud, masquerading as an antique.

Hours before he returned. Hours in which she had to try to think this thing through.

It serves me right, she told herself, *and it serves him right.*

They were out of step with the hurrying, ambitious, forward-surging world, she thought drearily. Why? The answers were easy enough — lack of character, inherent weakness, failure to conform. *Go on, list all the rest — laziness, dependence on the luxuries, wanting to have your cake and eat it, life-long. For love* and *money,* she thought bitterly.

She looked at herself as dispassionately as possible. It wasn't hard, she had been doing it ever since a plane spun downward, and a life went out in flames on a mountain top. Spoiled, softened, without fiber, dependent for more than twenty years on a way of life, fabulous and incredible, in which everything had been made as easy as dreaming. Even at school, the communal life, the discipline, had been a game to play; for, there also, there had been the little extras, the benevolent granting of privileges, the overlooking of this minor divergence or that. The money snobbery had crept in there, too. Terry was "allowed" the special treat, she was exhibited as schoolgirl hostess when guests came for tea, "and this is little Terry Austin." She had not recognized it then, the taint, the exemptions, and freedom. For she had never thought about money, not knowing its lack. Her friends had been selected because of their appeal, not because of their parents' solvency. It wasn't until after Mark Austin's death that she looked back and saw the hundred signposts.

A lily of the field, she toiled not, neither did she spin. And there was something lacking in her, in her character, something necessary and decent, which simply was not there. She turned her head and looked at her father's picture on the night table. A strong man, people said, and had called him unimaginative, ruthless. A poor boy grown into a man who took what he wanted. But one thing he had not been able to take — defeat, failure, the collapse of a private world. So he hadn't been strong, after all.

If he had faced it and seen it through, taken

his punishment, fought his way, if not back, then at least to some measure of success —

I would have been there, she thought.

But he had not wanted her there. He had not wanted to face her either, nor wished to take her with him into a painful and shameful abdication, the kingdom lost, the cheers silenced, the throne deserted.

So he'd left her to face it by herself and without any weapons except those which were accidental, her appearance, for one; and those which he had forged for her, the poise of a young woman who had always been secure, the self-control —

And all the amenities. She knew how to order a meal, how to direct a staff, how to greet a guest or take leave of a hostess; she knew how to walk as if she wore a crown, how to dress, how to smile, how to listen. But very little else.

With Chris it was different. He had been brought up in much the comparable manner during his early years, yet never feeling that he belonged, feeling on the fringe, believing that he had been deprived of something which rightfully belonged to him. The result was, in a measure, the same.

Chris hated the industry that had enriched his grandfather but not himself. You couldn't work for a system you hated. And he was not equipped for anything else.

Why? He was intelligent and attractive, he got along with people and had, she suspected, a capacity for concentration which meant a capacity for work.

The answer was, he didn't want to work.

She had already sensed in him an enormous restlessness. It hadn't seemed to matter at the time. During their stay at the Johnson house he had talked to her with increasing freedom about his navy service, and the men he had known. He had spoken sometimes as if he almost regretted that it was over and behind him, as if when the war ended he had lost a drive, an incentive to live, which was a little mad, as only his luck had kept him alive.

Excitement, living from one moment to the next, under an inflexible discipline which was beyond his control, carrying his first grave responsibilities, yet, in a sense, free of the other responsibilities — those of civilian life. She could see this dimly.

Nothing could have been more ironical than their encounter, one with the other; nothing more punishing. Somewhere something or someone had laughed, loud and long. For the attraction between them was as real as poverty and as rewarding as riches, for as long as it lasted. How long would it last, she wondered, aching all over as with a physical illness, how long could it endure?

Longer, no doubt, if the legend had not been just that — a legend of lovers cushioned on ease, protected by security, veiled from the harsher realities.

Sooner or later they must come to the end of this precarious road upon which they must pick their way with the utmost care, and then what would happen?

Anything could premise the end — an idle word spoken over cocktails, an item in a newspaper.

Or if, she thought, in sudden terror, *or if I have a child.*

You couldn't go on being perennial guests, charming adjuncts to someone else's lavish hospitality, you couldn't go on being as decorative and parasitic as the orchids she had seen blooming, with a baby. Babies weren't invited to make dinner conversation, take a hand at contract, play a set of tennis, dance with the difficult business partner. Babies didn't fit into the picture at all.

What was the ideal marriage? Companionship as well as passion, sobriety as well as laughter, a community of tastes, of beliefs, and of ambition — a gradual, steady building of something that would last.

She thought, *We have a community of tastes, none of which we can satisfy.* As for beliefs, she did not know what she or Chris believed. As for companionship, she had thought they shared it, but now she did not know. Companionship in a hotel suite, a country estate, a private South Sea island was one thing; it would be quite another in a cramped furnished room, a matchbox house in an ugly suburb, or — what had Chris said? — a cold-water flat.

If one of them had been different —

Her head ached violently, her thoughts spun in circles. She experienced a blinding contempt, more depleting than anything she had ever known; contempt of herself, shameful and sickening, contempt for Chris, with whom she had fallen in love; contempt, for the first time, for Mark Austin, whom she had loved for over twenty years, who had been the most generous, the most wonderful, the most admirable of parents.

She could not weep for herself, but she could weep for Chris and for her father.

Much later the telephone rang, and she answered it with an effort. She must have been crying for a long time, and then fallen asleep briefly. Her voice was hoarsened with tears, her eyes hurt and were swollen, her throat felt raw, and her head was a separate misery.

"Yes?"

"Terry? Is that you, Terry?"

She cleared her throat. "Yes," she said. "Mrs. Cotter?"

She recognized the light, hurrying voice of the older woman, who had been one of her father's many guests. He was lavish in his entertainment of the Americans who came his way.

Terry thought, *The dinner engagement is off*, and felt a pang of terror wholly out of proportion to the occasion.

Audrey Cotter asked, "Is your husband there?"

"Why, no," Terry answered, "he's gone out, but he'll be back soon. Why?"

She waited, trembling.

"Nothing — except I thought I'd have a word with you alone if possible. We're going down to Southampton tomorrow. Bill and I were talking about it. The staff has gone on ahead to open the house. These houses," said Mrs. Cotter in despair, "open one, close the other — "

A place in Asheville, a villa in Florida, the Long Island cottage, the Chicago apartment —

She added, "Have you any plans, Terry?"

"Why, no, not at the moment. I had promised one or two people — but then," she added, and found herself laughing quite naturally, "I up and married. We're going to

110

Chris's home in the Islands, of course, but we haven't decided when. Honestly, we haven't had time."

"Would it be too deadly," asked Audrey Cotter, "if you came down to us? We'd love it. Bill's so restless, you've no idea what happens to a man when he retires. It's dreadful. Terry, I hardly dare ask it, but this is our second season on Long Island, we don't know many people. Will it be too deadly for you with a couple of old fogies?"

They didn't know a great many people. They would like to. Terry Austin, Chris Russell, drawing-cards separately or together. Terry's mouth was a straight red line. This was the way she had to play it. All right, she would. And close to the chest.

She said vaguely, "I'm sure we'd love it, but, I don't know what Chris has in mind for the next few weeks or so."

Mrs. Cotter said eagerly, "Oh, a real visit, Terry — not just a week. I spoke to Bill, and he said I was crazy, that you'd be off on a honeymoon somewhere."

"Officially, we have been," said Terry, "and we haven't looked ahead for a day. There is no sense in getting an apartment, when we may go to Hawaii at any moment. And we can't keep the hotel suite, they just won't let you any more. My trunks are all stored at my friend's, Helen Lannis, and I've never even asked Chris where his things are."

Mrs. Cotter found it very romantic and said so. She added, "Well, talk it over with him, dear, and then tonight perhaps we can persuade you."

Terry hung up. She went into the bathroom to bathe her eyes, to get under a stinging shower. She thought, *Well, it begins. So far, so good.*

Chapter Five
Long Island Summer

The Cotter place, extravagantly built in the early twenties, had been designed with costly simplicity. The house, slightly bigger than a barn, was a wooden structure which sprawled in all directions, the bedrooms very large and en suite, and the dining-room so immense that it was small wonder the Cotters liked entertaining, whether they themselves were or not. The living-room was vast, and there were the customary playrooms and powder rooms, telephone nooks and far-flung porches. One of the features of the house was a mammoth bar and, in the cellar, the wine bins, as the original owners, keenly aware of Prohibition, had seen to it that no wine of theirs would ever taste of the cork.

This cozy dwelling was called the Cottage, and its shingles had weathered to a pleasant silver-gray.

There was a garden, informal, and another garden, formal, and then a private path to a private beach, ruffled into arching dunes and slipping down to the ocean, which ate at the sands steadily by day and by night.

The Cotters were nice people; they were also dull, pleasant, anxious to please, and friendly. Audrey was round as an apple, no matter what she did about her diet and no matter how her dressmakers pleaded. She was firmly laced, her bosom was ample and high. Her hair was probably gray and, improbably, chestnut. She had large hazel eyes, a button mouth, and the skin of a child. Terry liked her very much; and she liked Bill Cotter, who suffered from boredom, hypertension, and the inferiority complex of the self-made man, which sometimes expressed itself in tempers and arrogance. But he was a good sort.

There were no children, which had saddened these two for the thirty-odd years of their marriage.

On the first evening, after they had driven down, seen the house, been told about the hurricanes and what had happened to it and how Bill had picked it up for a song, Chris inquired, "What does Cotter do?"

He was tying his tie and looking in the mirror. The big room was all maple, hand-blocked linen, and bowls of roses. The windows were open, the air cool and fresh, smelling of roses and salt.

"Nothing, now," Terry answered. She was

opening a clothes closet. Her frocks hung there, some had been whisked away to be pressed. She was thinking, *They'll do; they'll have to.* She had taken what she needed for the country from the luggage at Helen's, explaining, "We aren't going to keep the hotel suite, we can't, they won't permit us. Darling, if I may leave this stuff here for a time — "

Helen had asked, "But haven't you any plans?"

"We're going to the Islands," Terry had told her, "but not, I think, until autumn. I've promised people — " She let her voice trail off and then added, "After these duty visits are over, perhaps we'll go out and stay on the Coast before sailing."

Now she took down a plain white dinner frock, quite unrelieved. It was fortunate that she had always preferred line and material to anything else in clothes. No extremes, no doodads. She could wear something a hundred times and no one would remember it. For the country old tweeds, worn to a soft blur, were always the best; and for warmer weather her wide full cotton skirts and embroidered blouses, as these were timeless. A fad now in the States but routine uniform back home.

Chris asked, "Nothing? He certainly does it more profitably than I can."

She said, "Oh, oil or something like that,

once. He sold out, went to Chicago and had a finger in various pies. Then he retired altogether. They go to Asheville in spring and autumn, to Florida in winter, or sometimes take a cruise." She added, "Chris, will you be bored?"

"Possibly. But don't be upset by the prospect. I shall sing for my supper."

They dressed and went down for cocktails. The pearls were like cream around Terry's young throat, the emerald on her hand a deep, angry green.

The dining-table had been reduced to its smallest proportions, but even so the four people seated at it seemed very far apart. Mrs. Cotter was laced into something black, sprigged over with sunbonnets, and Mr. Cotter in his dinner coat wheezed hospitably.

After dinner they had a brandy on the terrace and sat out there, Mrs. Cotter with a wool coat over her shoulders and Terry with her mink cape about her, and listened to the sea sighing, advancing and retreating. And Chris thought with a sudden nostalgia of the Pacific. This, too, was quite an ocean, but it wasn't his ocean.

The Cotters were *so* interested in the Islands. They had been there once, before Pearl Harbor, staying only a week between ships at the Royal. They had, they believed, met Chris's parents.

He made the correction. "My aunt and uncle, perhaps," he said.

"Oh? Well, at a wonderful party, a sort of native feast."

"A *luau*," he said patiently. He could imagine it, given for the visitors, complete with palms and hulas and the hostess wearing a *holuku*.

Now Audrey could remember who had given the party. "People named Peterson," she had told him; "they had a wonderful house on Diamond Head."

He said he knew it well. He did. He could close his eyes and walk through every room in it. But there was one room he'd avoid — not a room, but a *lanai* looking over the bright waters, haunted by a ghost he'd rather not meet.

But Terry was saying, "Of course we'd love to play." She rose as Mrs. Cotter did, and Chris came to his feet. He felt bewildered. He had been a great many miles away, and a number of years. He had been twenty-two again, miserable, and in love.

Terry pinched him as they followed the Cotters indoors. "Where were you?" she demanded. "Audrey asked twice if we wanted to play contract."

He said, "I sometimes suffer from amnesia."

Luckily, they cut each other as partners. They'd played before, and knew themselves a formidable team. Terry played an intelligent, calculated game. Mark Austin had taught her. Chris almost always held good cards and played with a wild sort of intuition. Together they were brilliant. The Cotters were not, and the Russells won. The stakes were low enough, a tenth of a cent. "I," said Chris firmly when asked what stakes, "am a miserable miser, and no gambler." This was as meretricious as anything he'd ever said, but the Cotters were pleased, it showed the right attitude. Cotter himself regarded inherited means with something that wavered between contempt and envy. He had come by his money the hard way.

Then they were getting ready for bed.

"Profit," said Chris, counting the gains; "not much but 'twill serve. We'll get through this yet, darling. Provided we always cut each other. We have to save a margin for losses, those we'll suffer when we cut lesser partners."

She wasn't listening. "Chris, what if they do take a trip to the Islands?"

"Who? Oh, the Cotters. Well, I'll ask you. What if they do?"

"You are very lavish," she said, sitting on the edge of her bed, "with your uncle Hugo's hospitality!"

"Why not? He is hospitable, when it comes to friends of the family, after, of course, a little editing and research."

"But what happens — in case? There must be other people you've asked or had to ask."

"A few. The Johnsons, of course. You know how it is. 'If you ever come to the Islands,' I say — "

"But what *happens?*"

"It's never come up before, aside from West Coast classmates. You don't understand the Russells, dear. No matter how much they dislike me, or, to put it more poetically, hate my guts, I'm a member of the clan. So my guests are their guests. And they don't go up to them and yell in their ears, 'Did you know that poor Chris has no money, none at all, owing to the poor judgment of his father?' No. Naturally, should the strangers stray out of the preserve they might meet up with someone, not in the family, who would be delighted to inform them. Come to think of it, though, we're related to half the people who, as the saying goes, count." He walked over, sat down beside her, and took her in his arms. "Let's worry about it when the time comes," he suggested.

She said tremulously, "They're awfully sweet to us."

"I know. Even to lending me golf clubs,

tennis rackets, and the rest of it; even to promising to find a decent horse, if I want to ride, or to putting the little car at our disposal if we want to go off by ourselves."

"I didn't realize," Terry said, "that it would make me feel so awful. I had twinges in Palm Beach but not to this extent."

"I told you I'd sing for my supper. You will, too. You will be both useful and decorative. We'll earn our bed and board and whatever else goes with it. You'll see. Now kiss me and shut up."

In a sense, she did see. People came calling upon the Cotters who had not called before. The Cotters and their charming guests were asked, and frequently, to dinner, to cocktails, to dance, to swimming shindigs. The Cotters were quite beside themselves with simple joy. Their servants came and went, and Audrey was in a furor most of the time, but the show went on. The Cotters gave parties and went to them. And they were not living in any temporary dream world either, as Chris told Terry.

He said, "They're swell people, Terry. After we've departed they'll still be in demand because people will have found out how swell."

It was July by now, and they had been on Long Island for several weeks. And Terry

120

said plaintively, "We are never alone, except at night."

"Do not belittle — " he began, and she flushed and threw a pillow at him.

"Except when we are dressing," she went on, "or resting or something. Chris, I swear to you, this must be harder work than being behind a counter!"

He looked at her oddly. "You're finding that out? I suppose it is; I've often thought so. Yet I prefer it."

"Being amiable," she said dreamily. "That dreadful old man, the other night. He's a — a *pincher*, but he's important to the Cotters."

"Shall I hunt him up and knock his teeth out?"

"Denture. No, you're not in a position to do that."

He said, "I'm not worried, although if I've guessed correctly the gentleman owns most of the real estate in Manhattan and is twice widowed."

"He said," Terry told him, "that he adored brides, they were so starry-eyed and sweet."

"Next time we meet him I must remember to fix it so that he sees a few stars," Chris answered.

After a moment she said, "I suppose we are

earning our way."

"Yes. And not doing too badly — at contract and, on my part, at golf. It all counts up, we can bank the monthly checks against our flight to the Pacific and still exit with graceful gestures toward the hired help!" He added, "And when *do* we exit?"

"You are getting bored!"

"Darling, a very little. Is it showing?"

He had put on a little weight, which became him. He was quite tanned now that the ocean was fit to swim in. He couldn't take it too cold, he said, and really preferred the swimming pools of the neighborhood. His eyes were blazing blue in his brown face.

Terry never tanned in the accepted sense. Her olive skin deepened in shade, the rosy undertones were more apparent. She had never looked better, as Helen Lannis remarked when, during that July, Terry came to town and met her for lunch. Helen and Frank were going to New Hampshire for their vacation presently.

"I'm so glad to see you," Terry said. "It was a boon when Audrey had to come in to have a fitting and see the employment-agency people."

"You look marvelous. How's Chris?"

"He's fine, but getting a little restless."

"Then you'll travel?" asked Helen. "I was

going to say, why don't you come up to New Hampshire while we're there? It's a simple place, but you could have one of the cottages if they aren't all booked. It would be such fun."

It would be fun, thought Terry, looking at the good little face, the bright-brown eyes. She would love it — to let down, to relax, not to be on exhibition, not to walk delicately as Agag. To be with Helen and Frank. Just the four of them, eating, dancing, having picnics, talking.

But they couldn't. Hotel cottages didn't come gratis.

She said regretfully, "I'd love to, and so would Chris. But I've promised the Griswolds in Newport and the Davidsons on the Cape."

"That was before Chris," Helen reminded her. "Now, you don't have to — "

"Of course not," said Terry hastily, "but they keep writing me. They're thrilled about Chris, they want us both, and he is anxious to see something of the East before we go to Hawaii."

"I suppose so." Helen sighed, her small face grieving. "When you go, heaven knows when we'll see each other again!"

They sat in a restaurant garden, under a striped umbrella. They could hear the blurred sound of traffic, but a fountain splashed near by, the waiters moved about quietly, pretty women laughed, and ice clattered in the frosty glasses, tea, coffee, gin rickey, planter's punch.

Terry wasn't drinking. Too hot in town, with the asphalt melting and even the best turned-out women looking faintly wilted. She ate a big green salad and drank her tea. This was her luncheon. She had asked Helen. She had talked it over with Chris first. "Can we afford it?"

"Are you buying clothes this afternoon?" Helen inquired. She looked wistful. "I'd love to go with you but I have to keep my dental appointment." She shuddered. "Let's not dwell upon that. But how I'd love to see you on a buying binge."

"Audrey wanted me to be with her when she was fitted," Terry said, "but I don't think I'll get much — I don't really need it — maybe just one or two things. When I reach Honolulu, or just before, maybe in San Francisco, will be time enough. Helen, I feel so guilty leaving my trunks with you."

"Only sensible thing," said Helen, "I can ship them before you leave if you're not taking them on the ship with you."

"Chris likes to travel light," said Terry truthfully. "And we may go by air."

"It's been good seeing you, if only for a little while," Helen told her. "I can't bear to think of you going so far away, although, come to think of it, you almost always were! Maybe Frank will let me take a trip sometime, or perhaps he will get away, too. I've always yearned to see Hawaii."

"It would be wonderful," said Terry, and her eyes filled, unexpectedly, because it would have been wonderful but must be avoided.

"Have you heard from Chris's people? Since their cables, I mean."

"Yes," Terry answered, "we've had letters from his aunt and uncle, and cousin; and from other members of the family. A little stiff, some of them, but nice." She managed a smile. "His aunt Cordelia said she was holding a personal wedding gift for me, some family jewelry."

She did not go into details, the ponderous, congratulatory tone of Hugo Russell's letter to Chris, which had arrived a few days before, nor speak of the check it contained. The sum was by no means munificent, but Chris, looking at it, remarked, "If you hadn't been who you are, darling, it would have been for a hundred and not a thousand."

Cordelia's letter had been self-conscious. Welcoming a pig-in-a-poke, thought Terry, but at least a wellborn, well-mannered, and, of course, gilded pig. The letter from Jack

125

Russell had faintly entertained her. He had turned a graceful if heavy-handed phrase. He was anxious, he said, to welcome her to her little kingdom.

Well!

Helen was speculating about the jewelry. "What was it, did she say?"

"No; and Chris hasn't any idea, except that it's probably old."

"You'll like that," said Helen, "you've never cared for modern jewelry. Which is odd, as your father would have bought out Cartier's for you, and Chris would, too, I suppose." She sighed. "Poor me, with my passion for diamonds."

It's lucky, thought Terry, *that Helen knows how little I care about jewelry or she'd wonder. And unlucky*, she thought further, *that I can't say, "Well, come on down to Cartier's right now and I'll buy you a clip!"*

She said, "Sometime maybe we'll go trinket-shopping."

Helen laughed. And Terry thought, *I suppose she respects me for not making demands on Chris so soon. Yet she's wondering, quite naturally, if he's going to give me a settlement or an income.*

There was a way to halt, for a time, this trend of thought. She said, "Chris is awfully generous," and so, she reflected, he was,

126

within his limitations, "but until he goes home and talks to the family lawyers we won't have financial discussions." She took a deep breath. "He knows about Father," she added.

"You told him!" Helen's eyes shone. "It was best, it was right. Sooner or later he'd have to know. What did he say?"

"Oh, he was sorry on my account, of course. Further than that it didn't matter."

"Exactly what I would have thought. So you could have told him before and not gone through all the agony," Helen reminded her.

"And have him shy away from a possible fortune hunter, or is it huntress?" She thought, *Have him shy away, period!*

"What does he think now?"

Terry said simply, "But *now*, you see, he knows that I'm in love with him."

"You're sure, if he hadn't a cent?"

Terry looked up quickly, but Helen's face was open and sweet. So she answered, wanting to laugh because it was funny and sad and true. "Even if he hadn't had a cent — I'm sure."

"Then," said Helen, "you're happy; so am I, and everything's all right."

Terry said quickly, "Chris knows I told you. But I convinced him that there's no point in announcing the beggar maid, Cophetua angle, at this time, to anyone, not even to his family until we are with them. There would be so much *talk*, and I do hate it."

She's had her share of talk, thought Helen tenderly. She nodded. "There's no point in it, anyway," she agreed. "You don't know anyone here very well, after all, except us, and you're leaving for Chris's home soon."

"Yes. After Chris has had his little whirl."

Well, that was that. She left Helen and went to meet Mrs. Cotter and looked at a preautumn showing, "just for our clients," with envy. But she didn't need clothes, even if she could afford them. She regarded midsummer things with longing, but Chris's thousand wasn't for that. "For however we travel, air or ship, it has to be in style, Mrs. Russell, as once we reach the West Coast the legend is your burden, not mine."

Chapter Six

REFINED BLACKMAIL

When they left the Cotters they went to Newport. The Griswolds lived in a large, rather understaffed stone house and, unlike the Cotters, were firmly established in the not too shifting sands of Bailey's Beach. They were older than the Cotters and had a raft of married children and young grandchildren. Life was not too formal at the Griswolds', it was very pleasant, and Chris was enchanted by the rather staid domesticity, enlivened only by the small fry. He found it somewhat nostalgic, the twilight, he said, of certain elderly gods. They swam, they attended sedate dinner parties and dances, they went to the Country Club, and Chris observed the phenomenon of the Reading Room. They played contract, always with excellent partners for low stakes, and Mrs. Griswold gave one of her famous picnics for them, which was attended by three generations of families long in summer residence.

Nothing untoward occurred during the two

weeks they remained. Mr. Griswold asked Chris about the sugar industry, more as a courteous gesture than anything else. He had little personal knowledge of commerce. He had been educated as a lawyer, but had not practiced his profession, preferring to collect books and modern paintings and to employ lawyers to manage the Griswold estate. He was more interested in Mark Austin, because what he knew of him represented a sort of adventure and daring which he himself had never experienced. The Russell family was one thing, a close corporation which he vaguely understood, but Mark Austin was something else again. His meeting and his short stay with Terry's father, when the Griswolds had gone to Central America on one of their rare excursions, had been quite memorable.

Terry felt stifled at Newport among these courteous people who took so much for granted. Mr. Griswold, and also his thin, active, benevolent wife, bore out Chris's statement that the rich could dress as they pleased. Unless the occasion called for more formal attire, the Griswolds went happily shabby, and it was something of a shock to watch them emerge from their comfortable cocoons when it was correct to do so. The Griswold jewels were extremely well known, but Mrs. Griswold, aware that they did not become her and that it was vulgar to wear more than a good piece or two at a time, did not bedeck herself with them. But the good pieces were fantastically valuable, and Chris, discussing them in the old-fashioned bedroom assigned to him and Terry, commented that he wished he had been trained as a gentleman Raffles. He also commented that it was routine, was it not, the bad food at the tables of the rich; "Not Aunt Cordelia's," he added thoughtfully, "though of course she penny-pinches, too. Still the Island fare is another matter." And how devastatingly backbreaking the beds. "I get up here every morning feeling rather like a corkscrew," he said. "Let's go on to other pastures."

So they went to the Cape to the Davidsons', whom Terry liked very much, and who lived in a ramshackle structure outside a little town, practically on the beach. The Davidsons were her friends. They had never known her father. She had met them in England, when Kent Davidson was at the Embassy in a minor capacity. They were under forty, and had two nice leggy girls, and were also friends of Helen and Frank Lannis.

Their house was full of sunshine and laughter and everyone helped in the kitchen when the servants left, which was often, and lived in bathing-suits. Sometimes they went into the village in a battered station wagon to shop, and on Saturday nights to the hotel dances.

Kent Davidson, having left the government service at the conclusion of the war, had taken over his father's lucrative publishing business in Philadelphia. He was a good-looking man, with an enormous zest for life and a gift for living, which his wife shared. Charlotte was active as a buzz saw, thin as a whiplash. She was an excellent mother, a famous cook, and addicted to athletics. She trimmed Chris at golf, to his chagrin, outswam Terry, and triumphed over her husband at tennis.

"Wonderful woman," was Chris's reaction, "but she wearies me. Physically, I mean." It was noon, and he lay on the beach with Terry. The fog had rolled away, and the sun beat down. For lunch there would be the sort of omelette that Charlotte seemed to turn out with one hand, hot biscuits, beach-plum preserves, a green salad. For tonight she had promised them lobsters.

Her household staff consisted of two local apple-cheeked girls, who came whizzing up each morning on bikes and departed at night. In the kitchen they functioned as washer-uppers and assistants; but took over the rest of the house like twin whirlwinds, running a vacuum, making beds, beating pillows, and singing, as a rule, in harmony.

"I like these people," Chris went on, "best of all, next to Helen and Frank. But that Charlotte! Hikes along the beach, among the sand and bushes, bicycle trips, rowing, sailing — I never saw such a dynamo. Do you suppose she's that color all year round? She reminds me of home."

Charlotte was tanned to mahogany, and her brown hair sun-bleached in streaks. Her eyes were gray, startling against the tan, her mouth a wide scarlet slash when she remembered her lipstick. She carried with her the enviable atmosphere of a woman who is adored by her family, loved by her friends, respected by everyone, and relied upon by neighbors. She had gone through the London bombings without, at least outwardly, turning a hair, having sent her girls home to the States, and assured their safety. As for her own, she did not give a finger snap for that, if she must achieve it away from Kent.

She came out now, blinking in the sun, as she rarely wore dark glasses. She flopped down on the sand beside her guests, wearing brief red shorts and a halter, her thin body coffee-color.

"Man coming," she reported, "one of Kent's writers. I don't like him much — " she let the sand run through her slender fingers — "but we have to put him up. Temperamen-

133

tal cuss. Can't work in hotels, can't work at home — I suspect he has wife troubles or something — Anyway, he'll have the guest shack, and we won't be unduly bothered, only it was such fun just us. Terry," she told Chris, "is the most comfortable person to be with."

"I wouldn't say quite that," he began cautiously.

Charlotte laughed. She said, "You know, I don't like many women really, just Terry, Helen Lannis, one or two others. Even the slim ones so often have fat souls. But Terry — " she smiled at her friend — "her soul has a beautiful shape."

"The cover ain't bad, either," said Chris. But he patted Terry's hand, and Charlotte grinned.

"Who's coming in?" she asked.

"I am. Wait till you come to us in the Islands," he said, "and I'll show you some real swimming plus surfing that will satisfy your passion for knocking yourself out."

"It's a bet," said Charlotte, and Terry's blood froze, as it always did, listening to Chris and his casual invitations.

She watched them running down to the water's edge, too lazy to move, and thought, *This whole thing was a mistake. It might make a difference to the Cotters, to the Griswolds, to people we have met casually, if we said, "Look, we're a couple of fakes. Chris is the world's poorest relation, and I haven't a sou, comparatively speaking." But it wouldn't make the slightest difference to Kent and Charlotte.*

Yet with Chris the deception had begun long ago, and last winter, with her. And if there hadn't been the deception, she and Chris would not now be together on a Cape Cod beach.

It occurred to her that she hadn't asked the name of the writer who would occupy the big one-room guest shack set at a little distance from the house, beyond the place where Charlotte held the day-long clambakes to which she invited her neighborhood. The shack had a huge bed-living room, and fireplace, a miniature bathroom, with shower, and was usually occupied.

Its new tenant did not turn up for two or three days. He came by car, driving in just as the setting sun was red upon the water and pink upon the sands. Terry was playing Ping-pong with Kent on the big side porch when the car came roaring in over the narrow sandy road and stopped. A door slammed. Kent put down his racket and went out to meet his guest, as Charlotte came out of the house. Chris was off walking on the beach with the two youngsters and the spaniels.

The man who got out of the car was stocky,

powerfully built, and his hatless head was dark. Terry could not see his face, but there was something familiar in the way he walked. He came up the steps, talking, moving his hands rapidly, and she recognized him.

Charlotte said, "Terry, dear — "

Terry moved forward. *But there's no reason to be nervous, none at all,* she kept reassuring herself, while her face adjusted to a bright mask of astonishment and welcome. *Only it's just unpleasant remembering,* she thought.

Charlotte was making the usual presentations. "Mrs. Russell," she was saying, and then, "Roger Amenly."

But Roger had Terry's hands in his and was crying, "Terry — Terry Austin!"

"You know each other?" asked Kent.

"How long ago?" asked Roger Amenly. "Two years ago, wasn't it, when you turned me down flat?" He grinned at his hostess. "I hasten to add that I was between marriages, therefore, a bachelor at the time. But I've never recovered," he said. "I read of your marriage, Terry. How very fortunate — " he paused and added, smiling — "for Mr. Russell."

Conversation was general, exclamatory and scattered, bright and trivial as a shower of confetti. Roger Amenly kept Terry's unwilling hands in his, swung her around, and said,

136

"I wouldn't have believed it. You're prettier than ever, even prettier than I remembered. And I did remember!"

Charlotte was asking, "But where in the world did you — " and Kent was interrupting, "This makes it all very cozy," and Terry was trying to free herself, saying mendaciously, "How nice to see you, Roger."

Amenly released her with a quick, smiling glance of his very dark eyes. He looked at Charlotte and gestured widely. "Don't hate me," he implored, "for crashing your holiday. But if Kent wants the damned book he'll have to furnish the peace and plenty necessary to its delivery."

Kent said, "Sure. Let's unload the car, and then I'll escort you to the padded cell."

They went off, and Terry collapsed on a porch swing and said blankly, "Well, for heaven's sakes!"

"But you didn't tell me you knew him," Charlotte protested.

"How could I? You didn't tell me the name of your expected guest!"

"I should be out there," Charlotte said, "making noises like a delighted hostess. I am not. Let Kent do it. Amenly is his boy, not mine. Where did you know him?"

"He arrived in Central America with letters to Father," Terry explained, "more than two

137

years ago, I think. He said he'd come primarily to do a series of articles and to get material for a novel. But I've never seen his by-line on an article, much less a book. I'd never heard of him before, nor since. I thought later that he must have been a phony."

"Nope," said Charlotte, sitting on the porch rail, swinging her brown legs. "At that, I wouldn't know about his Central American work. I do know he's written for years, under various pseudonyms, for obscure publications, and never made the grade. A year or so ago he turned up in Kent's office with the manuscript of a mystery novel. It was of the hard-boiled type, a corpse on every page, a detective who drank his way through the case, plus bedroom scenes in detail. Not my cup of poison; I like the better-mannered sort. However, Kent published it, it was successful and sold to the movies. He used still another pen name on it — Hank Howard."

"I read it," said Terry. "It scared the daylights out of me. I never dreamed it was Roger Amenly's."

"He's saving his own name, for he still wants to write what he calls serious and important stuff. Well, to each his dream. Meantime he makes a living. You don't like him, do you?"

"No."

"Good. Was that just conversation, that airy bit about your having turned him down?"

Terry said uneasily, "Naturally."

"Come again? You can tell old Aunt Charlotte. I won't tell Kent. He never tells me about the private lives of his writers — nothing that I can't read in the newspapers later — so I like to hold out on him once in a while."

"I had to be nice to Amenly, Charlotte, see that he went sight-seeing and met people who could be informative. Father was busy and, some of the time, away."

"Did our fascinating Roger stay with you?"

"In a manner of speaking. Everyone stayed with us, Charlotte. They came like homing pigeons, rushing down gangplanks, leaping out of cars, planes — we ran a species of de luxe hotel. Father liked it."

"You are sparing of detail. About Roger, I mean."

"There's nothing much. He went off on trips we'd arranged for him, came back again. We were just headquarters."

"What about the turning down?"

"Nothing. A routine gesture. Both his and mine."

"I dare say," Charlotte commented, "that practically every man you ever met asked you to marry him, if free, or to wait for him, if not. And not entirely because of Mark Austin, dear. What was Roger's matrimonial status at the time?"

"He was divorced."

"The present Mrs. Amenly is number three," said Charlotte. "I had them to dinner last spring. She is blond, lively as a carnival. Kent says she's an idiot but I rather liked her, if only because she makes Roger squirm. They've been married six or seven months. But it's no go, which is why he packed up and came here. He told us in front of her, that night at dinner, that she throws things when annoyed. I could wish she'd connect, but fatally, only his book does sell, and the next one will outsell it."

Terry said hopefully, "Perhaps we won't have to see him much."

"Meals," said Charlotte sadly, "and when inspiration flags, which I note, with most writers, is often. Writers afflict me. Of course, I was trained while Kent was in the diplomatic service, so I'm a perfect wife for a publisher. But the things I go through! We never have a season here without geniuses — the kind who forget meal hours, say, 'Don't bother about me, I'll just get myself a snack,' and then leave the kitchen in a shambles at the damnedest hours; also the kind who sleep all day while you tiptoe around the shack and shush the dogs and the girls. Or those who work all night, have to have coffee boiling on a hot plate, sandwiches, and liquor. One of 'em wanted vodka and Cokes, to work on. Then there are those who go to sleep on phenobarbital and wake up reaching for the Benzedrine. Peace, it's wonderful. But I think the most exasperating type is he or she who sits around, notebook in hand, waiting for a clue, a bit of dialogue, or a gem of wisdom to drop from your unwary lips. Of course, there's the kind that talks only about itself — come to think of it, they're *all* that kind. And once we had a woman here — you'd faint if I told you who she was — who lived on cigarettes, coffee, and chocolate peppermints. She burned holes in all my best sheets. She went walking in the water by moonlight. She played Wagnerian records — she took one machine over to the shack — at two in the morning!"

Terry was laughing, and Charlotte said, "Well, laugh. I have to suffer. Kent takes the month off, you know, flies down week-ends when he can, which isn't often. I have to stay on and hold the clammy hands of his writers. Here comes your one true love."

Chris was coming toward the house, the girls beside him, the spaniels a tangle of black and gold and beige about his feet.

"Blast!" said Charlotte. "If only Marie or Louise were older and you hadn't met Chris first, what a son-in-law he would have made!"

They came up the steps, damp and sandy, the dogs out of hand. Charlotte shushed them and shooed her girls into the house to dress. "You, too, Chris," she said. "You'll take cold."

"Not me. Charlotte, your kids are like you, wonderful and dynamic. They forget I'm an old, old man."

He put out his sandy hand and took Terry's. "Come along," he said, "while I alternately shiver and burn under the shower."

"Look pretty," Charlotte advised him, "as an old beau of your wife's has just turned up. What in the world is keeping Kent?" she inquired. "Surely they aren't discussing chapter six at this hour."

Terry and Chris went around the porch and into their room. "You shower first," she said.

"Okay." He put his hand under her chin. "What old beau?" he asked.

"He wasn't. His name is Amenly, he writes mysteries under the name of Hank Howard. I didn't know that till just now. I knew him briefly at home; he had a letter to my father."

"Something's troubling you," he said. "Old beaux must be a dime a dozen. What's with this one?"

"Nothing, except I didn't like him." She looked at him, disturbed. "And when we met

142

just now, I wondered if he'd heard anything. Of course he wasn't long in Central America, he had no friends there other than those he met through us, but he might have kept in touch with someone."

"Skip it, darling. You're imagining things. And what if he has heard rumors? He'd hardly mention them."

"He might."

"Rumors are neither proof nor evidence. Nor dinner conversation. If he says anything to the Davidsons they'll slap him down fast. And you forget I'm here."

She watched him go off to the shower, she heard the cascading of the water, heard him singing above it. He had a pleasant baritone, now exercising itself in the nostalgic "Song of the Islands."

Terry opened the clothes closet, took out a cotton frock, and put it over a chair. She took off her shorts and shirt, put a silk robe about her, and lay down on the bed.

She thought of Roger Amenly.

She had forgotten him, she'd written him off as an unpleasant experience. In a sense, the first. Fortune hunters, yes, old and young, but never one like Amenly. With the others she had been equipped to deal. Her father had told her bluntly, before she was sixteen, that men would be attracted to her. "By your looks," he said, "for you are going to be, if not a beautiful woman, then very nearly so. You will have enormous appeal. In addition to your looks there's my good luck and hard work. It all adds up. It won't be difficult to separate the sheep from the goats. There will be a man, or men who will fall authentically in love with you. You'll know it when the time comes. And if you love in return, do not too much disturb yourself by wondering if he would still adore you if you lived in a hall bedroom and earned twenty-two dollars a week. You don't. So speculation is idle."

She had not liked Amenly at their first meeting. He had an easy, practical charm which she distrusted. She had seen as little of him as was compatible with common courtesy and her position as hostess in her father's house. And then, before she expected him, Amenly returned from one of his trips into the interior. Mark Austin was absent from home, which Amenly had known. He made a gesture in the direction of all hotels, telephoning from the Austin house. But they were full, he reported. "I know you did not expect me until next week, but I've nowhere to go," he said.

Terry fixed that. She found a place for him through friends in the Consulate, but not before the unpleasantness.

He was entertained by what he termed her

reactionary notions. "Enchanting, and complete with duenna," he said. "Really, my dear, you're a big girl now. You haven't always been behind high walls."

They were in the patio, she sitting there, her face bright with anger, while he walked up and down. She could, at this distance, recall his eyes, the way he moved his hands, the way he walked, his shoulders hunched. Then he had turned and come back to stand before her. He had said, "I'd marry you, you know. Not that I approve of marriage. I'll even send ambassadors to your father, bearing appropriate gifts — one typewriter, somewhat battered, a couple of pounds of bond and manila paper, six erasers, two of which function. I also own two good suits, a handsome alligator brief case won in a poker game, ten shares of stock in a defunct mining company, a cash balance of six hundred eleven dollars and thirty-seven cents, and debts to five times the amount."

Just at first she had been mildly amused. But it appeared that this wasn't just Mr. Amenly's line. He had pulled her roughly from the long chair and kissed her equally roughly before she knew what was happening. He'd said, "The marvelous part of it is that I'm crazy about you. I suppose they all tell you that. Many of them mean it, no doubt. But how many are honest enough to add that your circumstances, as well as your desirability as a woman, would greatly sweeten the bitter pill of matrimony? We could have a good time on your money. I could even write the books I want to write, and while it is futile for a man to promise to be faithful to his wife, even the loveliest living creature, it is far less difficult to be true to one's bread and butter."

She thought, *It's silly to be upset because of that. It didn't upset me then. It just made me mad!*

But Amenly brought back a time which was lost; and another country. She thought, *Besides, the wench is dead.* Well, that wench was, secure and confident, able to dismiss a man like Amenly with a candor to match his own; and able to forget him.

Chris came out, girt in a towel, and said, "Your turn, Mrs. Russell."

When they were about to leave their room Chris held her back. He said, "Wait a minute, darling. Let the ice melt in the shaker, Kent cry that he is starved, and the girls gobble up the potato chips. I'm learning to read your mind. When we've been married fifty years you won't have to talk. You'll just look at me, and I'll say, 'Yes, dear, I'll put out the cat,' or

'It's time for your hot milk,' or 'If you insist at our age, walking in the moonlight — ' "

"Chris, I do love you."

"Of course. You don't want to leave this room, do you? You don't want to see this what's-his-name or names."

"I distrust him. I don't know why, exactly."

"Because he was in love with you? He was, I take it?"

"It's a nice way of putting it. No, he wasn't really."

"The Austin legend, which wasn't a legend?" He was silent a moment, thinking his own thoughts to which she had no access. Then he said, "I don't know how our hosts would feel about it, but if you like I'd be glad to take him apart and reassemble him, with bits and pieces missing."

"I wouldn't like."

"Perhaps you are blowing this up a little more than life-size, Terry. What were the gentleman's intentions?"

"Honorable, as the saying goes. Everyone's were in those days," she said, and laughed, but her eyes remained clouded.

"You're married," said Chris, "remember? Papa will handle it if the appearance of an admirer means *pilikia*."

"What's that?"

147

"Trouble." He kissed her again and asked, in a different tone, "It doesn't wear off, does it?"

"No, Chris."

"Then we're still lucky, we're all right." He opened the door. "Come on," he said, "let's have that drink."

During the evening she thought, *I'm an idiot. And I hate this. I hate it, always imagining things.* Amenly had regarded Chris's height enviously. "They grow them tall in your Islands," he said before dinner. "I have always longed to go there. Didn't I read somewhere that you owned one? Fantastic, if true."

Chris put down his cocktail glass as Charlotte mentioned that dinner was waiting. He said, "Yes, my family does have an island. It's very tiny."

They went into the dining-room, which was big, mostly windows, and contained little beyond the table and necessary chairs. The local help officiated, bringing in the platters of cold lobster.

Amenly was interested in the Russell island. "I suppose they call it that?" he asked.

Chris shrugged. "It has a name," he said. "Naniola."

"Very picturesque," said Amenly, cracking

148

a claw. "What does it mean?"

Terry knew. She knew a good deal about Naniola by now. She said, and smiled, "It means 'beautiful life.' "

"Oh," said Amenly, an eyebrow raised. "The good, the true, the beautiful." He surveyed Chris. "You are very fortunate," he told him, "in more ways than one. I hope someday to see Naniola for myself."

"That would be nice," said Chris pleasantly, and Roger looked at him and grinned.

He asked, "Are you returning soon?"

"Before autumn."

"I have some friends in Hawaii. By the way, where is your island situated?"

"Between Maui and Hawaii," Chris said. "Why?"

"I wonder. My friends live in Honolulu. Perhaps you'd know them. I'm certain you would. Like everyone else they're engaged in growing sugar and pineapples. The name is Peterson."

Chris sat beside his wife, and she could sense a withdrawal in him as if actually the chair had become vacant. He said, "I know the Petersons very well."

"I don't, alas," said Amenly. "My acquaintance is with one of the boys — he isn't a boy, of course, except compared to me. Must be about your age. The middle one, I believe. Tom."

"Tom and I were in school together," Chris said. He asked, "Have you seen him lately? I didn't know he'd been on the mainland."

"Ran into him in Los Angeles in the spring," said Roger, "during my wedding trip. His sister was with him, Mrs. Alex Gurney. A very beautiful young woman, by the way. Is there Hawaiian blood in the family?"

"Oh, yes," said Chris carelessly, "a long way back, like mine."

Kent snorted. "Viking blood more likely, by your coloring, Chris."

"I just didn't happen to inherit." Terry saw Chris's mouth twitch a very little with personal amusement. "My brother," he added, "had very dark hair and eyes."

"How interesting," said Roger politely, "and I recall that Mrs. Gurney's given name is Hawaiian."

"Her first name is Gerda," Chris said, "her ancestry also being Nordic. But most people call her by her middle name, which is Lilia."

"I didn't meet her husband," said Roger; "he wasn't with her."

"Busy man," said Chris. "He's a plantation manager." He added, "We'll be seeing the Petersons and Gurneys before too long. Any message?"

"Just that, yes, if I ever get my book done

I'll take them up on their invitation."

The rest of the evening held no alarms. Roger went off to the shack. He was tired, he said, and would turn in early. And the others played contract for a time and then went to bed.

Chris said, "I don't like the ex-boy friend, either."

"Funny," Terry commented, "that he should know some Island people, too."

"Not very. Only the Russells stay home. Everyone else travels."

"Peterson?" she said, trying to remember. "Someone else spoke of them. Oh, I know, the Cotters, remember?"

"Yes."

"Who are they?"

"Old friends, kissing cousins, now and then a Russell marries a Peterson or vice versa. I grew up with this lot."

She asked, "Do you suppose he'll go out?"

"Who? Amenly? I don't know. As for Tom, he'd invite the guy who sat next to him at the movies. I told you that the Islanders are notably hospitable. The Petersons are no exception. I pinned Amenly down somewhat after dinner. The acquaintance is quite slight, one of those bar-session things, and 'Let's all have dinner together' at whatever hotel they were all staying. Don't give it another thought."

She said, "Chris, hadn't we better leave soon? Oh, not because of Roger, that is, not altogether. But Charlotte is afraid he'll stay on until he finishes the book. Kent said he could have the shack for the balance of the summer. She told me tonight that she hoped we'd stay, she couldn't endure him unless we did after Kent leaves."

"And what did you say?"

"I said we couldn't impose for so long, and besides you wanted to see more of this part of the world before we go for good."

He ruffled her hair with his big hand. "As long as we aren't imposing I like it here, darling. And if we stayed on for a bit, that would bring the time about right. We could travel, without sparing the horses, and get home during September. Not that it's the best month in the world," he said.

"I hate — " She paused and then said it, the ugly word. "I hate sponging on Kent and Charlotte!"

"But we won't be, if you see Charlotte through her ordeal by Roger. I told you we'd work for what we got."

"I didn't know it would be like this," she said forlornly.

"No."

"And when we do reach the Islands," she said, "we can't stay indefinitely."

"We'll meet that when it comes up."

"What will your family expect?"

"They'll expect that you and I will buy or build a lavish place somewhere, a ranch, and perhaps a town house, plus a beach house, and settle down to a happy, idle existence. And they will say, 'Chris always fell on his feet.'"

"This time he fell on his head."

"I tripped," said Chris, "over my heart."

"That's sweet of you, and fanciful, and perhaps it's even true." She leaned against him. "But you can't put off the evil day forever," she warned.

"Which evil day?"

"The day upon which you announce that we can't buy or build anywhere, not even a little grass shack or whatever it is they live in."

"The day will never dawn," he said, "as we will return to the mainland, not having quite made up our minds, in order to accept a few invitations. Quite a lot. You've no idea the people you meet in your travels."

They remained with Charlotte after Kent had returned to business commending his wife, his children, his dogs, and his writer, in the order named, to their care. "I'll get back," he said, "when I can. Meantime, stiff upper lip, carry on, and all that sort of bilge. I shudder to think of my long-distance telephone bills when Roger gets in a tight spot and wants me to hold his hot little hand by remote control."

But it wasn't too bad. Amenly kept to himself, often not turning up till dinnertime. Charlotte saw that he had coffee, liquor, and enough food to sustain life in the shack, cheerfully sacrificing her miniature bar icebox. But sometimes he joined them at lunch, often for a swim before dinner or, if the work did not go well, at noon.

He was an entertaining man, he had been all over the world and had known a great many curious, interesting places and people. Chris speculated as to his age. Kent had said forty-odd, but Charlotte and Terry thought him younger. "Nearer fifty, or I'm a monkey's uncle," Chris told them. "What about war service?"

"Bad heart or something, he couldn't get in," Charlotte answered.

"Hm," said Chris, "overage, I dare say, heart or none. Didn't he do anything?"

"Some sort of propaganda work," Charlotte said vaguely. "I remember Kent's speaking of it when we first met him."

Gradually Terry's tension relaxed. Amenly spoke of the Austin house, asking her if she still owned it, and enthused over its remembered beauty. "Loveliest place I ever saw," he told Chris and Charlotte, and when Terry answered, "No, I have no property in Central America now," he nodded and reflected, "What would you do with it, you and Chris could hardly occupy half a dozen homes?" He spoke also of her father's death, saying, "I was sorry to read of it. He was a remarkable man." But all this was in the first few days, and after that he said nothing more. So, she thought, *I was imagining things.*

August was sun and fog, the smell of salt marshes, long stretches of sand, and the gulls crying. August was wild flowers in the wind, a golden moon, and stars over the water; August was clambakes and picnics, and the village alive with summer guests. August was fishing and swimming and cocktails on the porch in the evening. August, if you thought about it, was almost perfect, with Charlotte for friendship and Chris for companionship and love. But the clatter of Amenly's typewriter cut sharply through the long, lazy days, during which the Davidson girls came and went, noisy, healthy, and loving, and the spaniels tracked wet sand into the house and on the furniture, and no one complained, not even when they brought in a dead fish or two.

Kent arrived for a week-end and went away again; people came to call or to spend a day, the girls had school friends to share their big bare room, with its four built-in bunks and ship's clock. And on Saturday nights they went to the hotel dance.

Amenly, too. He liked resort hotels, he said, when he didn't live in them, the pretty women, the men who appeared week-ends, the honeymooners, the kids. He liked to dance and meticulously divided his time between Charlotte, her tall girls, and Terry.

Just before Labor Day, "You avoid me," he told Terry, as they danced to a good swing band on a crowded floor. It was very warm, and people crowded the porches, the doors stood wide and the French windows. Chris went by with Charlotte, his fair head bent, his mouth smiling.

"Why should I?"

"I don't know. Are you an unforgiving person? Yet, what was there to forgive? You must have refused a hundred men, bent upon establishing a claim to your lovely person and your father's money."

She said, "I'd forgotten your — prospecting, Roger."

"Good. Of course, that's why you married Russell. He's very attractive, by the way. He is the logical candidate, the Prince Charming, with good looks to match your own, and dollar for dollar as well."

"Really, Roger, this is in very bad taste."

"Sorry." He was silent a moment and then, "Do you know a man named Luis Lopez?" he asked.

"I don't think so." Her heart shook with premonition. "It's a common name," she said.

"He doesn't know you. But he knew your father. I met Lopez in Mexico toward the end of my unsatisfactory honeymoon last spring."

"Well?" she asked coolly.

"He told me about your father's death. It seems that members of his family lost a good deal in the crash of that plane." He looked at her closely. "You're very white, Terry. Suppose we go out on the porch?"

Chris and Charlotte saw them leave, and Chris said, "What's up, I wonder? She'd never leave lights and people of her own free will with our mutual friend."

"It's warm in here," Charlotte suggested.

"Quite. Shall we join my wife?" he asked.

But someone cut in, so Chris went off by himself to look for Terry. He did not see her on the porch, which was crowded.

They had walked across a lawn, down a flight of steps to the dock, and now stood there looking into the glittering water. A boy and girl rose from a bench and scurried away, annoyed at the intrusion. The little waves lapped at the pilings, someone was playing a

157

guitar in a boat far out, and from the hotel they could hear blurred voices, laughter, and the sound of music.

Roger said, "I brought you out here to say, more power to you. You pulled it off. I take it people don't know."

She said resolutely, "No; with the exception of one very close friend."

"Charlotte?"

"No."

"And Chris?"

"Naturally, Chris."

He said musingly, "It's a remarkable story; the rise and fall of a man like Mark Austin. I have much of the background, fortunately. It did not occur to me to write it until I saw you again. I admit I wasn't particularly interested in Lopez's cries of vengeance and easy Latin tears. He was quite drunk on tequila most of the time I was with him. But when I encountered you, I began to remember your father, yourself, the way you lived, and the singular arrogance that permeated all your kindnesses."

She thought, *I felt it, I knew it,* and was glad that the fear was no longer nebulous.

She said, "No one would print it."

"Why not? Mark Austin was a well-known man, a contemporary historical figure. It beats me why the story hasn't been broadcast, or the rumors, at least. I suppose the various governments were not anxious for the publicity, there were too many people involved. So, a plane crashed, a man died, his daughter sold her holdings and went away."

"I had none to sell."

"A euphemism. Lopez was delighted at that. Unless, he said, she managed to cache some of her this-and-that father's ill-gotten gains in the States. A blunt man, Lopez, but speaking in clichés."

"I didn't manage."

He said, "I wonder how much it would be worth to your husband to keep this out of print? It would make a colorful magazine article. The facts could all be checked. No libel suits could ensue. It would be the truth. I still have the notes I made when I visited you and could easily amplify them. The rest is easy; everyone knows Mark Austin's beginnings and a great many know his end."

"What do you mean, how much would it be worth?"

"Russell," he said casually, "is a rich man." Then he laughed. "I'm not a blackmailer, Terry, in the accepted sense. I make a good enough living now, and am likely to make more. Apart from having to pay two women alimony and a possible third coming up, I have very little need for money. But I would enjoy a change of scene after my book is written. A trip to the Islands, for instance."

She said evenly, "Chris has already asked you."

"I want you to ask me, and I mean it. I might do some articles with the Hawaiian background; also it would give me a setting for a mystery. Murder on Naniola — a good title."

They heard footsteps and turned. Chris came toward them, tossing his cigarette in a burning arc into the water.

"Hi, you two," he said cheerfully, "does this call for jealousy or a drink?"

His tone was light and even, but he came close to Terry and put his arm around her. And Roger said, "A drink, certainly. I'm afraid you have no cause for jealousy, Chris. You're very fortunate. We were just talking about Central America and Hawaii."

Terry felt Chris's hand grow heavier on her shoulder.

"Hawaii?"

"You say it well. If I tried for that faint *v* sound I would merely seem affected. Yes, I have promised Terry I'll come out this autumn. If Kent doesn't give me sufficient advance I'll work my way across."

"That's fine," said Chris. "We'll be on the dock waiting, with songs and garlands. Let's have that drink. I think Charlotte is about ready to go home."

They went back to the hotel together. And an hour later, when they were alone, Chris spoke to his wife. "What happened there on the dock?"

She told him. And after a moment he said, "I'm sorry, dear." His face was broken with pity for her. And then, "Try not to believe him. I don't. What magazine would — "

She said, "Think straight. It's a legitimate story, like those of the robber barons; as legitimate as Jesse James or a cattle rustler. My father was well known; he made a fortune and, in his later years, by dishonesty and bribery, many people were ruined when he died. Time has elapsed, there would be interest in such a story, and now that things are straightened out and those who were implicated have vanished from the various scenes there would be no rebuttal at all."

"But he can't do it, Terry. For your sake."

"For mine," she said, "and for your family's. Have you forgotten them?"

"Yes. You're my family, Terry."

Long after, he drew her close to him in the darkness. The night pressed in at the open windows, they could hear the sighing of the water.

He asked, "Not asleep?"

"No."

"Are you crying, Terry?"

"I'm wanting to, but I'm not."

"Funny people," he said, "the Russells. Holier than thou, that's Hugo and his sterling son. I dare say there was sharp trading back in the old days. But if so no one was caught. They wouldn't like Amenly's projected article. They'd like it even less than learning that I hadn't fallen on my financial feet, after all."

"That's what I thought."

He said, "Play it close to your chest, darling. This is one more thing we have to risk. We'll start West next week, I'll wire about reservations. We'll go by boat if possible. Passages are heavily booked. But perhaps a string can be pulled. And we'll implore Mr. Amenly to follow us as quickly as possible. Somehow I don't think he will. But we'll chance it."

"Chris, I'm afraid."

"Don't be. It's going to be all right. I'll talk to him tomorrow."

He did so, invading the privacy of the shack before midmorning, as the sun streamed in and the typewriter rattled and the pages of manuscript lay on the floor.

"Amenly."

Roger turned. He looked tired and rather old. He said, "Oh, hello, Chris. Take a chair, take two."

"No, thanks. Terry told me of your conversation last night."

"How unexpected of her," said Amenly, smiling.

Chris said shortly, "It's pretty absurd, isn't it? Or do you carry melodrama and threats into your private life?"

"Sometimes, when it pleases me. Do sit down. You make me nervous prowling."

"Were you serious when you said that you were thinking of writing about Terry's father?"

"Perfectly. He's news, he was fabulous, a superman. Are you offering me a bribe not to write it?"

"No."

"Pity," Roger said. "I love to bargain."

Chris said, "I will not have Terry made unhappy."

Roger said softly, "I heard quite a lot about the Russells when I was in Los Angeles. They'd just given a swimming-pool to some charity or other. Very good people, very upright. No scandal. I dare say they might be upset."

Chris said, "It would give me enormous pleasure to break your neck, and I doubt if anyone would care."

"I agree with you, though Kent would, selfishly. He counts on this book, poor as it is. It will sell, too, and to Hollywood. Which

163

reminds me, I am going to Hollywood after I leave here."

"I haven't the least idea why you suddenly want to invade the Islands, Amenly, nor why you can't pick up and go as any tourist does who has the price of passage and of a hotel room."

Amenly wheeled around, straddling his chair. He said, "I'll be frank with you. I have a reason for going. It has nothing to do with you or Terry. It is mainly concerned with the Petersons."

"Who have already asked you to visit them?"

"I'm afraid I wasn't wholly truthful. The invitation was withdrawn. And I don't want to go out as a tourist," he said plaintively. "What a shocking idea! I want to go out as a guest, under the best auspices and for excellent reasons. Well?"

"And if you could you'd be interested in writing articles with a Hawaiian rather than a Central American background?"

"Of course."

"Very well," said Chris. "When you've made your plans, cable me. As I said before, we'll meet you at the dock."

He went out quickly and closed the door behind him, and Roger sat for a moment smiling and then returned to his work. The typewriter clattered, and the sun slanted in, and he thought, *I can do a good day's work*.

Chapter Seven
MEETING THE FAMILY

Early in October, from their Honolulu home on the lower slopes of Tantalus, Mr. and Mrs. Hugo Russell issued invitations to a large tea and a smaller dinner, both in honor of their nephew Christopher and his wife. These functions were to take place about two weeks after the young Russells arrived from the mainland by air. During those two weeks Terry was supposed to rest, become somewhat acclimated, and while resting meet, with great informality, various members of the family resident on the island of Oahu or flying from the other islands to get a look at the bride.

Their verdict appeared unanimous and satisfactory. Terry was — or at least appeared, some added cautiously — lovely to see, charming in manner, and quite unspoiled. Chris, they told each other, was, as usual, excessively fortunate. Stated Cousin Laura Amberton, "That boy would fall in a sewer and come up with a pearl in his hand!"

The sewer she did not define; the pearl was,

presumably, Terry.

The reason that they had flown to Hawaii was the discovery that weekly sailings were booked heavily far in advance, and cancellations were infrequent, hence a remote possibility. Chris had been disappointed. He had looked forward to introducing Terry by the indigo-blue path of the sea; planning to rouse her when the first pearly shape of land swam up from the spectacular waters, to stand beside her at the rail and present her, as if they were gifts, with the southernmost tip of the Koolau Range, the round, lion-hued appearance of Koko Head, and finally Diamond Head itself, fabulous and altogether wonderful.

Approached by sea, the mountains and valleys, the colors and the astonishments were unforgettable, he said.

But, as they could not sail, he consoled himself with the practical thought that flying was less expensive, provided they could make quick connections and not have to wait over on the West Coast. This they had done, reaching their remote destination with incredible ease and speed, clocking the many miles — five thousand-odd — hour after hour, first over the wide land and then over the water.

Cordelia Russell, clinging to tradition in the face of an altering world, even her own world, was frankly disappointed. Meeting people at

167

the airport was not the same at all, she told Terry that first night at dinner. "Such a charming custom," she said, "going out to meet the ship, your arms full of *leis*, and the band playing, the singing — I am sorry you missed it, Terry."

Terry said she was sorry, too. She spoke mechanically, forcing herself to interest and warmth. She was very tired. The hurried departure from the Cape, driving with a friend of Charlotte's as far as Boston, and going on by train to spend a few days with Helen Lannis, while repacking was done and the reservations secured, and finally the long flights had wearied her. But her fatigue was not purely physical; it was rooted sullenly in her spirit.

When they had gone to their room, "What do you think of them?" Chris asked.

"I don't know, Chris, it's too soon. But they seem very kind."

The bedroom was cool and spacious, heavy with the fragrance of flowers, the *leis*, cream-white, ivory, rose-pink, red, deep-yellow, and the baskets with strange bright shapes blossoming stiffly from them, the vases filled with bloom. The room and the *lanai* that opened from it looked as if impermanent gardens were growing there.

"Put on a robe, come out on the *lanai*," said Chris. "It's something to see, isn't it?"

They stood there together and looked seaward. There was nothing to impede their view. Below them the lights of houses and streets shone, and above them the stars. The stars were crowded in a blue-black sky, the stars were scattered on the sea.

He said, "It smells so different — it *is* different."

"The flowers are wonderful," Terry agreed, but she was conscious that her head ached.

"I don't mean the flowers, I mean the air itself. You must have some impression of the family. Aunt Cordelia, for instance?"

Cordelia Russell was a handsome woman, very tall and slender. She wore her skirts long, year in, year out. She wore her face, year in, year out, as if it were a mask, as, indeed, it was. Her nose was high in the bridge, her voice somewhat shrill in pitch, and her dark-blue eyes superb with the abundant white hair. Her husband was no match for her. He was shorter by a head, fighting a losing battle against flesh, his gray hair thinning.

"She's quite beautiful in an austere way," Terry said.

"She hates me," said Chris amiably, "and she wonders why you married me. Do you?"

"No."

"Any reservations? Did she say anything about my grandmother's jewelry?"

"As a matter of fact, she did, after dinner. They hadn't expected us as soon. She said she would get it out of the safe-deposit box later."

"Better late than never." Chris's lips were a straight line. "It should have been my mother's."

Terry said nothing. She sat down in a long chair and rested her eyes on the view. It was healing, it was magnificent.

Chris sat down on the foot rest and lit a cigarette. He asked, "How about old Hugo? You had him wrapped around your little finger from the moment he met you."

"He's nice," said Terry.

"And my estimable cousin?"

"He, too."

"Is that all, for heaven's sake? I expected — oh, I don't know what. I could hardly wait to get here with you alone and do a little dissecting."

"It's too soon, Chris, I hardly spoke to them except in the general conversation. You know how that went — why hadn't we come sooner, how was our trip? They were sorry they couldn't be at the wedding, all that sort of thing. And the family news, in which I had no share, not knowing even the names or status of the people. Your aunt Cordelia explained as best she could. I am worn out trying to climb the family tree in all its many branches."

"Poor infant."

"And of course your aunt and uncle talked about my father and their visit with him."

"I know. I tried to change the subject. It was tough. But you were wonderful. In the library after dinner Hugo slapped my back until it caved in and told me how lucky I was. Jack agreed gloomily."

"And are you?"

"God, yes, I'm giddy with it. You see, I dreaded coming back. Perhaps I would never have returned if it hadn't been for you. And now, being here — "

He was silent, and she thought, *How homesick he has been and how he has fought against it.* It was not like her own homesickness, which was not for a place, really, but for a person, a way of life, familiar patterns now lost to her. But these Islands drew Chris to them, as to a mother whom he loved and with whom he had bitterly quarreled, or as to a woman, once beloved, who had given him nothing but misery and beauty but to whom he was forced to return. And thinking this, she experienced sharp jealousy, not of any person but of a locality.

He asked, "Do you think Jack and I look alike?"

"Quite a lot, a family resemblance. You're

taller; he's darker and more heavily built. He hasn't your charm, but he's very good-looking."

"Better-looking than I am? Say yes, and I'll break your neck!"

Terry yawned. She said, "Some people might think so. I don't. Does that satisfy you?"

"I suppose so. As to charm, I concede but do not feel it personally."

"Why hasn't he married? He must be quite a catch."

"An understatement. You know what a catch he is." He waited, but she was silent. He went on. "As you'll hear this anyway, I'll tell you first. Jack and I were once in love with the same girl. She was very young and I not much older. She knew which side her bread was sugared on, so she took him. Because of her youth, it wasn't announced. Then they had a terrific row and broke it off."

"Because of you?"

"If you do that often I'll burn you for a witch. Yes, I suppose so. Yet for no good reason. She wouldn't marry me, no matter what."

"Who was she?"

"She was Lilia Peterson — remember, our friend Amenly had something to say about her? Some time after the engagement was broken she eloped with a man named Gurney.

You'll meet her at all the parties and around. I think you'll like her."

"I won't like her. Should I be jealous of her — now?"

"No." He got up, disposed of his cigarette, pulled her to her feet, and kissed her. "Come to bed," he advised. "Tomorrow's another day, and heaven knows you're going to need all your strength to cope with the Russells."

During the first ten days Terry learned somewhat to accommodate herself to Cordelia's routine. Only tourists, in Mrs. Russell's opinion, slept late and retired in the small hours. Only visitors or newcomers — the *malahinis* — devoured Island life in large doses, over a week, a month, several months. The old-timers — the *kamaainas* — knew better than that. Night life, except for sedate entertainment in the home, was spurious and labeled for tourists only. Of course, she told Terry, the Islands had greatly altered since the war. It was tragic but could not be avoided. And so many people from the mainland had come before the war to build or buy homes which they inhabited for part of the year, bringing with them the regrettable tempo of mainland living. In recent years many Islanders spent more and more time away from the Islands. This was a custom of which Cordelia did not approve, but one which had infiltrated even into the family itself. Of course, for many years the sons of the family had been sent to the mainland when the time came for their university education. It was considered wise to give them the change, to permit them to see how the rest of the world lived, in order that they might return more than ever content to remain at home. Some had even gone to Europe. Hugo, and his father before him, had made a species of Grand Tour. And, of course, the younger Russell men had served in both wars, the government providing a rather different Grand Tour, all expenses paid — *Return not guaranteed*, Terry thought, listening.

Cordelia explained that hospitality was a matter of pride and tradition. The Russells had entertained every visitor of any real importance who had come to Hawaii. "Some of them quite charming," she admitted. In the main, her life was centered in the family, in civic and charitable obligations; as for her husband, he was in business and politics, "of," she added, "the higher type."

Terry learned that the household rose very early, and therefore rose with it. And as there were no real social events as yet — merely the various members of the family stopping in by day and evening, little was demanded of her beyond looking pretty and listening attentively. It would be some time before her trunks would arrive, and she went with Cordelia to supplement her wardrobe, buying carefully, the knowledge of what she could spend written indelibly upon her mind. Cordelia was delighted at this evidence of thrift and lack of ostentation. She herself did not patronize the smart, expensive shops. Her sensible frocks were made for her by a dressmaker, her suits by a Chinese tailor. But as Terry had to have something at once, Cordelia guided her to the good, old-fashioned stores, which did not cater exclusively to the tourist.

"I need only enough to tide me over," said Terry, who had learned that only the mainlander paraded the city streets in shorts or beach dress.

Cordelia was enchanted. It looked to her as though Chris had found the right wife. She wished only that Jack had seen this girl first. She had never thought she might welcome an outland daughter-in-law, and had, for years, promoted various suitable matches for her only son, none of which had come to anything. This disturbed her sense of power and irritated her. She thought, each time she watched Jack being merely courteous to a suitable maiden, *It's all that woman's fault.*

On the fourth day after her arrival, Terry

encountered that woman, at Gump's. Cordelia had taken her to Gump's, not to buy but to look. "Do you like jade?" asked Cordelia, and picked up an ancient carved figurine of enormous value. She added that her husband's collection — "has he shown it to you, my dear?" — was quite good. But did not comment that it was one of the finest private collections in the world.

Terry saw the tall young woman first, talking to a saleswoman. She watched her for a moment idly. Thinking she had never seen a more beautiful figure or such heavy auburn hair, and thinking, too, that the large dark eyes were in sharp contrast and the shape of the face and modeling of the mouth extraordinarily exotic. She spoke impulsively to Cordelia.

"What a beautiful woman."

Cordelia glanced up and her face altered slightly. She set down the jade figurine and said, "That's Lilia Gurney — she's a remote connection."

Lilia had seen them and came over, walking with a light, free grace and smiling. She said, "Aunt Cordelia," and then, "Isn't this Chris's wife?"

The introductions were made, and Lilia said, "I was going to call — but not yet, as I wanted to give you time. Thanks for your

176

invitation, Aunt Cordelia. Alex and I will be there." She kept hold of Terry's hand and added, "You've no idea how we've been wondering about you."

Terry said, smiling, "I've wondered about you, too."

"Impossible," said Lilia. "You've never even heard of me."

"Oh, but I have," said Terry, "from Chris and" — she hesitated a bare fraction of a second — "from a friend, Roger Amenly, who met you and your brother in Los Angeles, wasn't it, some time ago?"

She had no idea why she said that. It had simply flashed into her mind and watching Lilia's expression, a sort of withdrawal, a cautious alertness, she thought, *She is the reason, then,* the reason why Amenly wished to come to the Islands under, as Chris had quoted him, "the best auspices."

"Why, yes," said Lilia, "I remember him." She explained briefly to Cordelia. "A writer Tom and I encountered in our hotel." She smiled again and made her excuses. She must hurry, she had a hundred things to do, she and Alex were looking forward to the party, and do give Chris their love, "and," she added, "our sincerest congratulations."

She went out, and Cordelia looked after her. She said, half to herself, "What upset her? I've known that girl since she was born. I know her very well indeed."

Driving home, she referred to Lilia Gurney again. She asked as they drove through narrow streets, as Terry watched the flow of color and life, fascinated by the various racial characteristics, by the old, beautiful Hawaiian women carrying themselves like banners, wearing with dignity their *holukus* and flat, big *lauhala* hats, "What on earth did you say to her, Terry, to upset her?"

"To whom?" She had not been thinking about Lilia. She hadn't wanted to, especially; not now, at any rate.

"To Lilia."

"Did I upset her?" Terry wondered aloud. She turned and looked at the older woman. "It couldn't be Chris, could it? That was a long time ago," she said calmly.

To her astonishment Cordelia's color rose. "Chris?" she asked, and Terry nodded.

She said, thinking that it was time, "Chris told me about her, Mrs. Russell."

Cordelia said plaintively, "Could you not call me Aunt Cordelia, Terry? Lilia does, as you noticed, yet I am about a fifth cousin several times removed!"

"I'd like to," said Terry pleasantly. "He told me about her and Jack. That she and Jack had once been engaged," she went on.

178

"Boy and girl, calf love." Cordelia shrugged. "Personally I was pleased when it came to nothing and she ran off with Alex Gurney. He's fifteen years her senior, a good, hard-working man, I have known his people all my life."

"Chris and Jack were both in love with her," said Terry calmly. Now was as good a time as any to let Cordelia know that there were no secrets, none at all.

"Chris was a child," said Cordelia crossly, "and so was Lilia, and Jack not much more. Alex manages a plantation, which you'll see, as your uncle is very proud of it," she added. She was silent, and then said, as if it were a major crime, "Lilia has no children. She thinks far too much of her figure." She went on as they began to climb to the house, "I can't imagine why Chris thought that — episode sufficiently important — "

Terry said, "Nothing's unimportant to me where he's concerned. I know all about him, Aunt Cordelia. And about his father and mother."

Aunt Cordelia's nose twitched, a mannerism with which Terry was to become familiar. She said, "Chris is very like his father. Restless, unwilling to settle down. If Robert had lived — He told you about his brother, our adopted son?"

179

"Yes," said Terry, moved to sudden pity. She thought, *Chris was right, she loved his brother far more than she does Jack*. For Cordelia's face had altered, broken briefly into lines of grief and tenderness. And she was saying, "He — he was a most lovable boy, Terry. Have you ever seen his picture? I have some snapshots and old photographs, and there is a portrait of him you will see — Such a waste, so unnecessary." She added, in a firmer voice, "His death was a great shock to us all, a blow — "

From which, thought Terry, *she will never recover*.

She asked gently, "Did he look like Chris?"

"He looked like his father," said Cordelia. "Chris is like him but not in appearance. Robert looked like him, but his temperament was quite different." She did not speak again until they reached the house. Then she said, "Some of the Maui Russells are coming for tea this afternoon, Terry. Perhaps you would like to know more about them — I'll tell you at luncheon."

They lunched alone, on the big *lanai* with its wonderful view, deftly served by the Filipino butler and the Japanese maid. Chris had gone off with his uncle and cousin after breakfast. He deplored the necessity privately to Terry, but he was, he added, on his most exemplary behavior. They wished him to see alterations in the offices and to take him to one of the Cehu plantations in which Russell interests predominated. She wondered now if it was the one which Alex Gurney managed. Lilia had said nothing to indicate it.

At lunch Cordelia sketched the bewildering ramifications of the family, stressing the Maui branch. She asked, setting down her glass of iced tea spiked with pineapple fingers, "Terry, do you think that Chris would be content to remain at home?"

Terry's heart lurched. She answered cautiously, "I don't know. He hasn't mentioned it. I felt that this trip was in the nature of a visit."

"You are, of course, in a position to do as and live where you please. So perhaps I should say, would *you* be content?"

"If Chris was," answered Terry. Now she could speak the truth, and wholly. "Wherever he wants to be I'd want to be, too," she said.

Cordelia looked somewhat embarrassed, other people's emotions embarrassed her almost as much as her own. She did not like to think about her own. She was devoted to her husband, fond and proud of her son. But only twice had her heart conquered her intelligence, only twice had she experienced a total emotional involvement, the first time so

181

destructive and catastrophic that for years she had refused to acknowledge to herself that it had ever occurred, thrusting it deep into her subconsciousness, building around it a walled prison of excuses, belittlements and evasions. But the second time was different; then there was nothing of which she need be ashamed, she could be selfless and candid about that, for the second time it had been, as she repeatedly informed her husband, her "duty."

Many interests and attachments had been her duty, but only one had worn so smiling and beloved a countenance.

She said, "Very proper of you and quite unselfish. If, as I infer, you have Chris's best interests at heart you must realize that he should settle down, however — " She hesitated briefly, she was not one to come out and say crassly, "however much money you have for him to waste and enjoy." But the implication was there, and Terry, used to implications, received it silently. So Cordelia went on smoothly. "However much temptation there is for him not to settle down. If only he would interest himself in some phase of the family business. There would be, I am sure a modest place in the office, to start — how far he went would naturally depend upon him. We don't tolerate figureheads, however close the family connection. You could buy a place here, I know of several now for sale which would be suitable, and build or buy a beach cottage for relaxation —" Her voice trailed off as she reviewed sites and situations in her mind.

Terry said evenly, "Chris hates being confined. He doesn't like office work."

"Yes, I know," said Cordelia, and sighed. "Though I had hoped that he'd got over that. But work on one of the plantations would not entail confinement. Quite the contrary. And it would be good for him."

Terry said, smiling, "It's a little early, isn't it? Perhaps after he has been here a time — not that we can impose upon you for long."

Cordelia said, "I don't understand what you mean by impose, Terry. We are all one family. If you accepted just the family invitations that will come to you, and have indeed already come, you could spend a year in the Islands, during which you could, perhaps, make up your mind and help Chris to make up his."

Terry said, after a moment, "We'll see, Aunt Cordelia."

She was impatient for Chris to come home, but he did not come until dinnertime, not until the Maui cousins had had their tea, taken stock of the new relative, and departed. She saw him briefly while he was changing. There wasn't time for much conversation.

"I met Lilia Gurney at Gump's," she said. "Did you go out to whatever plantation her husband manages?"

"We did not. What did you think of her?"

"She's quite beautiful. I spoke of Roger Amenly. It appeared to upset her."

"Perhaps you upset her," he said, with a slight grin, "and Aunt Cordelia always does. They dislike each other. As for Amenly, forget him. Why should he figure?"

"He wanted to come out, remember — as a guest, not a tourist; and the invitation to visit Lilia Gurney or her brother, whichever it was, was withdrawn. Remember, he told you that? There's something there, definitely."

"I can guess," he said carelessly. "Roger made a pass at Lilia, she told Tom. I have no doubt that Tom socked him or something. He's impulsive that way. Naturally Amenly hasn't forgotten, and he wants to get even. One way to do it would be to come out under distinguished auspices." He laughed shortly. "He won't do it. That was just an idea. He's a nasty little man, really."

"Chris, wait a moment before we go down. I had to spend some money today."

"That's bad news."

"Not much." She told him how much, and why. She added, "You were right, your aunt thinks we should buy here, that you

184

should go to work."

"Even a grass shack, of which there are few left, comes high. I could fish, you could learn to make poi," he suggested.

"She's serious about it; she suggests that we visit all the relatives even if it takes us a year."

"Good God! What a dismal prospect!"

"And then make up our minds. She said, if not in so many words, that no matter how much money I had, you should not be permitted to drift any longer."

"That's my aunt who said that," said Chris solemnly. "Good old Cordelia. As a matter of fact I have been under considerable high-pressure salesmanship from both Hugo and Jack all day. They could use another hand in the office, which heaven forbid, or on one of the plantations. I reminded them, this was pleasure, not business, a honeymoon, a visit. They allowed as how they'd give me a little time. But for the honor of the family and all that they kept at me. Hugo said I could retrieve myself and, I assume, my father."

She said, "We'll have to go down now, Chris."

He swung her around till she faced him. "You're annoyed," he said. "You can't have become — corrupted so soon? You'd like me to say, 'Sure, I'll stay'? And if I did? What about the place we can't buy, the beach house we can't build? Things will look different then to the clan. Heaven knows they have half the money in the mint. But that doesn't prevent them from wanting the other half. If you were persuaded to do a little investing, it would be ever so nice, and all in the family. Had that side of it occurred to you?"

"Naturally."

"Then powder your nose and come along. You're not a girl who makes up her mind quickly. You look things over, you don't rush into them. That's a spirit which the Russells will find commendable. Stretch it out for all it's worth, Terry. Every day we can bring ourselves to spend here under one family roof or another is money in the bank — provided they don't know it."

Writing to Helen at the end of her first week, Terry said that she felt like a child holding a kaleidoscope to her eyes and watching the bright patterns shift and fall, a multitude of moving shapes. Everything became impressions, nothing remained the same. *It's a wonderful place,* she wrote, *I'm beginning to love it. I'm not allowed to rush around and sightsee, I'm supposed to become acclimated. Chris's aunt never rushes and she accomplishes more than anyone I ever knew. She runs this big house and, I am told, half a dozen others, and she's on in-*

numerable committees. She entertains a great deal, mostly family and close friends. But she always has time to rest, to oversee her gardens — I've never seen anything like them — and to keep a hand on the reins. She's the head of the family, in an important sense. Her husband is dominated by her except in business. He's a kind man, dull as ditchwater, and his entire conversation is statistics. If I talk to him about the mixed races here, he breaks them down into groups, and when, as yesterday, we went out to one of the plantations I was dizzy with facts, figures, exports, tonnage, irrigation, and employment. I acquitted myself well enough. After all, the sugar business is not new to me.

Jack, she went on, is a pleasant if slightly pompous young man looking something like Chris but utterly unlike him. Both his and his father's interests seem terribly limited, but then I haven't known them for more than a week so I shouldn't say so.

Her pen seemed stiff and moved sluggishly. It was hard to write to Helen. The things she felt, and of which she was afraid, she dared not set down on paper. More than that she could not, bound by her promise to Chris. She could not write, *Here we are, it is fantastically beautiful, everyone is very kind, and I am terrified —*

She and Chris had almost quarreled over

spending their last days in the East at Helen's. It was true, as he pointed out, that Helen had implored her not to stop at a hotel. *Who knows how long before we will see each other again?* she had written to Terry, at Cape Cod. *Please try to persuade Chris to stay with us.* And it was also true that staying with Helen would save a hotel bill.

Terry had told him, "Under different circumstances I would not hesitate."

"You went directly to her," he said, "last spring. How different were circumstances then?"

And she had cried out, losing her temper, "Very different." She had said, "It's like the sets you read about in Hollywood studios — wonderful, luxurious houses, all false front, no substructure. Nothing back of them — just what you see, like us!"

He had been going for his morning swim with Charlotte's youngsters. She remembered how he had looked, the towel about his shoulders, his hair ruffled from sleep, as he stood at the screen door and said, "You should have thought of all this last spring. But you didn't know about my false front then. Only your own."

Now she picked up her pen again and ended her letter, with the expected reassurance. *Everything is wonderful,* she wrote, *and we are so happy.*

Which was, she reflected, stamping the thin envelope, too charmingly girlish. But it would, she hoped, satisfy her friend.

As far as façades were concerned, in the Islands, and for the moment at least, she had only her own to consider. For everyone here knew about Chris. He had no face to save. His face was quite familiar to them, that of the moderately black sheep, the indigent relative, the restless, good-for-nothing member of the family, "so like his father." But Chris had deviated from the distressing paternal pattern. His father had made a very bad marriage and Chris a very good one!

Terry went out on the *lanai*. A light slanting rain was falling, but the sun shone below and on the sea, a spectacle of which she never tired. It was probably not raining all over the city, she reflected. Jack had told her that it rained on one side of the street and not on the other; there were one-shower streets and two-shower streets, he had explained gravely. She was accustomed to mountains and to sea, to alternating cloud shapes and sudden rain. But here they differed from what she still called home.

Last night Chris had borrowed Jack's car and driven her to the summit of Tantalus, a terrifyingly twisted and steep way, but worth it. She had sat there in silence, leaning against him, watching the continually shifting views, and when they had parked near the top she had lost herself in wonder, watching the lights to the west shining from Schofield Barracks and Pearl Harbor and to the East from Diamond Head and Koko Head. There lay the valleys, in formless outline, Manoa and Pauoa — and she could see dimly the white tracing of the surf on the sands, the other tracing at the reefs. But the rest was all immensity of sky and the glory of the stars.

She had been up there by daylight, but by night it was another world, no more beautiful, perhaps, but more frighteningly so. They had not talked much. They had sat there with his arm around her, and after a while she sighed, and he bent, wordlessly, to kiss her.

And she thought, *Whatever happens, I'll remember this always.*

When Chris spoke, he said, "It's hard to believe now that for so long there were no lights."

In her letter to Helen she had tried to describe this drive by night with Chris. And she had failed. There were no words.

Cordelia knocked and opened the screen door. All the bedrooms had screened as well as ordinary doors in this great house. She asked, "Have you been resting?"

190

"Oh, yes, and writing letters."

Cordelia said, "I am driving over to the beach house — it doesn't belong to us, really," she explained, being meticulous, "it's a joint family holding. It was built by Chris's grandfather. We use it seldom, your uncle and I, but Jack, of course, more as business keeps him here in Honolulu. We have caretakers out there, an elderly Hawaiian couple. The wife was in the family a long time; she looked after Jack and, when he was with us, Chris, and, of course, Robert. Perhaps you would like to come and meet old Kaleki and her husband, Moki?"

They went by way of the Pali, which Terry had already seen, up Nuuanu Valley wearing rainbows like scarves, and between mountains alive with waterfalls. From the Pali itself Terry looked out upon the rock walls, the peaceful land beneath, the bays beyond. The wind tore at her, as the car stopped to afford her the ever-alternating view, the wind was wild and unceasing, it blew here always as in the days of Kamehameha's victory.

They drove on down the curving, abruptly descending road, and Terry said, "I thought I was used to mountain roads, but this and the road up Tantalus — "

"You'll get used to them," said Cordelia. She sat beside Terry and knitted calmly. She was always knitting. The brown, smiling, skillful chauffeur took the car down the tortuous way, and Cordelia said soothingly, "We'll come back the other way, Terry, by Koko Head and the shore."

It was a pleasant afternoon, except for Cordelia's gentle questioning — mainly about Terry's father. "I remember him so well," she said, "and that beautiful house. You did not keep it? What a pity. Chris would have enjoyed it, also." She added that she and her husband had in their long married life taken only two long trips, one the cruise that had terminated in the visit to Mark Austin, and the other when they went to Europe, "to bring Chris home," she said. "You know, of course, that he was in Paris when his parents died?"

"Yes. He just said he had returned, he didn't tell me that you — " She broke off, conscious that she had said too much, and Cordelia said dryly, "Probably not. For he did not wish to return with us. He was only a twelve-year-old boy, but very stubborn. He stayed with the Consulate people who befriended him until we came. We took Robert with us, for the change, and hoping that Chris would become more amenable if he saw his brother again."

"He was little and alone," said Terry

192

quickly, "and he must have suffered terribly from shock."

Cordelia patted her hand. "You don't need to defend him, my dear. In retrospect it seems long ago and far away. And now, I am sure, he has found himself — with you. The right wife, a family, responsibilities — these are what he has always needed."

Terry said nothing. She was remembering the Maui cousins. One of them was a little deaf and had raised her voice when speaking of Terry, who was, she thought, out of earshot. But Terry was out on the terrace admiring the orchids and clearly heard Cousin Sophie say, with satisfaction, "A very nice young woman. You say her father's success was recent? One would not believe it. She has none of the earmarks, she is quite unspoiled, very like the Family. One would never dream — "

She had ceased abruptly. Doubtless someone had choked her off, indicating Terry's presence on the terrace. But probably, Terry thought, the forthright old lady would have said, or at least thought, "one would never dream she had a cent." Which was pretty funny when you thought it over.

Chris had prepared her for this when the question of façade had arisen between them again, as it did, shortly before they left New

York. "No one," he had said, laughing, "will expect you to live up to the Austin legend. At least, they'll hope that you won't. People with great means come to the Islands, Terry, as tourists, as buyers of winter homes — 'New money,' my sainted family calls it, if, indeed, it mentions it at all. Security is in their bones and blood. They don't speak of it, even to one another. They do as they please and have what they want, but you'd think they plucked houses from trees and ran them on moonlight. They are consciously unconscious of the golden spoon, they don't talk through or around it; they swallowed it, every last one of them, at birth. Display is vulgar, says my aunt Cordelia. She spends anything she wishes for what she wishes. But there are a lot of things she doesn't wish, and therefore she doesn't spend in order to acquire. You'll learn after you've been with her awhile."

In a way, this attitude was fortunate, and the thought occurred to Terry a number of times during the first days. None of the Russells would *expect* her to rush out and buy houses, clothes, or start a jade collection. If she had, they would have been disappointed in her.

So far it had been easier than she had believed possible but the road on which she was set had heights and depths and unexpected twists and turns as terrifying as those leading down from the Pali. She woke each morning to the golden haze of light, a little more anxious than when she had gone to bed. Chris, on the other hand, was content to let things ride and said so. "Stop fretting," he told her. "Take it a day at a time." He added plaintively, "I'm helping, am I not?"

In his way he was, as none of his family had ever seen him more amenable. He paid informal calls on old friends, he went with Jack or Hugo on tours of inspection. He was sometimes gone all day. He told Terry that he was being talked *at*. "Oh, nothing definite, but it lurks," he said. "I'm permitting it, I'm listening. They know me too well to dream that I'd fall in their arms, crying, 'Here I am, the prodigal son, kill the fatted pig and let's have a *luau!* Take me, make something useful of me, set me to timekeeping, promote me to assistant manager, help yourself to my beautiful wife's money, buy a slice of pineapple, another stick of cane, build a couple more mills.' Yes, they'd be very suspicious if I showed signs of weakening in a week or two. So I'll let them talk, I'll let them work on me for quite a while, darling, quite a while. Until we get too bored," he added reflectively.

It amused him, Terry thought. He had never before been in this position or, she cor-

195

rected herself, this apparent position. In a sense it gave him temporarily the upper hand, with laughter in the sleeve as a fitting accompaniment.

Yet every day she woke to dread, and presently the two weeks had gone, and the Russells gave their parties.

Chapter Eight

A Wonderful, Terrifying Day

On the morning of the Russells' tea and dinner for Terry, Chris remarked, "Henceforward to be known as the Day of the Great Acceptance." He added that everyone had accepted, to the point of standing room only.

"And I," added Terry, "am also accepted, to coin a phrase, or for the time being."

She looked at Chris, who had just got up, and asked, "What if it rains?"

"It won't. Or, if it does, always remember that it's liquid sunshine. Hasn't Aunt Cordelia told you there's no word in Hawaiian for weather? Anyway, it wouldn't dare. I was up at sunrise and out on the *lanai*. You slept peacefully. Me, my head ached." He yawned. "I shouldn't go out with the boys, I'm getting too old. While you and Aunt Cordelia were discussing tatting last night and Uncle Hugo was writing in his diary, I was being entertained by my dear cousin and his pals. A sort of belated bachelor dinner — remember?"

"I couldn't forget," she assured him. She

thought that Chris was a little too unconcerned. Perhaps he was nervous. She asked him, "You aren't nervous, are you?"

"I am always nervous," he assured her, "when more than six people are assembled. How about you?"

"I'm so scared that my jaws ache," she answered truthfully.

"You don't look it. You look very lovely, sitting up in bed. Perhaps you should have had a *levee* instead of a tea."

She thought, *I never look it.* She had learned concealment the hard way; it would stand her in good stead today.

It was a beautiful day, from sunrise to sunset, all through the brief dusk, the rising of the moon; a day which had been ordered, a specially woven tapestry of gold and green and blue; a day of moving shadows, the shadow of palm and banyan, the shadow of clouds. The trade winds blew, and their burden was fragrance and music. The time came, people came with it, women in pretty frocks, as bright and delicate as the skillfully massed flowers, as the bloom of the gardens, and the orchids in the greenhouses; and Terry, standing beside Cordelia, offered her hand, smiled, and spoke her piece.

Pleasant people, friendly, flattering — if most of them had come out of curiosity, they didn't exhibit it. Terry had seldom seen so many gathered together upon a private occasion — young and old, they filled the rooms — the drawing-room, the library, the music room, and the long *lanai;* they walked upon the terrace and in the garden. They ate, drank, admired and felicitated the bride, congratulated the groom, and fell easily into small, intimate groups, greeting their dearest friends, slight acquaintances, and sworn enemies with equal fervor. And the Hawaiian musicians played all through the afternoon, building a background of melody, the old songs, sweet as the ripe cane, plaintive as the mourning dove, nostalgic as remembrance of the past. And everyone said to everyone else, "What a beautiful party!"

After the majority of the guests had come, Terry went circulating among them with Chris, in obedience to Cordelia's direction. "You have been standing still long enough, my dear. Chris, take Terry around and see that she really meets people." And after a while they went out on the terrace, and for a moment Chris stood still, oblivious of chatter as persistent as the mynah birds, inclining his head and listening to the music. Terry did not know the song, it seemed to her woven from the same sweetly mournful pattern as the others, but it seemed to reach him secretly, and

199

when he turned to her and they walked on, his eyes were clouded.

"What is it, Chris?" she asked, low.

"Nothing. When I'm away from home and hear so-called Hawaiian music in hotels or on the radio I hate it. It seems corny and is for the most part faked, stepped up, distorted, a carbon copy. Yet it always disturbs me. I don't know what they played just then, but it's old and pure, it belongs."

She said, "I loved it, darling."

He took her hand and held it, and people watched them, the girl with the smoke-black hair, a crown-flower *lei* about her neck, the sunlight on her yellow frock, and the tall young man, as blond as the legends describe the Hawaiian god Lono. "What a handsome couple," the guests said to one another; and some said, "Pity it couldn't have been Jack," and someone commented, "Usually a man is lucky to marry a girl with looks or one with money, but Chris Russell seems to have hit the daily double," and the woman with whom he spoke answered, laughing, "I knew those trips to California had more to do with Santa Anita than with business!" And a young man who had been with Jack's party last night at the Royal Hawaiian wondered aloud, "Will they stay here? Personally I think they're crazy, with the whole world to choose from."

He was, as it happened, an employee of the Russell interests and not happy about it. And Lilia Gurney, as Chris and Terry approached her, overheard.

Lilia was wearing white, and a big hat. She was, at all times, a lovely young woman. She cried, "Look, Chris, there's Alex. I was beginning to think he wouldn't get here."

Alex Gurney was too busy a man to drive into Honolulu for a daytime social occasion. But he had been able to come late, in time to take his wife home. He greeted Chris, his good smile warming an undistinguished face. "It's swell seeing you," he said, and looked at Terry, smiling. He added, "Chris is a lucky man, Mrs. Russell."

She said impulsively, "Couldn't you both be — less formal?" She liked Alex immediately. Not a big nor a good-looking man, she was instantly aware of dignity, sincerity, and quiet humor.

Lilia said, "We must be going now, I'm afraid. Terry, you'll come see us — perhaps later when you're able to get away for a weekend? It would be such fun. Chris, do persuade her." Her eyes, on Chris, were candid and affectionate, and Chris's reflected her honesty and warmth. And Terry thought, *Why, I like her, and I needn't have worried.*

But she hadn't worried, really. There was

nothing to worry about in that department, at least not yet.

Jack came up, crying "You aren't leaving, Lilia?" and Lilia said, "But we must," and the conversation was scattered and general. But Terry saw Jack's effort to keep from looking at the other woman and she thought, startled, *He is still in love with her.*

The Gurneys left to find Cordelia and Hugo and make their farewells. Others departed, a few latecomers came, and people exchanged pleasant gossip, made appointments, drifted from one to the other. There were legislators among the guests, and a very small percentage of mainland people who now made their home in the Islands; one visiting Hollywood celebrity who had been brought by his host, several beautiful women of mingled races, one Chinese-Hawaiian, the most exquisite creature Terry had ever seen, and there were also officers, those of the army and the navy, a judicious sprinkling of gold and silver bars, oak leaves, eagles, stars — And a woman's high-pitched voice remarked, over the other voices and the dreaming music, that uniforms certainly dressed up a party. And someone else said somberly that there was a time when uniforms were a damned sight less dressy and their wearers weren't drinking tea or high-balls in a garden — and not so long ago.

When finally it was over and the guests had gone, and sudden darkness fell like a cloak of dusky feathers, Cordelia patted Terry's hand and said, as to a child, "You acquitted yourself very well, my dear."

Hugo agreed. He was on his way upstairs to rest. His feet hurt, he said, and his face was stiff with smiling. Terry said, "Mine, too." And Jack, wandering in with a highball glass in his hand, asked, "When's dinner?"

"Not, thank heaven, until nine," his mother informed him. Several members of the clan were already beneath this roof where they would remain for a night, two nights, for as long as it pleased them. Some had taken up temporary quarters in their own Honolulu houses, some lived on Oahu, and by now Terry had met them all.

She went upstairs to rest and then to dress for dinner, and looked at herself in a long mirror. She took off the *lei* and looped it over the dresser. Tonight she would wear the gardenia *lei* that Jack had brought her.

Her dress was not new, and she had lowered the hem. But it was soft, fluid silk, very pale-yellow, and cut on classic lines. It became her very well. Jack had been moved to flattery earlier in the day. He had said, "You were pretty two weeks ago, Terry, but it seems to me that you grow more so every day.

203

The Islands agree with you."

She was lying in the tub, having extravagantly scented the water, when she heard Chris come into the bedroom. He called, she answered, and he whacked perfunctorily on the bathroom door, entered, and grinned at her from the doorway. He looked, she thought, tired.

"Go 'way," said Terry lazily. "I'll be out of here in a moment and you can soak. I'm worn out and you must be."

"I'm still on my feet. You look like a kid with your face scrubbed and shining and your hair pinned up like that. Well, so far so good. Everyone who rates with Cordelia came to look you over and wonder how I managed to delude you. Cordelia's tickled to death, in her restrained way."

"I only hope I get through tonight."

"You will. Chin up and all that sort of thing. What are you wearing?"

"I've decided — on the gray dress."

Chris asked, "You don't mind?"

"I mind. But it's the prettiest dress I own." she ran cold water over a washcloth and held it to her eyes. "I have to wear it sometime," she said.

"Forget the other time," he told her and came to lean down and lay his cheek briefly against her hair. The door closed and she was alone, and she lay back in the tub and thought about the gray dress.

Chris had seen it, she had brought it with her in the big wardrobe case. She had hung it in the closet at the Cotters', and he had asked, "Why don't you wear that?" and she had told him.

The dress had been made for her in New York at the shop which kept a model-form of her measurements, after she could no longer get things from Paris. She had drawn a rough design and selected the material from swatches air-mailed to her, the finished frock had been flown to Guatemala. It had been ordered in time to wear at a formal dinner her father was giving. The last, the last at which, secure and without premonition, she had presided as Mark Austin's hostess.

She thought again, *I must wear it sometime. I'm being very silly.*

Yet when, later, she put it on, she was shaking. She felt its sliding weight and texture, she saw in the mirror the reflected sheen, the muted color, which was like her eyes, but lighter, neither quite gray nor quite leaf-green but a mingling of these. She remembered the first time she had worn it, which was also the last, and how Maria had exclaimed, calling her dove, and heart's darling, and most beautiful.

Her father had liked it, too. When she came down the curving stairs, there he had stood looking up and smiling at her.

This was a picture dress, high fashion then and now. It was fashioned of a heavy satin, obtainable at an outrageous price. The long skirt was very full, the bodice tight, the waist diminished to fragility. It was a dress which covered her to her hands, to her throat, having a small, turned-down collar, and voluminous sleeves ending tightly at the wrists. There was no ornamentation on it except the antique small buttons at wrists and down the bodice; and these were of gold.

With it, she had thought to wear part of the set of amethysts that had been her mother's. She opened her jewel case and put them on, the brooch, the pendant earrings, the matching bracelets, and the big ring in which the stone was the color of a dark wine, like the sea at the horizon here in Honolulu.

Chris said, "I don't dare touch you, damn it. You're very beautiful, Terry."

"Distinguished," she corrected absently, "and striking. Never really beautiful, Chris."

But she was not thinking of him, she was looking into the mirror as if hypnotized by her own reflection. Yet she was not seeing it, nor thinking of this house, nor of the people in it, nor of this night, and this land, an island set in

206

the sea. She was thinking of her father and of Maria. She had not written Maria since leaving New York. She would wire tomorrow, and Maria's nephew would reply for the old woman, in his curious mixture of school-taught English and remarkably formal Spanish. And then she was seeing candles flickering on the dark wood of a long table, on lace and linen, on the shining crystal and the wine in the glasses. She was seeing Mark Austin, far down the table from her, laughing, his head thrown back. And the great cool *sala*, the patio beyond; and hearing the music; not the music of the steel guitar but that of the marimba.

"Come back to me!" said Chris sharply.

Terry turned and smiled, but he saw that her mouth was unsteady and her eyes sorrowful — and moved quickly to put his arms about her. "To hell with the dress," he said. "Terry, darling — "

But someone knocked, and Cordelia asked, "Are you dressed, may I come in?"

So, at dinner, Terry did not wear the amethysts but the garnets which Cordelia had come to give her, together with the rest of the jewelry in the old leather box. "I have divided it," she said, "half for you, Terry, half for Jack's wife — when he acquires one."

She was distressed, but pleased, when Terry

moved to take the earrings from her ears, unclasp the bracelets, unpin the brooch. She said, "Oh, don't take them off, Terry, they are lovely. Are they family pieces?"

Her mother's, her grandmother's, Terry explained and showed Cordelia the other things, sapphires in ancient settings, a pearl dog collar, many of the pearls black with age, the light cross of tortoise shell and pearls, the heavy cross of crystal, the onyx, the jet, the rose-cut diamonds. She said, putting them away, "I've never cared much for modern things, you know."

Cordelia was delighted. She had quite normally expected that Chris's wife would possess the costly customary glitter in abundance. But here was a girl of discernment, one who would appreciate her garnets, and the matched sets of turquoise and of topaz. She put the shabby case in Terry's hands and said, "I am glad that you will like wearing these."

Twenty-six people sat down to a family dinner that evening, and the musicians played on the *lanai*, and later, under a moon sliced from silver and hanging pendant from the sky, the Hawaiian women came to dance. Two or three were young and very pretty but the others were old, or middle-aged, heavy and tall, with great dignity and beauty. They danced, not the hulas the tourists know, but the old hulas, which were prayers and tranquillity, rejoicing and thanksgiving. And sometimes they danced only to a drum, struck by the oldest of them all, and at the end she sang for them — not a song, but, Chris whispered to Terry, "a *mele*, a chant." The old woman sat, her body swayed, her hands moved, and the chanting was as if the soul of a people had spoken.

Terry's eyes were bright with tears, and people saw and were pleased, and thought, the young men with envy, *I hope he appreciates her.*

This was the night when all of the clan who could come had done so. The oldest was not there, Josiah Russell, but he had sent a gift.

They had all brought gifts. "For your house, when you have one, Terry," or, "Wherever you go, to remind you of the Islands." There were very old poi bowls, carved from a single piece of wood, polished by use and age, patched by skillful hands; gifts of linen, of woven *lauhala* mats, of crystal etched with ginger blossoms and the bird of paradise flower. And Hugo had something for her, a string of gem jade beads, heavy and cold, and from Jack a *lei* of crown flowers, carved from ivory.

So, because they were kind, because music

sang, and the scent of blossoms was wonderful in the night, because Chris looked at her with ardor and tenderness, Terry felt, for the first time since that morning in New York after her marriage, secure and relaxed, lulled to a quiet, miraculous happiness.

Chapter Nine

An Unwelcome Visitor

After that they made the house on Tantalus their headquarters and began the round of visits. There would be rains and Kona storms and drops in temperature, but for the most part the sun would shine. Was Terry afraid of high altitude? She must visit Great-uncle Josiah Russell on the Big Island, on his cattle ranch run by a grandson. It was three thousand feet high and cold at night, she must take warm things. Terry explained that she had lived for years in high places, at five thousand feet — for instance, in Guatemala. Did she like swimming? She must go to Cousin Laura's beach house on Kauai. And had she been to Kona? Kona was still old Hawaii, she could drive from Josiah's ranch and spend the day.

Jack said, "You should have a car," but Terry asked, "How?" and he agreed it was tough and took a long time. Meanwhile they could use his, and he would drive his father's. And so they had a car in which to explore

Oahu, to drive to this person's for tea or for dinner, for a day at the beach or on a plantation. They spent one such day with Lilia, in the attractive house that Alex Gurney, as manager, occupied. The cane grew tall, toward its maturity, toward the day when it would ripen, the tassels dance in the wind, mauve and gray, and be immolated in the flame of its burning, be struck down, cut, and taken to the mill.

But she hadn't seen it all, and she must, they cried. She had not seen Mauna Loa and Mauna Kia, crowned with snow, nor looked up at them in the spring through the lilac-blue haze of jacaranda blossoms in someone's garden. She had not ascended to Kilauea, past the red bloom of ohias and the giant tree ferns, to look into the cup of fire, where Pele slumbers, waking at intervals to pour forth her molten lava. She had not seen, on Maui, the high broken shape of Haleakala, which is the sun's house, yet over which the moon rises bright as day. And she must watch the fishermen by night in the flare of torches, or by day, casting their nets. She must know Kona, which is still old Hawaii, and see the waves break on the black lava, and ride on dusty roads, thick with jacaranda, hedged with hibiscus. Nor must she forget the rainy coast of the Big Island, the cane rushing down the flumes, the waterfalls, the rainbows, the broken coast line.

So all this she saw, as the weeks went by and she flew, always with Chris, occasionally with Cordelia, from island to island, high over the water which was milk and jade, sapphire and turquoise, emerald and indigo and wine, and beneath them the moving shadow of their wings.

Between their visitings, when they were back at the house on Tantalus, Terry made or received calls with Cordelia, attended church, visited hospitals and museums, and served for Cordelia's charities. Cordelia was charmed with her facility with the needle. So unusual, she said more than once, boasting of it gently as if she patted Terry's head and gave her a bon-bon for good behavior.

No one pressed or hurried her, but everyone they met or visited asked, sooner or later, "When are you going to find a place?" or, "Have you and Chris decided on anything?" and, "Did you know the Elwood place is on the market?" Sold to mainlanders before the war, it was for sale again. "It would be ideal, it's out Diamond Head way, so if Chris should decide to go into the office —"

Chris, if present, merely smiled and said nothing, except "It's up to Terry," which placed the burden on her, and she became increasingly adept at evasion, replying that they had not yet come to a decision.

No one questioned that. This was a land in which the resident was active, conducted his business, made, as a rule, a profit, but did not hurry, especially when, as in this instance, there was no necessity. Only Jack Russell speculated. He said privately to his father, "You'll see, Chris has no more intention of remaining here than I have of leaving. He'll amuse himself until he's bored, then he'll put Terry under his arm, and they'll be off, God knows where. I wouldn't be in her shoes."

"You're not apt to be," said his father with heavy humor. "Well, it would be a good thing if he'd decide to stay. If anyone can make a man of him, she can."

"It's a little late, isn't it? If, perhaps, he'd married a girl without money? But then, of course, he wouldn't."

"They're extremely happy."

"Maybe. But he hasn't changed," Jack said.

By January, some four months after their arrival, the weekly boats were bringing their load of sun seekers, vacationers from New York and Boston, from Chicago and Hollywood, from Maine and Connecticut. In January, Charlotte Davidson wrote to Terry:

Roger Amenly's wife has procured her divorce. There were all sorts of repercussions, as she's a garrulous gal. I enclose the clippings. Roger's book is on the spring list, Hollywood has bought it from manuscript. But he has vanished from our ken, for which heaven be praised. (Remember how grateful I was when he departed suddenly from the Cape, a couple of days before you did? And how when I said, "I'm sorry, Roger," he retorted, "You lie, dear, you have always disliked me"?) Anyway, all communications go through his agent, who wrote Kent that Roger had rented a hideaway, at La Jolla, in order to write what he — Roger, not the agent — termed an important book. Which will flop, said the agent sadly.

Terry showed the letter to Chris, who remarked, "And that disposes of our little friend. See how you got steamed up over nothing — which goes for me, too. He was sore; his pass wasn't completed, so he took refuge in vague threats and menacing gestures. Forget it." He forgot it a moment after and said, "I wish we weren't going to Lilia's for the week-end."

"Why?"

"I don't know. I'm getting — oh," he said vaguely, "fed up."

This was what she had feared, and lately had realized. Four months is a long time to

215

wear the mask, to sit behind it smiling and amiable. She felt sharply the antagonism between Chris and his cousin, between Chris and Cordelia. It rarely came to words, but it was there. It was as if Jack were watching Chris for a signal, a misstep, as if Cordelia weighed him day after day in the balance. Chris had long since given up his early pretense of interest in the business preoccupations of his uncle and cousin. He had exhausted all that in the first two weeks. Now he did not go to the office or visit, except socially, a plantation, whether of cane or of pineapples. He went off on his own concerns or remained with Terry. And it was beginning to bore him.

Terry had become cautiously intimate with Cordelia Russell. She was a little afraid of, but liked her. She had learned real respect for what she felt was Cordelia's integrity. *But,* she argued with herself, *she hasn't been fair.* Why Robert and not Chris — why Robert in preference to her own son? She could not understand this, the sorrow not exhausted, the idolatry that could not be concealed. Nothing in the photographs Cordelia showed her appeared to warrant it, nor in the letters which, after a time she brought out and gave Terry to read. Boyish, unremarkable chronicles written from college and during his war service.

"The snapshots and photographs don't do him justice," Cordelia said, "he was a very handsome boy."

Yet not so handsome as Chris, nor even as Jack, thought Terry, holding the lifeless representations in her hand. Bob had been taller than Chris, in most of the pictures he was a little stooped. And he was quite dark, with thick black hair and, she judged, brown eyes.

Cordelia asked on one occasion, "Chris told you about him?"

She answered warily, "Yes, Aunt Cordelia."

Cordelia said after a while, "I see. He told you that Robert drank? To the end of my days, I shall never know why. He had so much to give, he was given so much." She added, clearing her throat, "If it had been Chris — "

Terry thought often of this conversation, which took place shortly after Christmas — an "old-fashioned" Christmas, with the clan gathering, and the traditional carols and plum pudding, the exchanging of gifts and the overeating. She had dreaded Christmas; it had entailed the most careful shopping and expenditure. But Chris had told her that they would not expect her to go overboard; in fact, they wouldn't like it if she had.

Cordelia had liked Terry's gift. "I thought,"

217

said Terry, "you might like it better than anything I could buy." It was a mantilla, one of several which had arrived in the trunks and had belonged to Terry's mother, black lace, delicate and old. Cordelia had been quite enchanted. Perhaps because after a fashion it linked her with Terry's past, she became thereafter, somewhat more outspoken.

So she said — "If it had been Chris." She regarded Terry steadily. She said, "You love him, and see no fault. And I find none, Terry, but his restlessness, his lack of roots, of attachments, his unwillingness to put his hand to the plow — all the Russells have worked, and worked hard, and all the men of my family — these things we have never been able to understand. No, that's not altogether true. In these things he is like his father."

"And his mother?" asked Terry quietly.

A curious expression flickered over Cordelia's face. She said, "She was besotted about her husband, and to the exclusion of her children. I never knew her well. None of us did."

She added that Chris had great potentiality for good and, "We count on you," she said.

Terry did not repeat this to Chris. No secrets, he had warned her. But if he knew that Cordelia had discussed him he would hate it, he would say, "Pack your things, and we'll be off. We can get to the mainland, go some place cheap for a while. There's a town in Mexico you'd like." She knew he would say it, he had already done so once or twice. But the day would come when he would mean it. And she was happy here.

Not wholly happy. But she could be. She was at home in the Islands, bemused by them. She liked many of Chris's relatives and their friends. If she could be here on an honest footing, she thought, if she could be here not as Mark Austin's daughter but as herself?

They went to Lilia's for the week-end; she had a dinner party for them; it was gay and entertaining, and Terry liked Lilia very much. She had liked her from the day they met, and more each time thereafter. She was fun to be with, friendly and amusing, and she had an enormous vitality, a capacity for enjoyment which was engaging. Terry said as much, driving out to the plantation, and added, "I expected I'd hate her."

"No one hates Lilia."

"I should. You were in love with her."

"Long ago and far away," he reminded her.

"You're fond of her still."

"Naturally I was fond of her before I fell in love with her," he said, smiling.

"Yet you were sharp about her, Chris, even

a little mean. You said she knew which side her bread was sugared on."

"I merely coined a phrase. Her family knew, let's say. They, like myself, are on the poor-relation roster. Jack was preferable to me. Besides, Lilia was a kid, hardly eighteen, and didn't know what she wanted."

"She must have wanted Alex."

He shrugged. "He was pitiably in love with her." He paused, and Terry thought he would add "too." But he did not. "And, I expect, after that blazing row with her family, he seemed a refuge. Perhaps she was in love with him, who knows? She was plenty mixed up. There was talk of having it annulled, in solemn family conclave. But an elopement was scandal enough. Besides, they all knew Alex; good, steady, reliable guy, Island-born, and a worker. She might have done worse. Also he was a close friend of her brother Tom's — and Tom, older than Lilia and with a head on his shoulders despite his bad temper, made their parents accept the situation. I dare say he's made her a good husband, as husbands go."

They remained at Lilia's until Monday, and Sunday night Cordelia telephoned at about ten o'clock to tell Chris that a cable had come for him. "I thought," she said thinly over the wire, "that it might be important.

Shall I open it, Chris?"

He said, "Yes," standing there in the wide square hall, and looking to the *lanai* where Lilia, Alex, and Terry sat talking.

Cordelia was silent, he heard the rip of paper and then her voice again.

" 'Sailing next week hope convenient for you and Terry,' " she read. " 'Grateful for invitation and looking forward to seeing you.' "

She paused, and Chris said, "What's it signed?"

"Roger —" she hesitated, and then, "Amenly. Perhaps I do not pronounce it correctly."

He said, "Hell," clearly, and Cordelia said, "Really, Chris —" and Lilia and Terry glanced up across the *lanai* to the hall.

"Sorry," said Chris. "Yes, it's Amen, pronounced as in prayer — thanks, Aunt Cordelia."

She said he was welcome and hung up, and he stood there a moment waiting, wondering, in a blind sort of disgust and anger, how he had been so stupid as not to foresee just this. And on the *lanai* Lilia said, laughing, "Did he actually say 'Hell' and then 'Amen'? What in the world did he mean?"

Terry said, "I can't imagine." But she could, as Chris moved out to join them and looked at her in warning.

And then he said evenly, "Believe it or not, we're having a guest."

"We can't," said Terry lightly, her hands cold. "We *are* guests."

"My error," said Chris. "I tossed invitations around like confetti." He looked at Lilia and asked, "You recall him, Roger Amenly?"

"Of course," said Lilia. Her face did not alter much, and Alex, looking at his watch, for it was his bedtime, asked lazily, "Who is he? I never heard of him."

"You must have, dear — not that you ever listen," said Lilia. "The man — a writer — whom Tom and I met on the mainland." She added thoughtfully, "Tom doesn't like him, Chris, and neither do I."

Terry said, "No one seems to like him." She spoke deliberately, to give Chris his clue, and Lilia, too, if she needed one. "I'm afraid it's my fault," she went on. "I asked him. I knew him at home, when he visited my father."

Lilia's eyes were eloquent. They spoke to Terry's, they said, *It's you, then? But you can take care of him or Chris can.* She breathed deeply and smiled at her husband. She said, "Time for bed, Alex."

"Pity the poor manager," said Alex, "up before dawn. Are you coming out to the crossing tomorrow morning, Terry, to see me set an example?"

"Don't," advised Lilia, "it will kill you. When the whistle blows, turn over and go back to sleep."

"I'll come," said Terry. It wasn't hard to get up in the soft darkness on Monday morning. She had slept very little. She had asked Chris over and over, "But *why?*" and he had said, "God knows, except that it's Lilia, of course. Not that he can make any headway. She stated her position clearly enough, didn't she?"

"But we can't have him. I mean, it isn't your house, what will your aunt say?"

"She'll say that a guest of ours is, of course, her guest. She will hope for the best, she'll expect it from a friend of yours. Are you going on record there?"

"Yes."

"Then she will expect him to be courteous, amiable, aware of the beauty of his surroundings and the importance of his hosts. If he were presented as my friend, she'd worry."

Terry said hopefully, "Perhaps he won't stay long."

"Who has not stayed long if he could?" inquired Chris. "With the thousand and one things to show him, as you've been shown, and people crying as they've cried to you, these past months, wait until you see spring and the shower trees, wait until *Lei* Day, and wait until Kamehameha Day, wait until you have seen the Russell stronghold. The Russells' island. For the Russells rarely go there until the spring, you know. I heard Aunt Cordelia planning a trip, for two weeks, she said, or three, with Jack and Hugo coming when they could — by plane and by boat. No, Amenly won't leave on the next sailing or the one thereafter. He'll stay. He'll get material for a book. I can hear him say it. Stop worrying," he added, "there will be a way, some way. Go to sleep."

But she did not sleep and rose in the darkness and in the sudden pouring rain to go to the crossing with Alex and watch the workers converge and the trucks rumble away into the fields.

They drove back to Honolulu on Monday afternoon, and Terry said, "It's stopped raining."

"Yes, some time ago. What is really on your mind?"

"Nothing that I didn't tell you last night, Chris. And that's still there."

"Play it my way. I'll send a wireless to the ship, a day or so after the sailing. Let's hope he won't be on it."

"He gave no address in the cable, purposely. He'll be on the ship, Chris."

"All right. Attack is better than defense, and to disarm is better than either."

"But what does he *want?*"

"Lilia."

"That's fantastic. He was on his honeymoon when he met her and Tom!"

Chris laughed shortly.

Terry said, "Very well, we'll assume it. Yet I can't believe it. I know him better than you do. He isn't capable of wanting anything very much, and certainly not for long."

"You merely mean that in your case the villain ceased to pursue. My darling, one swallow does not make a summer or even a satisfying thirst quencher."

"Please be serious, Chris."

"I was never more so. Let's look at it dispassionately. When, before we left Cape Cod, you told me the details of your acquaintance with our prospective guest, what did these amount to? That he somewhat reluctantly asked you to marry him, and you refused. After he left, you had a letter or two from him, reproachful but hardly tragic. On the literary side, you said. Then silence, and lots of it. What would have been in it for him if he'd kept on annoying you? Your father was a powerful man, your position tenable, so he picked up his marbles and went home."

"Well?"

He asked patiently, "Can't you see that it's different with Lilia? She's married, she was away from home when she met him, and something singularly unpleasant must have happened. Tom probably stepped in and crowned him. *Not* with flowers."

"You said that last night; I still don't get it."

"As I see Amenly, the picture's clear enough. He's a little guy, no longer young. He has had, to date, three unsuccessful marriages. In his intervals of freedom he has probably tried to marry advantageously. You, for instance. Did you think you'd be the only one? Of course not. In or out of freedom, he's amused himself, and when it comes to the intention dishonorable, a married woman's much safer — provided she's clever and discreet and her husband either indifferent or remote. Amenly has been busy for most of his adult life trying to prove something to himself. The psychologists are not dumb, Terry. They have plenty of valid explanations. I don't know what's eating him — I'll never know, I dare say. Whatever it is, it probably has its roots in a feeling of inferiority. He hasn't been successful professionally until recently, either. And even this success isn't the one he wants. He makes money, but has no prestige. Remember, Charlotte wrote that

Amenly had said he was going to write an important book? He never will, he's too shallow, too preoccupied with himself. He's finally made some money but it wasn't only money he wanted. He isn't even at the top of his specialized field. I asked Kent. His stuff is derivative, it belongs to a school he didn't found."

"What has all this to do with Lilia?"

"I don't know, but I'll make a guess. Amenly's honeymoon was over, probably before it began. He was bored with the third Mrs. A. Lilia is a very attractive woman. She was married. Her husband was a long way off. Maybe Mrs. Amenly was bored with her bridegroom. Yes, that's it. He'd sold her a bill of goods, no doubt. So he had to go on proving to himself that he was irresistible, the great lover, the uncommon man. Lilia was the proving-ground. Only it didn't work out. It's one thing to have a proposal of marriage refused, another to lose out on a proposition. Lilia wasn't having any, and Tom said scat, with painful accompanying gestures."

"How do you know?"

"I know Tom."

"Go on," said Terry.

"Amenly was still sore, if not literally. He never expected to see Lilia again, the casual invitation to visit Tom was withdrawn — an invitation tendered, no doubt, during the first day or so when they were pals, over a shot of bourbon. So he had to write her off as a failure. Then you turned up — another failure, by the way, which added insult to injury. And you turned up married to a Russell." He grinned and added, "Of course, when he meets the Russells in their own bailiwick, particularly Christopher John Russell, he's going to be very astonished — and pleased. But to return to his meeting you. He had something on you. You don't think he was just sitting in the shack concocting murders, do you? I have a very well-founded idea that he made cautious inquiries. It wouldn't be hard. He could remark to Charlotte, for instance, that it never failed, the alliance of the privileged, as exemplified by Mark Austin's daughter and a Russell. Whatever she said would be enough to inform him that she didn't know about your father. There was also the newspaper comment. One and one could add up to a lot. It wouldn't be hard to figure that your friends were in total ignorance of your father's financial and personal status at the time of his death. He probably didn't bother to make inquiries about me; if he did, they would have availed him nothing in that section of the country. So he saw an opportunity to come here under, as he remarked, the best auspices, and to get even with Lilia — and Tom."

She said, "I know. I agree to a point but I still don't see why."

"A woman scorned," said Chris, smiling, "is admittedly a hellcat. But a man of Amenly's type — oh, brother!"

"It's ridiculous," she said firmly.

They were silent, and Chris thought his own thoughts. Lilia had spoken to him last night. They'd been alone, and she'd said, "I'm thinking of going to Maui for a while." Her aunt lived on Maui, Lilia often visited her. But Chris hadn't let it go at that. He'd asked, "Because of Amenly's cable?"

She said simply, "I don't want to meet him again, Chris. And I'd be sure to. Aunt Cordelia will entertain for him, I can't always refuse; besides, he'll say he knows us. I can't risk it."

"For your sake or Tom's?"

She said, "He and Tom had a row, yes. You know Tom and his quick temper. But Tom was sorry afterward, he said they were both tight, perhaps Amenly didn't mean to be offensive. And Tom's devoted to you, to all the family. If Roger Amenly were your guest he'd behave himself."

"You'd better tell me the truth, Lilia."

She said, "I was a fool. I didn't mean to let it go so far."

"How far?"

229

"Not that far, Chris, but he believed, he thought — "

She'd broken off then, and he'd asked sharply, "Why? why did you let him think — whatever he believed?"

"I was bored. Oh, it sounds so stupid, and it was," she said in exasperation, "but life had gone on here for so long in the same way. I felt as if it would be like that till I died. I looked in the mirror, I'd changed very little but I felt unattractive, as if there were nothing ahead for me."

"What about Alex?"

She said, with difficulty, "Alex is wonderful, everything that's good and kind. I don't deserve him. I never have."

She did not say, "I am in love with him." If she were she would not have come to this flat stretch of living, arid and desolate.

"Alex loves you very much."

"I know, I know. If we had had children — But that's stupid, too. I can't, Chris. You know medical statistics prove that it is much more likely to be the husband's fault — only 'fault' isn't the right word — than the wife's. But not in this case. But would things have been different? Surely children don't solve everything, do they?"

"I don't know," he'd answered. "Certainly in my parents' case, they constituted a problem."

"Alex made me take that trip with Tom, which we couldn't afford, to get me away, to give me a change," she said forlornly.

He said, "It seems that we haven't mentioned Amenly's wife."

"They had been living together for quite a while before their marriage. He told me so," she said dully. "He said she'd threatened him with some sort of nasty lawsuit if he didn't marry her. So he did, on the understanding that after a suitable interval she'd divorce him. He said she was willing, because she'd have a legal right to alimony or a settlement."

"Nice guy."

"Here comes Terry. She's such a darling. I hope she likes me and that you're terribly happy."

That was that. Chris could fill in the blanks. Lilia had once been in love touchingly and with candor, as he had been. The Petersons cried, what nonsense, at her age, she could not throw herself away, moreover it wasn't serious. But they hadn't worried about her age when Jack put in his bid. They'd simply said, how suitable, how delightful, but of course it couldn't be formalized as yet by an announced engagement. How had she felt about Jack? She hadn't told him, on the day she said, "I'm marrying Jack, Chris, when

I'm nineteen." That was the day Chris had walked out of the house on Diamond Head. He hadn't been in it since, until last week when the Petersons had a small family dinner for Terry.

He had seen Lilia once after that day, and at Naniola in the following spring, when she had cried in his arms and said, "But it isn't any use, Chris," and when he'd said, "We can run away," she cried harder than ever and told him, "They'd have it annulled; and besides, we haven't anything."

Jack had walked in on that little scene, and presently a sampan had taken Chris away from Naniola in, he remembered, something of a storm. And the storm had gone on after he left.

Jack wasn't marrying Lilia when she was nineteen or ninety. Convinced that her attachment to his cousin had been of the valentine and schoolgirl variety, he'd been willing to overlook it. But not hearing her say, "I don't love him, how could I?"

But Chris had nothing except a job which he disliked and at which he wasn't especially good. And after a while Lilia had run off, not with him, but with Alex, who had always been doggedly in the background, if without hope, and ten years older than Lilia. The Gurneys were not the Russells, but they were solid and frugal, respected and liked. Alex had a job he enjoyed, at which he was very good, and which promised him a future, not spectacular but assured.

Chris had never figured out why she'd married Alex, why she hadn't waited — for someone who would be right for her. Perhaps, young and emotionally immature, she had been sick of loving violently and being as violently loved. Perhaps Alex had represented the way out, the peace after the storm. She need give him so little to make him happy.

Terry said, "You've been awfully quiet for miles and miles."

He said truthfully, "I was thinking about Lilia."

"I know." She put her hand over his on the wheel. "Do you believe," she asked, "that there's something troubling her, more than just not liking Roger?"

He could not tell her. No secrets, they had said, but this was not his secret. He could say only, "I don't know what to think."

Chapter Ten
FORCED TO THE TRUTH

Roger Amenly leaned on the rail and watched the beauty and color approach and slip past, saw the high white finger of the Aloha Tower, listened to the chatter of his shipmates, and remembered Chris's wireless — *On the dock to meet you, as promised.*

The small boat came scooting out, the people came aboard, their arms heaped with *leis.* But not Chris — Chris would be on the dock. A reporter and a photographer made their way to Roger and said, "Mr. Amenly?" It was quite pleasant. They knew all about him, the travel articles, the Hank Howard whodunits. They asked where he was staying, and he answered casually, "With friends, the Christopher Russells."

He was having a very good time.

Did he intend to write articles about Hawaii, how long would he be here, was he planning a novel? Roger shrugged amiably. He couldn't say, really. He'd come for an indefinite time, and to relax. As to articles or novels, one never knew, but all material was grist to the author's mill. Yes, the coast line was very beautiful. Yes, Diamond Head was extraordinarily impressive.

Snap went the camera, scratch went the pencil. There were others aboard, more fashionable, more celebrated; Amenly had been something of an afterthought. The senator, the two Hollywood stars, the singer — these were really important.

Damn Chris, he might have come out in the small boat.

But Chris waited on the dock, and he carried a red-carnation *lei*. He said when Amenly reached him, "An indicated aloha," looped the *lei* around Amenly's neck and added, smiling, "I hope it chokes you," and presently led the way to the car.

"Terry sends her apologies," he said, and made no other excuse.

Driving through the streets Roger remarked, "I'll spare you the usual tourist exclamations. But this is quite a place, Chris. Where are we headed?"

"For my uncle's," said Chris. "Terry and I stay there when we're in Honolulu."

"I'm afraid it's an imposition," Roger began, with great correctness.

"It is, indeed," Chris agreed, "but my good aunt is always most hospitable. I'll have to warn you that she doesn't tolerate, even in a guest, the unquenchable thirst, an off-color story, or the type of profanity that is admissible in most places."

"Thanks. Have you seen Lilia Gurney?"

"Yes."

"Does she know I'm coming?"

"She knows. Terry and I were spending a week-end with Lilia and her husband when your welcome cable arrived."

"You're quite a boy," said Roger fondly. "Shall we swear an eternal friendship?"

"I'm not in the mood," said Chris, and calculated Roger's luggage — the suitcases, the inevitable typewriter, the trunk that would eventually arrive on Tantalus.

"I'll see her," said Amenly. It was not a question.

"Not, I gather, if she can help it," Chris retorted.

"Oh, you are in her confidence?" inquired Roger. "Yet she won't be able to help it — will she?"

The traffic was heavy, Chris put his mind upon his driving. He answered after a time, "I am not in Lilia's confidence. All I know is, she likes you no better than Tom does. If you see her, it won't be through any arrangement I make."

"I'm sure you're speaking impulsively,"

said Roger. "Anyway, women are much cleverer about these things. Perhaps Terry will be more amenable."

"Why," asked Chris, "and I inquire merely to make conversation, do you come where obviously you're not wanted?"

Amenly said, "This doesn't sound like bands playing and beautiful women singing in welcome. I might as well be on Fifty-second Street. But to answer your question. I came because it amuses me not to be wanted, by the charming Mrs. Gurney, her somewhat excitable brother, by you and Terry. You're all so damned smug," he explained equably, "it irritates me."

"If you think we're smug," said Chris, "wait till you meet the rest of us."

"So self-assured and integrated," Amenly went on. "Except, naturally, Terry. Her assurance was shaken for a while; then you came along and restored it permanently." He paused, and added gently, "I hope."

"What do you want with Lilia?" Chris asked.

"How crude. Would you be astonished if I said I fell in love with her, and find her unforgettable?"

"Yes and no."

"Meaning?"

"Meaning that she's a lovely young woman,

it would be easy for any man to fall in love with and remember her. But also that she is happily married. So you can't marry her — Even if you could, it would not be to your advantage. The Petersons have everything but money," Chris said.

"A rich man always suspects a poor man of mercenary motives."

"Have you never harbored them?"

Roger laughed. "Terry has told you? But who could blame me? Beauty *and* a fortune. But it was clairvoyant of her to turn me down!"

Amenly was comfortable in the house on Tantalus. He made himself agreeable. He was apologetic and almost self-effacing. Hugo said he wasn't a bad sort, and Jack was astonished by his intelligence. He hadn't believed that Chris would have a friend — well, Amenly was Terry's friend really — so interested in the sugar business, so anxious to see the workings, the wheels. And Cordelia commented that their guest was very nice. He waited on her, which she liked, although it confused her, as she was usually too busy. He even held her yarn for winding.

In the early course of his visit, Terry and Chris took Amenly dutifully from Waikiki to the Blow Hole, from beach house to the

Royal. He was never alone with them on these excursions. There was always someone who went along, sometimes Cordelia or, if she could not go, anyone whom they could press into service. "Do come," Terry would say to one of her new friends, "it's so much more fun when there's four!"

Lilia, they ascertained, was on Maui when Amenly arrived and Tom, where he worked and belonged, on Kauai. But Jack was a weak link in the defense, he talked by the hour to their visitor, over brandy in the library or out on the terrace or over a dinner table. Amenly listened, and Amenly said, "Big business has always been extremely interesting to me. I'd like to get enough material to do a series of articles on industry in the Islands. It's time someone did a good, and just, job, I think."

"Well," Chris told Terry gloomily, after Amenly had been in residence for nearly three weeks, "he has Jack hypnotized. Hugo, too, for that matter, and almost Aunt Cordelia."

Jack took Amenly with him on various business expeditions, a plantation here, another there, a trip to Lanai to see the pineapples, one to the cannery in Honolulu where some canning was done year round, although this was not "the" season, a flight to the Big Island, and a round of plantation viewing on Oahu.

Inevitably Lilia returned, she could not remain away forever, she had her very considerable duties at the plantation, and Cordelia dropped the brick at dinner one night. She'd met Harriet Peterson at the bank. She hadn't seen her in weeks. Her asthma was better, poor woman. And Lilia was home.

Amenly asked brightly, "That wouldn't be Lilia Gurney, would it? It's an uncommon name. Or, perhaps not, here. But if so, I met her and her brother in Los Angeles some time ago. It would be pleasant to see them again."

Cordelia assured him that it was, indeed, Lilia Gurney. She said, "I'll ask her and Alex to dinner. Tom's on Kauai, he's rarely in Honolulu."

Amenly did not visibly show relief but that he felt it Chris had no doubt.

Amenly thought, *It's too easy*, and for the fraction of a minute wished it were not, wished he could stay another week or two in this great cool house innocent of motive. He could be quite content with these friendly, stodgy people, at whom he could laugh a little secretly. Content, that is, if Chris were not there to watch him, and Terry, remote, pleasant, and unrevealing. He could not regard Chris without envy — he was luckier than Jack, he didn't have to work — nor Terry without rancor.

But Lilia Gurney had stirred him as Terry had not, as no woman had since, perhaps, the first. He'd fallen in love with her as he hadn't, in many years, with any woman, without reserve, with even a little terror, He had tried to rationalize it. *It doesn't mean anything except that you're getting old, so you're scared, you're trying to find your way back to something that no longer exists.*

For a brief time he had believed, with as near an approach to humility as was possible, that Lilia was interested in him. She liked being with him, enjoyed listening to him, laughed at his jokes. And once she had let him kiss her, regretting it at once and saying that, please, he must forget it. She was lonely, she said, looking away from him, and he had been kind.

But he hadn't forgotten. He had thought, *It's utterly insane but here it is. This is it. After my divorce* — He thought, *Lilia will get a divorce, we can be happy, I'm making money. I'll make more.*

This had seemed to him to be the most self-less decision of his life; perhaps according to his very dim lights it was.

He had thought about it, constantly watching Lilia, in the hotel gardens and at the pool. Watching, also, his wife, whom he distrusted and disliked. And then one night, unable to sleep, knowing that his wife slept heavily as sleep came easily in a little box of tablets, he went out on the balcony that ran past his room and Lilia's, found her door unlocked, and went in.

He didn't think of that often; nor of Tom, coming in from next door. He didn't think often of Lilia's face as she switched on the lights; nor of what she said; nor of his senseless frustration before Tom, hearing the raised voice, came in.

Unfinished business. If he hadn't forgotten, neither had she; also he could remind her. He wondered how her husband would react. Even the stupidest man — and he judged Alex Gurney to be quite stupid, would ask questions, but by that time Amenly would be on a plane or ship bound for the mainland.

So he listened, smiling, to Jack Russell saying, "Suppose I take you out to the plantation? It's one you mustn't miss, I'd planned it anyway. Gurney's done a fine job," and went on into methods, tonnage, and statistics generally, while his father agreed, and Terry looked at Chris, then away.

On the day Jack drove Amenly to the plantation, Chris telephoned Lilia. He said merely, "Amenly's coming out with Jack this afternoon."

He had called her while she was at lunch.

She thanked him and returned to the table. She had been an idiot to run away, a worse one to think she need run. She looked at Alex, who had. never failed her. Any failure had been in herself. Recognizing that, she could try again for success, in the important things. She thought, *What a fool I was not to tell him at once when I reached home.*

"Alex," she said, "could you spare me a little time after lunch? I want to talk to you."

When, sometime later, Jack arrived, having telephoned the plantation office, Alex was at the house to meet him and his guest. He made it quick and final, going out to the car and saying, "How are you, Mr. Amenly? Lilia has told me about you." He had no need to say more. Amenly understood, and the rest of the time there was as one of his recurrent dreams, the dreams in which he was going some place but never arriving, in which he tried to pack and couldn't, called a telephone number and received no answer, or in which he tried to run and something held his feet immobile.

Lilia said, at the door, "Hello, Roger." She added, "I can't make the rounds with you, Jack, I've a dozen things to do. I'll expect you back here for a drink." She could look at Amenly and not be ashamed. She was free. Alex had freed her.

The houses of the workers, the hospital, the

recreation center, the clinic, the mill, the cane fields — Roger made the right inquiries, exhibited proper enthusiasm. He wanted a drink badly. He had been temperate since coming here. He was a man who drank immoderately, except at certain periods. This might be one of them, he thought grimly.

He took only one cocktail in Lilia's house, looking at her sitting beside her husband, her eyes clear and grave, and his resentment and frustration grew. He watched Jack. He thought, *He's in love with her, I suppose.* He was wrong. Jack had, in his own phrase, got over Lilia long since; but she had spoiled him for other women. He knew where and how to find his own amusements, always discreetly. Not until Terry's arrival had he envied any man, not even Alex. But then, he'd always envied Chris, although what had there been to envy — except Lilia, once? He'd had more reason to envy Robert, but Robert was dead, and you didn't envy a dead man, or did you?

Driving back, Amenly, thinking of Chris and Terry, told himself, *They've sweated it out all day. And they'll know soon enough. From Lilia. I promise a bomb, I deliver a dud!*

He made himself sit through dinner; if he drank more brandy than usual, surely no one noticed. But Chris noticed and told Terry, "It didn't come off."

"What makes you think so?"

"I know it. We're playing golf tomorrow. I'll get a chance and call Lilia."

He did so, from the clubhouse, saying, "It's Chris. Is everything all right?" and her answer came instantly. She said, "I talked to Alex after lunch yesterday. There was no reason why I couldn't have, months ago, except that I was ashamed. It's all right, Chris, it's fine."

"He knows?" asked Chris. He didn't mean Alex now, and she answered, "He knew at once, as soon as he and Alex met."

"I'm glad, dear," he said, and went back to the others. Terry looked up, and he nodded slightly and put his hand on her shoulder, and Roger Amenly, looking at the drink he held, thought, *I'm drinking too much;* and then, *I'm sick of it here, sweetness and light, and people saying aloha and too many flowers and too much blue sky.*

But when he said he must think of making a reservation, he had imposed upon them too long, Cordelia expostulated. "We'd hoped to show you Naniola." She explained Naniola, the little island. They usually spent some time there in the spring. But perhaps they could manage a week-end now, she said brightly. Terry had never been there.

So they came to Naniola by air and by cabin cruiser, and the island rose from the sea,

245

rocky and high on one side and with long beaches and sheltered waters on the other. It had beauty and peace, and Terry held Chris's hand and wished herself alone with him.

The house was long, rambling, and not much to look at, with shabby comfortable furniture and its own lighting system, which sometimes did not work. The plumbing was antiquated, but the gardens were wonderful. The people who had been brought to Naniola long ago still lived there, or their sons and grandsons did. They had their own store and a dispensary. If any were ill, they were taken quickly from the island. They farmed, a small, contented group. The younger men had gone to war, and those who had returned were back again. There wasn't much to do, Cordelia explained, for visitors. Fish, ride — they had good horses — explore the island, which wouldn't take long, lie on the beach, swim.

Amenly hated the place on sight. Too small, too smug, too storybook. It had not even the interest of being forbidden. People came and went, many people. Naniola had been built for pleasure, long, long ago.

They'd brought meat with them, for refrigeration. They lived simply there, there was always fish, the vegetable garden and the fruit. Jack apologized. "We picnic on Naniola," he said.

That's all I lack, thought Amenly, awake in a vast hard bed in a big bare room, *a picnic.*

But there was a good cellar under the house and a storeroom with pre-war liquor. It was offered him, as to any guest, so he drank, watched Terry and Chris, resenting them deeply and with an increasing violence. There was nothing he could do to them, they were secure, they had everything. It did not occur to him that the older Russells wouldn't know Terry's recent circumstances. Her friends might not, but her husband and his people would. He could do no damage, merely strike to wound.

The opportunity came as a source of release when, on the second night after dinner, Hugo spoke of Terry's father. "Pity he couldn't be with us," he said, "he would have liked this place, I think." He did not know what made him say that, sitting there, looking at his nephew's wife, thinking, *What a nice girl, but I should talk with her, she must exercise her influence over Chris;* and then remembering her father.

Amenly was in that stage of drunkenness which is not immediately obvious to one's companions. He had had several cocktails before dinner, coming in, finding the shaker there and no one in the room, and several highballs after dinner, and he had eaten next to nothing, his resentment a hard knot in his stomach. And now he said:

"He would have liked it very much. Good old Mark Austin." He heard himself giggle, as a woman does, on a high note, saw Terry's shocked, still face, saw Chris rise and go over to stand near her. And added, striking out with that enormous sense of release, "Pity he was a crook, wasn't it — or that they found him out?"

"Amenly," said Chris, and saw that Hugo and Jack had also risen and that Cordelia, dropping her knitting, was coming over to take Terry's hand and say, "Terry, my dear."

"Well, he was a crook," said Amenly irritably, "and if he ruined himself he also ruined a great many other people. They didn't all take the easy way out — as Austin did. Didn't you know? Ask Terry, then, perhaps she knew all along."

The big, comfortable, shabby room was instantly alive with quick voices, brusque movements, gestures — the articulation of shock and anger, astonishment and humiliation. But although Terry saw and heard, fully conscious of the emptiness of relief — the sword falls, the blow is delivered, what else is there to fear? — she was also aware that for the split second, which is as years, time had halted and the past became indistinguishable from the present.

Her eyes obediently followed the unrolling film of the moment; she saw stupefaction on Hugo's face, she saw Chris's eyes bright with rage, and Amenly shrink back defiantly. She saw Jack's expression, and read it, correctly, as gratification. She knew that Cordelia was still sitting beside her on the huge divan heaped with mats and pillows, and she felt Cordelia's hand tighten on her own. She saw Hugo and Jack move, in unison, to step between Amenly and Chris, and she heard Hugo say, not loudly but sharply, "I'll take care of this."

And yet she was not really there at all, except in her body, which sat erect, unyielding, on the *hikiee*. Her hand was unresponsive in Cordelia's, and she had not spoken a word. She was a child again, running in a garden; she was caught up in her father's arms, his laughter was louder than the bird song, he was stronger than a hundred men — this mountaintop was next to the sky, these flowers bigger than the stars. She was a child who would live forever in this moment and this place. And then she was a girl, crying in a stateroom on a ship because she was going away from home. And now she had come home again, and Maria was brushing her hair, as she looked in a mirror, and along the corri-

249

dor outside someone hurried on noiseless feet and laughed — a little maid, a girl younger than herself, hurrying, soundless on the stone, laughing because she went toward love or sleep or mischief.

A parrot she had once owned, and which long since had died, asked querulously, *"Quién sabe?"* over and over; a dog she had not thought of in years barked, and a woman's voice, a voice she had forgotten, said, "I knew your mother, she was very beautiful"; and a man who had professed to love her said, "I promise you shall be happy."

She smelled pipe smoke and leather and the sweat of horses, and her father said, "What you want in this world you have to take."

All this she saw and heard, and yet everything in the room in which she sat beside Cordelia was as clear as still, unsullied water; the portrait of Robert Russell over the fireplace, the many flowers in heavy pottery bowls, the stained coffee cup on the table beside her, the carved wooden Buddha across the room, serene and smiling. Sounds were clear, too — someone passing by outside laughed, as the little maid had laughed long ago; and a far-off singing drifted in, the wind in the palms clapped small, dry hands, and the surf breathed against the rocks and beach. She could feel the heaped mats on the couch, her one hand pressing down upon them, she could feel the thin flesh, the hard bones of Cordelia's fingers around her own.

She was two persons and one of them had nothing to do with what was happening here, for nothing had happened to her of any moment, she was an onlooker here, a stranger; and the other went back in time to a secure world without a danger or foreboding.

And yet Hugo was saying, "I'll take care of this." It took so long to say five words, yet they were quickly said.

Terry came back to her integrated self with a wrench which was most painful and which she felt deep in her flesh, and Cordelia said questioningly, "Terry?"

But Chris spoke before she could form words in her mind. He said savagely, "Get out of my way, will you?" and moved quickly to brush his uncle and cousin aside. But Hugo said with authority, "No, Chris."

"He's to get away with it?" Chris demanded.

"Brawling is hardly the solution," his uncle answered. He spoke evenly, almost mildly, to Roger Amenly. "You are not yourself, Mr. Amenly," he said, "and while that is hardly an adequate excuse, we must accept it. I suggest that you will be more comfortable in your room."

He glanced at Jack, who nodded and put a heavy hand on Amenly's arm, saying, "Come along," without inflection. But Amenly pulled back and said sullenly, "Confined to barracks, I presume. That's *very* funny. I'd heard a little about you people over here — smug, patronizing, Victorian — but I couldn't believe it. Apparently I've upset an apple cart. I apologize. It never occurred to me that you didn't know about Mark Austin. Hell, what difference can it make? The Russells don't need money and are above scandal."

Jack reached out and took him by the shoulder. "Let's get going."

"Okay," said Amenly, "if it's an old Hawaiian custom."

He went toward the stairs with Jack beside him and did not look toward Chris or Terry.

On the big hearth a sweet-scented fire snapped and murmured and released its warmth against the slight evening chill. Its voice was drowsy and distinct. Jack and Amenly went up the broad curving stairway side by side. The living-room was two stories high; a gallery on which the bedrooms opened ran around it at the landing. There Amenly paused, pulling away from Jack to lean on the railing and look down at the quiet people. " 'You're nothing but a pack of cards,' " he said contemptuously, "so, as Alice also remarked, 'Who cares for you?' "

"That's enough," warned Jack; and those below heard footsteps and the sound of a door opening and closing.

Chris broke the incredible spell that held them. He came over to the *hikiee* and sat down, taking Terry in his arms, removing her, as it were, from Cordelia's jurisdiction. Cordelia folded one hand over the other but did not move away, and Hugo came to stand beside her.

"Terry?" said Chris, his voice roughened; and when she did not answer, he shook her slightly. "Damn him," he said, and then, "Terry, for God's sake!"

Cordelia said, with distaste, "There is no reason to be profane or melodramatic. Hugo, get Terry some brandy."

Terry released herself from Chris. She spoke quite loudly because it seemed to her that she spoke in echoing space and emptiness. What she now experienced was loneliness. What would happen to herself and Chris did not at this moment greatly matter. The world they had built and briefly inhabited together had been of mean, small proportions. In it they had found pleasure and not much more. Now it existed no longer, except in time, and was as remote as her former world.

She said, "I don't want brandy, thanks. And Roger told the truth. My father was dishonest. He ruined himself and the people who trusted him and killed himself because he could not face it." She looked from Hugo to Cordelia. "I couldn't face it either."

Cordelia began, "We won't talk about it tonight," but Terry shook her head.

"No," she said, "we'll discuss it now." Hearing a sound, she turned, looking up. "Jack's coming," she added. "He's in on this, too."

Jack came downstairs. He said, standing by the fire, "I persuaded our guest to retire." He grinned, remembering, and then looked at Terry. "Go on with what you were saying," he said, "or am I intruding?"

"Of course not. I'm not going to try to explain or excuse," she said. Her accent was quite marked. She had been thinking, if she thought at all, in Spanish, translating as she spoke. Now she forced herself to think in English and to speak slowly.

Chris said, "There's nothing to explain, Terry. Aunt Cordelia's right. In the morning we'll talk about it if you insist."

She folded one hand on the other, as Cordelia had done. "Now," she said again. "I'm sorry it happened this way, but it had to happen sooner or later."

Hugo sighed. He asked Chris, "You knew all this?"

"Naturally," Chris answered. And thought, *Well, I'm glad it's over, in a way*. And then he thought, *Poor kid;* and then, *What comes next?*

Terry said, "Chris didn't know it when he married me. He thought he was marrying Mark Austin's daughter. The Mark Austin people knew and envied and honored. Because I intended that they go on believing that as long as possible. So I came to New York and lived on a shoestring. A golden shoestring." She looked down at the emerald blazing on her hand and spoke to Cordelia softly, as if in confidence. "I had this," she said, and turned her hand, "and the pearls, I had clothes and furs and a legend. Chris, too," she said.

Chris spoke harshly, "Suppose you tell them the important factor — which was that we fell in love."

"Oh, yes," Terry said listlessly, "we fell in love. There's nothing incredible about it. And I had no training, I was not equipped to earn a living. I didn't, as a matter of fact, want to," she said coolly. "So it seemed to me that a good marriage was the only solution. Who could suspect me of a mercenary motive? When I fell in love with Chris I thought I was very fortunate. To marry for love — and into money."

"Chris!" said Jack, and laughed.

Chris said, "Shut up, will you?" He looked at his uncle. "Well, we both labored under a misapprehension. I thought I was fortunate, too."

Cordelia said, and her son and husband looked at her in amazement, "And weren't you — both of you?"

For the first time Chris smiled. He said, "In all my life you have never said anything so friendly, Aunt Cordelia."

"Let me tell them," said Terry, "from the beginning."

It took a long time to tell, sitting there while the fire sighed on the hearth, the wind rose, and the sea stammered against the rocks. She omitted nothing, neither her father's story nor her own, nor her decision, her meeting with Chris and her quite comprehensible mistake. Nor did she omit that morning in the New York hotel and their adjustment to the altered conditions. She said finally, "It could have gone on for some time, I suppose, if Roger Amenly hadn't come to Cape Cod and then followed us here."

"This will provide a great deal of amusement for a great many people," Jack commented.

Cordelia shuddered inwardly. The picture

was very clear. She thought, *But I liked her,* and almost instantly Terry said wearily, "When you seemed to like me, all of you, I was happy. But not entirely. Because how much of it was for myself?"

Jack said, "A lot. You're a very attractive girl." He went over to the table where the decanters stood and mixed himself a long, stiff drink. He added thoughtfully, "There's a way out of this with the minimum of gossip."

"How?" inquired his father.

"No one has really expected Chris to settle down here," said Jack, "so no one will be astonished if he and Terry decide suddenly to return to the mainland. Of course, the true picture will be exhibited, as Terry said, sooner or later. But for the time being no one will wonder. We can weather such dinner-table discussions as arise now — and later. It isn't the first time that we've — "

Chris broke in. "You're wonderful, Jack. Why don't we say it baldly? None of you has ever had any use for me and you don't come out of this much better than Terry and I do. For when I came home with, apparently, a rich wife, you killed not one but several calves. In honor, I suppose, of the golden — bull. By the simple process of marrying I had redeemed myself."

"That's not true," said Cordelia sharply. "We merely hoped that with the right wife — "

"But the right wife had to be able to club me into respectability with a checkbook?" he asked. "Well, whatever you thought you've been amiable, and I appreciate it. Jack's even been moved to envy, I think. He has always hated my guts, but recently he — "

"Chris!" said his aunt.

"It's true enough. When we were kids, I could beat him at almost any game, and then later there was Lilia."

"What has Lilia to do with this?" inquired Jack. He finished his drink and set down the glass. His face was congested with anger.

"Nothing," said Chris swiftly, "except as one explanation of why you and I, as the saying goes, have never got along."

"There's no point in past quarrels and recriminations," said Hugo sharply. "Whatever your and Jack's relationship, it isn't germane to the situation. It is true that you have been a disappointment, Chris. I have told you so many times. You were headstrong from childhood, you grew up rebellious and spendthrift. There was a place for you here and a future but you would not take it. I wrote you, if you remember, during the war. We were all proud of your record. I asked you to come home, but you would not. I recall your answer. In it you blamed me for many things, including your position, as you put it, of poor relation. It was not my doing. My father did not consult me when he provided for your father."

Cordelia made a quick, brusque gesture, very unlike her. She said, "I think we're getting away from the immediate problem."

"What problem?" asked Terry. "You don't have to save face just because you thought Chris had married a girl with money, do you? Chris thought so, too. He didn't know she was next to penniless and that her father was a thief." Her voice rose. "You're safe," she said. "What can touch you? Chris has never been one of you except by blood. I'm not one of you, either. As for my father, you knew him slightly, but what happened to him can hardly concern you."

"Yet it does," said Hugo. "You have pointed out that Chris is by blood a member of this family; and you are by marriage. Anything which concerns you concerns us."

Chris said softly, "Even the Russells and perhaps especially the Russells are not above disliking gossip — about themselves. When Great-uncle Josiah took a notion to marry his cook — "

"Chris!" cried his aunt. "Terry isn't interested in — "

"They ganged up on him and saw to it that he didn't," Chris went on calmly. "And there are other instances; such as the time when fourth cousin Amy's mother discovered that Amy was pregnant. They took a nice long trip to the mainland and when they came back Amy was properly married off. What became of the baby, if any, I wouldn't know. You met Amy, Terry, a proper young matron, very holier-than-thou. Maybe if they'd let her have the baby — maybe if Great-uncle had married the cook, Amy's disposition wouldn't have suffered nor old Josh's digestion. I could go on for hours — "

"Not," said his uncle, "tonight."

Chris said equably, "Well, there it is, Terry. We just don't like being talked about unpleasantly."

"Which we will be," prophesied Jack. "Surely you haven't forgotten Mr. Amenly. What do you propose to do about him?"

Chris said, "It's very simple. You and I tie him up with a bed sheet and hurl him off a cliff. Most effective. We regret it. He jumped or fell under the influence of strong drink. Who'd question it at Naniola?"

"I'd be gratified," said his uncle, "if you were less facetious. I am sure Mr. Amenly will prefer to leave in the morning. Jack and I will go with him, the rest of you will remain here until he has left the Islands. I am quite certain he will be willing to leave, and, I hope, on the first plane."

Chris laughed. "Amenly," he remarked, "is a stinker. But he's an adult stinker. He isn't, however, a Russell or even a remote connection, by marriage or otherwise; nor an employee who has been dismissed. He's a free agent. You can ease him off Tantalus but not, if he's become attached to our climate, on a plane. He can go to a hotel, he can stay as long as he wishes or can afford, and he can talk as much as he pleases to whoever will listen. It's going to make a very good story. So far he knows only one side of it. But practically anybody will enlighten him as to my standing in the community. Which should give him an unexpected belly laugh."

Hugo said, "I admit I hadn't thought so far."

"Console yourself with the realization that nothing can reflect upon you," said Chris.

Terry got to her feet. She was stiff, she ached. She said uncertainly, "I don't see what good all this is doing. Could we talk about it in the morning?"

She was purged, she was clean and empty. And Cordelia, looking at the young white face, experienced a pang of compassion against her will, against even her principles.

261

She said, "Of course. Chris, take Terry up-stairs." She tried to smile. "When you come down again, I think Mr. Amenly will have left," she added.

Chapter Eleven
A Picture of the Past

Some time later, Chris spoke. "Why don't you come to bed, Terry? You're only wearing yourself out, walking up and down or sitting there by the window. You'll catch cold."

"I'm trying to think."

"Tomorrow will do. It's almost tomorrow now. Besides, what is there to think? We'll pull out as soon as we can. This interlude is *pau* — finished."

She said vaguely, "My head aches a little. I think there's some aspirin in the bathroom. I forgot to bring any — "

She went into the bathroom, which was big, rather bare, very old-fashioned, and served also as a dressing-room. The shower was in one corner, sometimes it functioned, sometimes not. On one side of the room there was a big window, on the other a dressing-table with a medicine cabinet over it. She swung the mirror door open and found the aspirin bottle. There was no need to pull on the single light. The room was full of moonlight. She shut the cabinet door, looked idly into the mirror and stood, still looking, transfixed. The mirror reflected the moon in its silver entirety. The moon rode high, it was round and full and tiny, floating on the surface of the mirror a bright, remote world. If she picked up the hand mirror and held it before her she would hold this moon in her two hands, another world, a world of brilliant cold, of silvered death, of unbearable beauty and reflected, twice reflected, light.

"Terry? Are you all right?"

"Yes, of course. I'll be right there, Chris."

She returned the bottle to the shelf. It was not really her head that ached. It was her mind and her spirit. It was not a matter which concerned her palliation of drug.

She looked at the moon again. Another world. So many worlds, she thought.

Terry went back to the bedroom, took off her robe, and slid her feet from the straw slippers. She was cold suddenly, she shook with it. She got into the big old bed of carved koa and lay down beside Chris, her head against his shoulder.

"We have each other," she said faintly, "and yet — "

"Haven't we always, since the first?" He smoothed her hair back from her forehead. "I love you, Terry," he said.

"I love you. I don't think that they believe it."

"Of course, they believe it — about my loving you, at any rate. Who could see you and not believe? Anyway, does it matter what anyone believes?"

"Yes, in a way. I can't explain why."

It mattered to her. It made all the difference. There must be some way to make it clear to everyone that they had loved each other from the beginning, for that much must remain untouched and whole and decent.

Chris said, "We'll get away as soon as possible. After that, we'll manage."

"How?" Her heart grew quiet with caution.

"You won't like this, I expect. But once on the mainland, we can sell the jewelry. It will bring quite a lot, even with fluctuating values."

She thought, quite a lot; enough to live on for a long time if they were careful. When had Chris ever wanted to live carefully? You could do a number of things with the money the pearls would bring, and the green-eyed emerald — you could, perhaps, buy a small house and a share in a small business.

She could not imagine Chris in that house or that business.

She said, "We'll talk about it in the morning. Let's go to sleep now, Chris."

265

He slept after a little while, but she lay wakeful. The moon rode her downward course to her setting, the night was dark as grief, the night faded, as grief must fade, the sky was gray and brushed with gold, awaiting the upsweep of rose and carmine, the hot, fierce spears of the sun. And birds spoke quietly, one to the other.

When it was still very early, Chris asked, "Are you awake, Terry?"

"Yes."

"Have you been for long?"

"All night, a hundred years. Chris, it's no good."

"What isn't?"

"Whatever it is you've thought and planned. It won't be the same when we go back. Roger will go back, too, and he will tell the story over and over. To save *his* face. He'll tell it his way. By then he'll know about you, too."

"If I know Jack," said Chris, "he won't have to learn it in chance conversation, in a bar, on a beach, in a plane. Did you see Jack's expression when I spoke of Lilia?"

"You shouldn't have."

"I wasn't thinking about what I should or should not do."

"Chris, listen to me. We can't go back to packing and unpacking suitcases in other people's houses. Did I ever tell you about Jennifer and Bert Cranson?"

"No, and why should you at this juncture?"

"I'd forgotten them," she said, "until recently. I knew them in London, Helen and I met them on a house party. After a while I learned about them. Bert had an inherited, not very impressive, title. Jennifer had money, which she lost. They had just a tiny income. Bert took a job now and then, selling shares or getting new members of, say, a golf club. He was rather stupid, but pleasant. He could shoot and ride, play tennis and golf and, of course, bridge. Sometimes he and Jen met Americans and introduced them to important people, for a price; or Jen took the women to a dressmaker or furrier or jeweler, and Bert took the men to his tailor and haberdasher. They earned commissions, of course. Jen had great tact — I remember a very offensive man at that house party and how well she handled him — and the older women liked Bert. I suppose wherever they visited they had the most undesirable room in the house and that the servants despised them. Sometimes they stayed with children while the parents traveled, and they were always ready to fill in or help out — garden parties, funerals, weddings, debuts — half the thank-you letters or letters of condolence people in their little set received

267

were written by Jen, she wrote a pretty hand."

"I don't believe any of this, Terry. Are you drawing a moral?"

"It's true, and, yes, I'm trying to. When I met the Cransons they were in their late thirties. What's happened to them, besides growing older and more frightened? People didn't give big house parties during the war; they don't now. I remember someone saying that their only hope of an assured future was to attach themselves to a rich, disagreeable old woman, make themselves indispensable, however kicked around, and pray she'd die and leave them something."

Chris sat up, thumped his pillows into position and reached for the cigarettes on the marble-topped table beside him. He lit one and the sweet, acrid smoke drifted past, and Terry's stomach turned over.

"That's not a very pretty picture," he said. "I suppose you didn't intend it to be?"

She said, "I saw it only in broad outline. What had it to do with me then? Now I can fill in the outline."

"All right," he said evenly, "what do you want to do? You call the shots."

"Chris, let me say this first, and just once more. It was never any fun. I tried to believe it was at first. I never quite succeeded."

"So?" He was conscious of anger, of fear,

and of hurt. They had been together, wasn't that, in itself, fun? More than fun, wonderful and sufficient? He looked down at her as she lay there, her black hair loose on the pillow, her face very pale in the dim light. In a few moments the room would be flooded with the golden warmth, and then perhaps she would not look as if sometime during the night she had drowned in darkness.

"Go on," he said.

"I want to stay here, Chris. I want to know your people. I like most of them. I like your aunt and uncle. I can see the things you do not like in them but they aren't important. People who are very secure become somewhat arrogant, restricted in their thinking, and complacent. My father didn't because, although I didn't know it, he was never really secure. Also, people who have worked, as their people did before them, believe in work. At least, they do here. Chris, I respect your aunt and uncle. I could be fond of them. I could make friends. Lilia, for one. I could be fond of Lilia, too."

"That's all very well," he said uneasily, "I won't argue with you about the family. I see them in one light, you in another. But how can you, now?"

"Nothing has changed, and they were kind," she said, "last night."

"Kind! *Kind?* Because they didn't make a scene, throw us out? It's a little hard to throw people out of here, you know. Terry, you aren't thinking straight. Even if I wished to stay, how could we?"

"You could go to work," she said flatly.

He turned and put the cigarette in an ash tray.

"For whom? For my uncle, for Jack, provided they were willing?" He laughed shortly. "Come," he suggested, "try again."

"I am trying. There must be positions not controlled by your family. You have never looked for one. You worked under your uncle's direction, so to speak, and hated it. Not the work, Chris, I can see that now, but because you thought that they'd tossed you a job like a bone, that you'd been cheated."

"Wasn't I?"

"I don't know. I know so little about you really."

"That goes double," he said slowly. "And if I say, no, I won't stay here, that nothing would persuade me to stay?"

"Then I suppose you'll go away. And I shall, too, but not with you," Terry answered.

He pulled her up until she sat straight beside him, her shoulders against the headboard, her pillow slipping down. He asked loudly, "Just what do you mean by that?"

270

"What I said. There must be someone who would take me with them, to look after children on the trip, perhaps."

"That would certainly make for interesting conversation."

"Does that matter to you, too? This hasn't come overnight, Chris, just because Roger drank so much and struck out in resentment, because he dislikes me, or even because of whatever happened between him and Lilia. He thought you perfectly secure, but he knew that he'd hurt you through me. I don't really know why he did it and I don't really care. But ever since we met the Cotters that night, and said, yes, we'd visit them, I have been fighting clear thinking. I was like a child who believes that, no matter what has happened today, tomorrow will be wonderful, tomorrow will bring a miracle. What miracle? My father couldn't come alive again, to be the man he once was, the man I believed him to be — nor would your situation alter. But, no, I had to go on hoping for something, a sea change, a new world. I hadn't grown up. I'm just beginning to, Chris."

After a moment he said, "All right. We'll go back to the mainland together, and I'll find a job. There'll be something, I dare say."

"It has to be here."

"In heaven's name, why?" he asked angrily,

wanting to shake her because she was stubborn and ridiculous, wanting to kiss her because she was forlorn and unhappy.

"You belong here," she said. "I learned that, somehow, last night. You've lost something here, and it's only here that you'll recover it. This is your own place, these people are your own, no matter how you feel about them. It can't just be because a long time ago your father married someone his family didn't like, and in other ways estranged them. It's something in you. I know you aren't lazy, Chris, I know you are intelligent, I know that you could do many things well, and in some find a great deal of satisfaction. But you won't. You have told me often that you are restless. Perhaps you are, but that's too easy an explanation. Who isn't restless since the war? I don't know what has hurt you," she said slowly. "It can't be just because of Jack and your aunt and uncle, it can't be because of Lilia. At least, I don't think so. Maybe it goes back to a little boy in Paris, whose mother and father had died, who was alone and frightened."

"Will you stop talking like an amateur psychologist!"

"Very well. But if you throw your life away, that's your business, Chris. Only you can't throw mine away, too."

He said, looking at her as if he had never seen her before, "Let's get this straight, without touches of whimsey. If I don't stay here you will leave me, no matter where I go?"

"Yes."

I must *leave him,* she thought. *Otherwise, we'll go on drifting, and sooner or later we'll wake up, the drifting over, and we'll hate each other.*

"Where do you intend to go — in that case?"

"Don't look like that, don't be so hard. I'll go to Helen. Last night you said we could sell the jewelry, we could live on it. I won't, Chris. It can't buy anything I'd want that way. But I would sell it to buy something which would last — a training, perhaps, for some work for which I might be fitted."

"You could have done that when you came to New York."

"I know." After a moment she said, "I wish I had."

"But the solution was marriage. It can be still. There are other men. Do you want a divorce?"

She began to shake and, without volition, he put his arm about her. "Don't, Terry, don't. And don't cry — please don't cry. I don't know what in hell this is all about or what's got into you, but I do love you."

She was quiet for a moment, except for her weeping. After a while she said, "I love you, too, but it isn't enough. That's what makes me so frightened, and wretched. It just *isn't* enough. Not the way we've been loving each other. Because that should be only a small part of it — wonderful, but just a part. It's been like having an affair, I suppose. We have built nothing together, we've had nothing to build on or with. Either we stay together and try to do just that or it's no use, none at all."

"You talk like a schoolgirl," he said, and his face burned with anger and an unacknowledged shame for her, for himself. "An affair! Are you out of your mind?"

"Not any more. I suppose many marriages begin as an affair," she said drearily, "and then build from that. Some never get any further — those are the people who get divorced or the people who stay together and loathe every minute of it."

"Terry, be reasonable. It's all a little too simple. I go to work, the affair becomes a marriage. Is that why you think it would be?"

"No, of course not. But we would have a chance. And our self-respect."

"I haven't lost mine!"

"Then you never had it," she said sadly. "I haven't thought much about self-respect until lately. After my father died I was too busy protecting him, I thought. How could I protect him when he had destroyed himself — and I don't mean his death. What had it to do with me, my integrity, my value as a human being? He was my father, I am myself. What he did with his life is over. No, I suppose I was protecting myself, and not him. I couldn't take it, I couldn't have people look at me and — " She broke off. "Well," she said, "what I do with my life now is up to me, and has just begun."

Terry waited, but Chris did not answer. She looked at him, and he was frowning a little, his face remote, closed against her and secret, as a clenched fist conceals emptiness or treasure or is merely a waiting threat.

She said, "I'm going to shower, Chris," and got out of bed. Her back ached. She stooped for her slippers, took a toweling robe from a chair, and went into the bathroom. The shower functioned this morning, but the water was tepid. She let it run over her tired body and then turned the handle to Cold. That was better. She gasped, her blood tingled, her fatigue was momentarily dispelled.

She dried herself, put on her robe, and sat at the dressing-table to brush and arrange her hair. The mirror no longer reflected the miniature moon; it reflected only her face, the olive skin blanched, the eyes heavy and troubled. She looked as plain as was possible for her.

When she returned to the bedroom her face was carefully made up, and for the first time in months she had rouged her cheeks slightly.

Chris was standing by the windows looking out. He said, without turning, "Amenly has left, I think."

Now she remembered sounds of footsteps and muffled voices in the corridors earlier that morning. They had registered briefly on her consciousness but no more, she had been too intent upon her personal problems.

He added, "I suppose they'll send the boat back for us," turned, looked at her, and smiled. His face was a little drawn but for a moment it was open again and familiar. He added, "Don't worry too much."

But that meant nothing, exactly nothing, she thought, as she dressed and, dressing, heard the shower running next door. And presently Alika tapped on the door and said, "I have your tray, Mrs. Russell."

Alika was the daughter of the Hawaiian couple whose main duty it was to keep the house in readiness for the family, and who together with Alika and her sister came to help when the Russells were on Naniola.

Terry opened the door, and Alika came in. She was a pretty girl, and Terry remembered that in the spring she was to be married. She thought, *I wish her luck.*

Alika set the tray on a small battered table, as she had done on the previous morning. Later they'd had a big communal breakfast, but today, she remembered, only Cordelia would be downstairs. She asked hesitantly, "Is Mrs. Russell breakfasting in her room?"

Alika said yes. She added that Mr. Russell, Mr. Jack, and Mr. Amenly had left. Her dark eyes were veiled. She had still been in the house last night after dinner. How much she or anyone else had heard, who could tell? Or what they surmised.

She said, "Mrs. Russell says she will be downstairs in half an hour, and to ask if you would join her."

On the tray a pot of the strong, bitter Kona coffee, and the sweet golden flesh of the papaya, toast folded in a napkin, sugar and cream. When Chris came out of the bathroom, Terry was standing by the windows, her cup in her hand, and Alika had gone. She was thinking that when you are unhappy beauty is an added burden; she was thinking that she might never see Naniola again, set in a sapphire sea.

When Chris had dressed he sat down to drink his coffee and eat the fruit with its scattered black seeds of pepsin. He said, "Do sit down — the papaya is very good."

"I'm not hungry, Chris. And Alika said your aunt wants to see us presently. The others have gone."

"So?" He pushed back his chair and lit a cigarette. He had not, she noticed, done more than eat a mouthful of the papaya. "What are you going to tell Aunt Cordelia?"

"What I've told you — as much, I mean, as concerns her."

His chair fell with a crash which seemed louder than an explosion, and he went quickly toward her and took her in his arms. He said, "It's no use, Terry. I've been trying to see things without you. I can't. If this is the way you want it, this is the way it will have to be. Do you realize all it will mean? A little house on a big plantation, among people strange to you. Talk, gossip, speculation. You may fare badly at the hands of the women. You will be expected to take part in the social life of the plantation. It's a tight little world, in which you will not reign. You have been accustomed to reigning — "

"Not lately. Oh, Chris, Chris," she said brokenly, "as long as we are together, as long as we are really together — "

"For heaven's sake, put down that cup." But it was too late, the cup shook in her hand, the coffee spilled. He took the cup from her

278

and held her again wordlessly. He said, "I won't like it, Terry. But I'll do my damnedest."

For me, she thought, and for a moment was wonderfully happy. But how long would that last? She had given him a choice, yet if he loved her it was not really a choice. He could do nothing else if he loved and wanted her. She was repelled and astonished to realize the coercion of love, the compulsion, the weapon. It was a form of blackmail, after all. He would stay, he would do as she asked, not because he believed in or recognized a personal necessity, but because she asked it, because in no other way could he keep her with him.

So it would not be enough, she thought, wavering, almost ready to cry, "Never mind, it's not what I want, it won't work, it can't!"

Yet it was a chance, their only chance.

She said, when he had kissed her, "We mustn't keep your aunt waiting."

Cordelia was out on the enormous *lanai*. She looked as if she hadn't slept, and when they came out to her she regarded them gravely, without smiling. She said instantly, "Sit down, I want to talk with you. Chris, your uncle and Jack took Mr. Amenly off the island this morning; they will pick up the car and go to the airport. Hale will drive the car back and then return with the boat. We can leave tomorrow morning."

"Okay," said Chris, without question or comment.

"You've breakfasted?" she asked.

"Yes. We don't want anything now," said Terry quickly, "at least, I don't."

Cordelia nodded. And Chris said, with an attempt at a smile, "Did our friend go quietly?"

"I didn't see him, but I presume so. It really doesn't matter. Have you any plans?" she asked.

Chris spoke before Terry could answer. He said, "You may not like it, Aunt Cordelia. But we are going to stay on the Islands. I'm going to get a job. This will upset Uncle Hugo and it will be contrary to Jack's ideas. But if I don't, Terry says she will leave me."

"Is this true?" Cordelia asked Terry.

"Yes."

"Do you think it wise?"

Terry said, "Chris suggested that he find something to do on the mainland." She looked steadily at Cordelia. "But I believe that his place is here and that he will never be happy until he proves it to himself, no matter how deep his distaste or humiliation."

Chris flushed. He said, "Terry doesn't understand, she hasn't the remotest idea what it will be like."

"I don't care what it will be like," said Terry.

"You see?" Chris asked his aunt. "In a curious way I'm sorry for you and for Uncle Hugo. This must be the last thing you'd want."

"I can't speak for your uncle," said Cordelia, "and you can't speak for me. Even if I don't want it I agree with Terry."

"You do?" He was astonished beyond belief.

"Yes, as there's no reason why you shouldn't take your rightful place here —"

"My grandfather made that impossible," he interrupted.

Cordelia shook her head. "You made it impossible," she contradicted, "for even if your father's and your uncle's positions had been reversed, you would still have had to work for whatever authority you desired to reach."

His eyes were very bright. "Of course," he agreed, "and work hard, sweating it out, from beginning to end. But with this difference, that I would then be doing what was expected of me, as any man does who goes into his father's business. Not just a job given because of a family connection, a job landing nowhere."

She said, "That's stupid reasoning, and if Robert had lived —"

He said, "I had thought never to tell you this. He wrote me as often as he could. In his last letters he said he was not coming back, that after the war was won he would find something to do on the mainland. He said he had followed your wishes because of his gratitude to you but that he had always hated it. Which was, of course, why he drank," said Chris evenly.

"Chris," said Terry, her heart wrenched with pity for the older woman, "Chris, please don't."

"You loved him," said Chris inexorably, "you adopted him, you would have — if you could — set him above Jack in every way. He knew it, he was grateful, and he loved you. But he would rather have been with us, Aunt Cordelia."

She said stonily, "He was only a little boy when your father and mother died. You came home to us then; he would have done so."

"You don't understand," he told her. "We were a unit and belonged together. Sure, he would have come back here with me, and eventually escaped with me. He wrote me once that we could have been quite a team. Well, he escaped," said Chris.

Cordelia sat erect in the straight chair. She

said, "I knew he was not happy. I thought it would pass."

"He wanted to write, he wanted to paint."

"He could have done both," said Cordelia. "I encouraged him, I knew he was gifted."

"He didn't want to write or paint as a brace of hobbies," said Chris. "He was willing to be poor and obscure and a wanderer if he could have done the things he wished. I don't say that he had more than a second-rate talent for either. But it was what he wanted to do — and it was what he would have done had he lived. If Father had inherited equally with Uncle Hugo, it would have been the same." His face was taut and his eyes bleak. "But if that had been so," he said, "I would have been the one to stay and to follow the ancestral footsteps, not Bob."

"You?" said Cordelia incredulously.

"Yes."

"But you despised it, you worked only because we made you!"

"Which is why I despised it," he said, and Terry's heart shook with panic. She thought, *And now I am making him, and he will go on despising it.* Chris was still speaking. "Because it wasn't mine, because what I was doing was on sufferance, on tolerance, because I could see a hundred things I wanted to do and none would be permitted me," he said.

283

"Feeling this, you are willing to try again, with conditions unaltered?" Cordelia asked.

"They aren't unaltered. I realized that this morning. For the first time in my entire life I have someone who believes in me." He looked at Terry. "Or don't you?" he asked. "I think you must, otherwise you would not ask so much of me, darling."

Her eyes were wet with tears. She said, "I do believe in you, Chris."

Yet she had not, in his sense, until this instant; she had believed only that what they had of love would survive and mature if they worked together for survival and growth.

Cordelia asked after a moment, "Have you any idea what you want to do?"

"No. I haven't thought that far except that I don't want to ask Uncle Hugo or Jack to help me." He shrugged. "I dare say they will tolerate us under the family roof until I find something — if only for the sake of appearances. I thought Alex Gurney might know of something despite," he added, "his Russell tie-up."

Cordelia asked, "Why don't you see Hammond Mannering?" The shadow of a smile crossed her face. The Mannerings were very important people, as important as the Russells, with as many interests. Great-uncle Josiah's deceased wife had been a Mannering.

Hammond Mannering and Hugo Russell were of the same generation. They worked together for the common good of the Islands' industries. They had gone to college together. They were intimate friends, who rather disliked each other.

He said, surprised, "I hadn't thought of it."

"Do so, then. Hammond was fond of your father," Cordelia said. "He will want to do what he can for you. Chris, is there anything you care about except Terry and your vanity?"

"Vanity?" he asked. "What do you mean by that?"

"Pride, if you prefer, but I think it's vanity, which is quite different. Whatever it is, it is perverse. You were too proud to remain here, yet not too proud to live by your wits and on the careless bounty of strangers."

His face stung with the rising blood. He said, "You'll never understand, Aunt Cordelia."

"I dare say. But is there anything you care about?" she persisted, and Terry answered for him.

"He cares about people," she said. "He cares what happens to them and why."

She thought of his patience with Dick Johnson, partly because of Bob, but not wholly. She thought of the things he had told her of the men in his outfit; and of the count-less times since their arrival in the Islands when she had seen the warmth that went out, not to his old friends or those of his family but to others — the laboring men with whom he stopped to talk when they were at the Gur-neys', the people who served them here and in the Tantalus house, the fishermen at Kailua, on the Kona coast, the old men dreaming in the sun, playing cards on the rickety porch of a battered store, the barefoot, brown chil-dren, the workers in the coffee plantations, the woman nursing her baby beneath a jaca-randa tree.

"Who doesn't?" Chris demanded, staring at her.

"Lots of people," said Terry.

Cordelia said briskly, "We'll return tomor-row, and of course you will come home with me. When you have found a position, there'll be the question of furnishing your house."

Terry turned the ring on her hand, so that the big emerald was hidden. She said, "We'll manage."

"But Chris has quite a lot of furniture," said Cordelia. "It's stored in the attic. It belongs to his parents. They left it when they went abroad. It's plain and good, some of it quite old." She added, "And I can help you with the rest."

"Thanks," began Chris, "but — "

"Wait a minute." There was a white line around her mouth. She said, "I am not being — patronizing. Which is what you think, I suppose. I owe you a good deal, Chris. I've never wanted to acknowledge it, I thought that your way of life canceled the debt. But I have begun to think that you would not have chosen that way had it not been for me."

"I don't understand," he said soberly.

"I could have taken you," she said, "as well as Robert. Your father expected me to."

"I don't believe it. Bob wasn't strong, so they left him with you."

She said with great bitterness, "They wanted no one but each other, Chris." She took a long breath and said, "You have wondered why I preferred Robert to you, why, as you remarked, I set him above my own son. I will tell you, as I owe you that, too. I was in love with your father, and he, I believed, with me. We had grown up together, and falling in love was as natural as breathing. When he was old enough we would marry, we said. My parents knew, and his parents. But he went away to college and on his return he met your mother." She paused and then said, "So I married your father's brother, Chris. He loved me, he was good, he was kind, he was a man who accepted his responsibilities. Your

287

grandfather virtually disinherited your father, not only because of his marriage and your mother's divorce but because of me. He had no daughters and he was fond of me. You," she said, "grew up too like your father for my comfort — restless, careless, lacking a sense of responsibility, and secret," she added slowly, "something hidden in you, and remote. You walked like him, your smile was his. Robert looked like him, but his nature was different. I could look at him and think to find in him all your father was not."

"Aunt Cordelia — " He was greatly moved, knowing how much this had cost her, but she shook her head. She said, "I've had a good life, a far better one, I suppose, than if things had been different. Only I used you as a sort of whipping-boy. Every time you failed, every time you hurt or disappointed us, I congratulated myself that you were not my son. Can you understand that?"

He shook his head slowly, too bewildered to answer. But Terry understood; she did not speak, but Cordelia saw her eyes. And Terry thought, *It was because she felt that Chris should have been her son that she could not forgive his mother. With Robert it didn't matter. She could see his father in him physically, but Robert had none of the qualities that had hurt her, and which Chris had inherited.*

Cordelia said, "I never thought I would tell you, Chris. It seemed too great a humiliation. Also, I never wanted to tell you until now."

He said indistinctly, "I'm glad you told me." He was trying to realize that he had always been drawn to her. He had been critical of her, he had made fun of her, and he had blamed her for his brother's unhappiness. But not until this moment had he known that, much as he had loved his brother, he had been jealous of him, feeling excluded and an onlooker.

He spoke suddenly, in a loud, startled voice.

"It wasn't the will," he said incredulously, "it wasn't the money, it was *you*, Aunt Cordelia. I had to rationalize my feelings somehow, so I said it was the money, it was the resentment of the disinherited. I couldn't admit even to myself that it was your affection for Bob that I resented. You see, I knew about my father and mother, I knew that they loved me with what was left over; they were gay and kind and fun to be with, but I wasn't necessary to them or anyone. And when you came to Paris and took me away I thought — Well, there was Jack, of course, and there was Bob, but I believed you might have something left over, too. And then I found you didn't."

She put out her hand to him, and he took it

and held it, and Terry took his other hand, and he sat there between them like a man who is bound and yet one who has found his freedom. And no one spoke until, after a long time, while the wind applauded in the palms and a blue sampan put out from the beach and the water glittered in the sun, Chris asked, "May we have lunch early? I'm starved!" and was horrified to feel Cordelia release her hand and put it across her eyes and begin, very painfully and most unfamiliarly, to weep.

It was raining next day when they reached the house on Tantalus, but then on Tantalus it often rains while the sun shines below and the valleys are filled with rainbows. And Terry, hearing the straight falling rain as she moved about unpacking the suitcases, thought of Naniola in the sunshine encircled by the sea, and of Chris and herself walking along the sand or climbing the high steep hill, and coming back to stop and talk with the Naniola people in their little houses and to dine alone at the long candlelighted table. For Cordelia had said, "You will have things to talk about, you two, and plans to make, and Alika will bring me a tray in my room."

They had talked it out all that afternoon, and after dinner, and late into the night. So that his childhood and boyhood came clear to her, and she looked at the picture with compassion. A psychiatrist could explain it, she supposed, the resentment and heartbreak that the child could not acknowledge and so had substituted another resentment, comprehensible to him and quite satisfactory. She could see him, as he had once expressed it, wandering the world over, with the parents who fed and clothed him, filled the needs of his growing body and mind and who were utterly engrossed in each other. But all the time the pull for Chris was toward home, and when Cordelia came for him, a twelve-year-old boy suffering from loss and shock and loneliness, home was embodied in her. But she had failed him, and there was no home.

"You see," he told Terry, "I'd always thought her quite special. I suppose kids distrust a lot of emotion, especially when it's trigger-quick. My mother was like that, beautiful and bad-tempered, gay and melancholy. My father knew her moods, he loved them, even the bad-tempered ones. But she was wearing, as a mother. Aunt Cordelia was always the same, she didn't embrace you one moment and push you away the next. I rarely heard her laugh but never saw her cry — until today. And she was so fair always — when Jack and I got into rows, for instance. I used to pretend I was sorry for Bob stuck in the

Islands under her strict discipline. But I envied him really. Kids like discipline, if it makes sense, they feel more secure under it. I had none. I was permitted to do as I pleased. There were just certain regulations in exchange for which I had my freedom. I must be well-mannered, I must be clean, I must study. My father tutored me sometimes, and sometimes I went to school, wherever we happened to be. Other than that I was left to my own devices, to grow up as best I could. So I used to say, when I thought of Bob, 'The poor kid.' But I knew I was the poor one. And then when I came home, when I saw how much Aunt Cordelia loved him, how much more than Jack — not that she ever showed her favoritism in the usual ways — I understood that I had come home to a place and not to a person or people. It was as simple as that, so I grew a sort of shell and manufactured a grievance. After all, I was only twelve and not thinking very straight."

"You haven't thought straight ever since," she said.

"No. Then I fell in love with you," said Chris, "and I thought, *Now I am necessary to someone.* But last night, and this morning, when you said you would leave me — "

"I had to say it, I would have had to do it!"

"I know. I believed it, only for a moment.

For what you wanted was to build, and without me you could not," he said.

Well, here they were, on Tantalus, and when the time came they would leave it and live on their own mountain, she thought fancifully. Cordelia had warned them, "It will not be easy." Nor would it. And Terry thought, *I don't want it to be easy.*

Hugo and Jack came home in the midafternoon, as they usually did unless they were on a trip somewhere, and they had drinks on the *lanai* and big pitchers of iced tea with pineapple fingers, and for Terry, who loved it, the strong, iced Kona coffee. And Hugo, when they had been served, looked from one to the other and said, "As I said on the telephone, there was no difficulty, none at all."

Jack jingled the ice in his glass. He said, "Mr. Amenly had the grandfather of all hangovers. He was most apologetic."

"Where is he?" asked Chris.

"At the Royal. He spoke of staying for a time. But I doubt it," Jack said, and grinned. He added, "There are ways in which he can be made uncomfortable, and I think he knows it."

"By blackmailing," inquired Chris politely, "in your private club, Hawaii Nei?"

"If you wish to put it that way," said Jack. "You must understand, of course, that there's nothing to prevent him from buttonholing the first acquaintance or stranger he sees and confiding in them."

"I don't think you will run into him," said Hugo, "but if you do — "

Chris said, "If we do, it won't matter." He set down his glass. "I've made an appointment to see Mr. Mannering tomorrow morning, Uncle Hugo. He thinks he has a job for me."

His cousin's jaw went slack, and Hugo cleared his throat. He asked, "You intend to remain here? But surely — "

Cordelia cut in. She said crisply, "Of course he intends to remain. Why shouldn't he? Terry likes it, she wishes to settle down here."

Jack laughed. "What's the angle? I thought you hated the sugar business — or any other business, for that matter."

"I thought so, too," said Chris amiably. "It seems that I've been mistaken."

Hugo said, agitated, "If you really feel that way, I am sure that I could do something; that is, if you insist."

"Thanks," said Chris, "but if I get a job it will be as much on my own as possible. I'll even ask Mr. Mannering to try to forget the slight family connection."

Jack said, "Wait a minute. There must be an angle." He regarded Chris a moment and then shrugged. "The one I expected? You'll stay unless there's an inducement to leave? Is that it?"

"No."

Jack got to his feet. He asked, "Then what in hell is it? We don't want you here, any of us!"

"Sit down, Jack," said his mother sharply. "You are quite mistaken. I want Chris here, it was I who suggested that he see Hammond Mannering."

"You?" said Hugo, as if she had turned and bitten him. "You?"

She said, "Chris is willing to go to work and to take his responsibility as a married man. This is his home. He has as much right to it as you, Hugo, or Jack."

Jack said merely that he would be damned, and his mother raised her eyebrows. She said, "You were content enough to have Chris come home — "

"Because I thought he would go away again, and live happily forever after on his wife's money!"

"That's enough," said Hugo heavily. "Your mother is perfectly right. This is Chris's home. If he wishes to remain there's nothing more to be said."

"Plenty will be said," Jack reminded him.

"What exactly?" inquired Cordelia. "That

a young man returns with a wife and goes to work? Is there anything unusual in that?"

She rose, remarking that she was going to her room, and standing, looking out over the gardens to the mountains and to the sea, she spoke quietly. "There will be very little gossip, Jack, and none for long. No matter what Mr. Amenly has said or will say. What can he say except that Chris married Mark Austin's daughter? We knew that, did we not? If other people assumed that Terry's father died a rich man, does it follow that we assumed it? If they learn now that he died poor and dishonored, does it follow that we did not, all of us, know that, too? Mr. Amenly is a stranger; also his word is not especially reliable. Our friends will take our word. And we will not even have to give it."

She walked out of the room and after a moment, Terry followed her up the stairway and knocked at her door. When she went in, Cordelia was lying on a chaise longue, and Terry said, "I shouldn't have come up, you want to rest."

"No, sit down there at the foot."

"Thank you for saying what you did."

"It was simple enough. I should have said it the other night, at Naniola. But then, of course, things seemed quite different."

"Very different. Yesterday when Chris and

I were alone, it was mostly of you that he talked."

Cordelia looked at her. "I've had quite a while to realize what I have missed and what I have lost."

"Not lost, Aunt Cordelia."

"Yes. It should always have been Chris, of course, but I wouldn't let it be. It's too late now. I can't even return to the uncomplicated affection I might have felt for him when he was a child, because it was never uncomplicated, you see. Nor can he feel about me as once he felt. I know how he felt now, I knew it when he said, 'It is you!' He is no longer a child, and an adult outgrows his parents or his substitute for them if he's to be happy. That's the way it is." She looked at Terry thoughtfully. "And the way it must be with you," she added, "for you must outgrow your dependence on your father."

"I have," said Terry.

"Not wholly. You can't go back, Terry, to the way things used to be, any more than I can go back and be a young woman again. But Chris and I understand each other now. We can be friends. And because we can be friends, he must let me help him wherever and whenever I can." She smiled a little. "At least you and I need have no reservations. I liked you immediately. I thought I would

297

have wanted a daughter very like you."

"You didn't feel it the other night at Nan-iola. I could feel you *not* thinking it."

"Only for a moment. I am a conventional woman, I have been for the greater part of my life. I have grown to see things in quite formal and definite patterns, I'm afraid and by choice, I think. It's so much easier and less disturbing. But once I detached you from what you called the legend, and looked at you as yourself alone — I found I felt no difference toward you, Terry."

Terry rose and went to the head of the couch, bent down, and touched her lips to Cordelia's cheek. She said, "The way Chris and I feel now, we don't need anyone on our side. But that doesn't keep me from wanting someone, and being grateful when I have found you."

Chapter Twelve
THE CHALLENGING FUTURE

Lei day had come and gone. The shower trees dripped their rainbow colors, the poincianas were crimson parasols. On this mid-May morning it was hot on King Street, and crowded. Terry walked slowly from the library, where she had stopped to return some books, across the palace grounds, and on to the bank. She was by now accustomed to the traffic and the throngs of people of all races, but she would never tire of the surge and flow, of the old men with flower *leis* about their hats, of the Hawaiian women who still wore the *holuku*, of the elderly Chinese who had not followed the younger generations into Western ways of dress.

At the bank a pleasant young teller, half Chinese, half Portuguese, cashed her small check. She thanked him, put the money in her purse, and looked at her watch. She had time to go see Jack before lunch.

She left and walked to the office. It was not a high building, but it was big, and built around a court, patio-fashion. Flowers bloomed in the court, trees bestowed their green shade, a fountain splashed into a pool. Jack's office was on the first floor. She waited briefly in an anteroom and was then admitted.

It was cool here, too, the room was large and pleasantly bare, except for the fine desk, the comfortable chairs, and utilitarian files. There were enlarged photographs of plantation scenes on the walls, a Kelly etching, and a picture of Naniola from the air.

"Well," said Jack, "this is an innovation."

It was the first time she had been here since her arrival in the Islands when Hugo had taken her through the offices.

She said, "I come under the white flag."

She did not display it. She wore a cotton frock, in a pale, soft green, and a brimmed white hat, and around her throat the *lei* of carved ivory that Jack had given her.

He asked, "Was this trip necessary?" and picked up his hat from the polished surface of the desk. It was a Panama, wreathed with a feather *lei*. He turned it over in his hands and put it down again.

"I think so. You haven't been to see us."

"I didn't think I'd be welcome."

She said, "We'll both welcome you."

"Both?"

Terry sighed. "It wasn't sensible of you to

300

go to Mr. Mannering, Jack. Whatever you said could make no difference. He recognized Chris's sincerity, he was willing to give him a chance."

"It was foolish, I admit it." He leaned across the desk. "Maybe I believed I had your best interests at heart."

"I doubt that. Jack, I'm meeting Lilia at her mother's for luncheon, and then she'll drive me to your mother's, where I'll stay for a while. Doctor Kalen's wife brought me into town, she'll stop for me at teatime. When I see Aunt Cordelia I'll ask if she and Uncle Hugo will come to dinner Saturday night. It's my first real party. I'm not much of a cook, though I'm learning, and Mrs. Kalen is lending me her Kazue for the evening. She and the doctor will be there, Lilia and Alex, and the Langers are coming."

Kurt Langer was the plantation manager, and Jack remarked thoughtfully, "You catch on fast, don't you?"

She said mildly, "For some time I was my father's hostess. It wasn't hard, I had ample help. It isn't hard now, in different circumstances. For everyone is extraordinarily kind."

"I understand that Alex undertook a mission for you when he went to San Francisco back in March?"

"He sold my emerald ring, yes, and at a good price," answered Terry. She repressed the quick rise of anger. "Although I have no idea how you knew. Not that it was a secret. It's pleasant not to have secrets."

"I overheard a conversation between my mother and father, quite inadvertently."

"It doesn't matter." She straightened her shoulders. "Jack, Chris doesn't know I've come here. He wouldn't like it. If you want to tell him in order to create a disturbance, that's up to you. But for some time I've wanted to ask you to do something for me."

He said irrelevantly, "You're a very pretty woman, Terry."

"If that could be of any influence, thank you," she said, unsmiling. "Will you listen?"

"For five minutes," he agreed.

She said, "I want to ask — No, I'll say it more strongly, I want to implore you to put nothing in Chris's way."

He interrupted. "I? But how could I possibly — Chris fights under the Mannering banner, so to speak."

"Mannering or Russell, what does it matter? You're all in this together. You can make trouble for him if you wish, as I suppose you've always wished — a word here, another there, a half-truth, a reminder, a prophecy. These travel, they reach the right — or wrong

— ears. As of now, Mr. Mannering is very pleased with Chris. He works hard."

"A timekeeper, I believe," said Jack politely.

"As timekeeper, which you know. And he is well liked." She held one hand in the other, hard. She had not expected this to be easy. It wasn't. "Jack, whether you admit it or not, Chris has one great gift, the gift of friendliness, of understanding, of clear thinking where people are concerned — "

"Since when?"

"Since always. Oh, not in relation to himself and his family, very few have *that*. But in relation to strangers and to the people with whom he works. The men like him. There is a future for him and he has been promised it eventually."

"What future?"

"To confide in you seems the height of folly, but I must risk it. Mr. Mannering has promised that after a time Chris will go into public relations, into personnel work. It is the place for him if he earns it. I think he will. Nothing is more important than the relationship between labor and management. He has a goal to reach. Your mother sees this and your father is beginning to, and would do nothing to jeopardize it. On the contrary, I believe he will do all he can to help. The whole dreary business of our coming here and what happened afterward was a shock to him; and a greater shock came when Chris refused his offer of assistance and went to Mr. Mannering."

"Kind offices of my mother," said Jack.

She went on, without replying directly. "But he, at least, did not remind Mr. Mannering of Chris's sins of omission or commission. I think he is rather proud of Chris now."

"Am I supposed to be?"

She said, "You're being very difficult. Why?"

"It goes far back. Why should it be made easy for him? Chris always had everything."

She said softly, "Of course, I remember. He beat you at games, and Lilia fell in love with him."

"Kid stuff," he said quickly; "that isn't it at all." He looked at her, frowning. "What's wrong with me anyway?" he asked. "I work my damned head off, I am as presentable as most men, I don't drink too much too often — yet I walk into a room where your husband sits and feel like a kid with a bloody nose."

She said, "I don't think there's anything wrong with you, Jack," and smiled at him, feeling for the first time a sense of compassion, "except that you once *were* a kid with a bloody nose, and your mother probably said it

304

served you right if the fight was fair. Which I suppose it always was. As for Lilia, you haven't forgiven her, either, although you are no longer in love with her, any more than Chris is."

"I was hoping he was, when you came here. I couldn't figure out why, otherwise."

"But he wasn't. He's very fond of her and so am I. He would go to any lengths to help or protect her, as you would if she asked you."

He brought his fist down on the desk, and she jumped. He said, "But she didn't ask me, damn it!"

Terry's eyes widened. "So that's it, too," she said. "How did you — " She caught herself up in time and was silent.

He said, "You may as well know that during the week Amenly stayed here until he wangled a plane reservation I saw him. I ran into him in a bar. He was plastered. He forgot my share in his abrupt departure from Naniola, and he didn't know, when he rang up people he'd met and who'd asked him to come see them, why they were so terribly busy. Nor that I'd had a hand in that. Not," he added hastily, "for Chris's sake nor for yours."

"Naturally."

"Anyway, I took him back to the Royal, sat out on the *lanai* with him, and listened to his maudlin maunderings about Lilia. I would

305

have knocked his teeth out except that it made
no sense. If she'd told me — "

Terry said, "There wasn't much to tell.
Tom took care of Roger, you know, on the
mainland. It went on rankling, so when he
saw an opportunity to come here as our guest
he seized it. I don't know what he expected to
accomplish. And I didn't know then what had
happened between Lilia and Roger, Jack.
Chris didn't tell me. But now, long ago, Lilia
did. You see, she told Alex, too. So it wasn't
Chris who fought the foolish little dragon, it
was Lilia. By telling Alex she drew the
dragon's teeth, if dragons have teeth, and put
out the fire."

"Amenly didn't mention Alex, he kept
muttering about Chris and his interference."

"Take my word, it wasn't Chris. Not that
he wouldn't have interfered had it been necessary."

"I feel like a chump," said Jack. "A lot of
good bourbon — for which I paid — went
down the Amenly hatch."

"Back on Naniola," said Terry carefully,
"the day you left, your mother told Chris that
his greatest fault was vanity or, if he preferred, pride. It must be a Russell trait. You
have it, too."

"Me!"

She said vigorously, "I sometimes think

306

that the old missionary blood — it had to be strong stuff to accomplish all they did, no matter what side of the record you've been reading, and I've read it all, I spend my spare time catching up on what went on a hundred or more years ago — I sometimes think that after a few generations it turned neurotic. Look at Chris — " She hesitated, there was not much she could say without hurting Cordelia, but there was a little, and she could soften, even falsify it perhaps, for a good purpose. "Most of Chris's difficulties," she said finally, "have been from jealousy he wouldn't admit, of you, who were so secure in your parents' affection, and of his brother. He hadn't much of a life as a kid. He was always homesick and conscious of his lack of roots. He envied you yours, and later, your cleverness, your success. He envied Bob. Yet he need not have done so, because Bob wasn't happy. Chris has known that for some time. Yet all the while you envied him, I don't know what; his gypsy life perhaps, the medals — which are forgotten now — his freedom, and finally the rich wife! Well, you were wrong. He wasn't satisfied with his life nor his freedom, and the rich wife didn't exist. I suppose the trouble is that he admired you enough to believe that he dislikes you. You two have just carried the old feud into your adult lives."

"Chris admire me? You're crazy! He thinks that whatever I've done has been handed me on a silver platter."

"He never thought that," she said gravely, "for he knows enough about this business to know that it couldn't be so. Also he knows your father. If he could believe that, he wouldn't care. But he knows that, given the start — and no one can find fault with that, can they? — you've made yourself very valuable, quite by your own efforts. He wants to be valuable, too. It's the old struggle again, but not for mastery this time. Help him to win it, in ten years, in twenty years. And you can help, simply by not trying to hinder. For you have something Chris has never had, you have self-confidence."

He shook his head. "You're all wrong. He was always the most cocksure, the most arrogant — "

"That isn't self-confidence," said Terry, "it's the opposite." She looked at him and spoke a whole truth. "Jack, if you had been born a poor man you would have made your way. Not quite as soon, but as surely. You would have believed in yourself and your job, whatever it was. You didn't need the Russells, you needed no one but yourself. For the job comes first with you. Everything else is subordinate to it. Lilia would have been, any woman you might have married, any woman you will marry. I discovered that about you very soon. I dare say Chris will never go as far, nor that the job will mean as much. But he can go a long way, and I'm going to help him. And now it's been more than five minutes."

He rose as she did, and held out his hand, and she put her own into it. He asked, "How did you know I'd be alone here?"

"I knew Uncle Hugo was at an H.S.P.A. meeting," she said demurely. "So I phoned your secretary."

He released her hand. "Okay, Terry. I'll drive over Saturday night to dinner."

That was all, but it was, she thought, enough. He would not speak of this to Chris, there was every reason why he should not.

She felt very tired, as if she had been engaged in a struggle. She would be late meeting Lilia. She must commit a small extravagance.

The boy who drove her taxi had a carnation *lei* around his hat, too, and his racial mixture was one which defied her. The tourists were flocking into Honolulu, you saw them on the streets, you could see them at Waikiki, lying on the beach, or trying, usually without success, to master the art of *he'e nalu* — surf riding; you could see them evenings at the hotels and clubs, dancing to a Hawaiian orchestra, or going out to a *luau*.

But she was not a tourist.

The Petersons' old house on Diamond Head was a vast wooden structure, pleasant and old-fashioned, set in lovely gardens and dreaming in the sun. It is much drier on Diamond Head than on Tantalus. Today the top of Tantalus was wreathed in clouds, and rainbows were like scarfs in the valleys.

Lilia was waiting for her with Mrs. Peterson, a big handsome woman who suffered from a slight cardiac ailment and who shortly after lunch excused herself and went upstairs to rest. And Lilia and Terry sat there talking. They had seen each other quite often, the two plantations were not very far apart, and Lilia had come over to help when Terry moved into her little frame house on the wide plantation street.

They talked of places and of people as the lights and shadows shifted on the sea and a plane went roaring overhead.

Lilia said, "I still can't get used to the sudden sound of planes. For just a minute I'm back in a nightmare."

She was back in it now, the terror, the rage and anguish, the blood and the courage, the betrayal and panic, and the marvelous sense of unity. She added after a minute, "I wish you'd been here before the war. It has changed so greatly — I don't mean just physically."

It was impossible for Terry to know, no matter how much she had heard of the war years.

Terry said, "I've a project. They're helping me at the library. I'm reading all I can about the Islands, past and present. It isn't enough to pick up a few words, which every tourist learns, or to manage the train of the *holuku* your mother gave me, or to get my local geography straight. I want to belong here after a while."

Lilia said, "You will, I know. I haven't seen you in, how long, a couple of weeks? So I haven't told you we are going to adopt a baby. Alex and I. It may be a long time before we get one, but we'll wait." She smiled, looking, Terry thought, particularly beautiful. "How about you?" she inquired.

Terry flushed. She said, "Not quite yet. Of course I didn't even consider it until recently. Then, the last thing we should do was have a baby. Hostesses hire baby sitters, but if you came for a week-end to sit with your own baby —" She shrugged, and went on, "But after I learn how to keep house properly, after Chris is more settled, and after —"

"Don't wait too long."

"I shan't. I suppose I couldn't plan to have my first child born on Naniola," she said. "No, I suppose that's out of the question. But

I'd like it. Naniola," she said, " 'beautiful life.' "

After a while Lilia drove her up Tantalus. It had rained, but now the sun shone again, and Cordelia was waiting for them. She said severely, "You're late."

"Not very. Are Uncle Hugo and Jack home?"

"Not yet. Why?"

Terry asked, "Would you all come to dinner Saturday night? Alex and Lilia are coming, and a few others. It's an occasion."

"What occasion?"

"Our wedding anniversary."

The anniversary of their marriage. But they would not have been married for a whole year when Saturday came. They were just beginning to be married. It took a very long time, a marriage did. Lilia's, for instance, and Cordelia's.

Mrs. Kalen came in, voluble, round, brisk. The wife of the resident doctor on the plantation, she had been one of the nurses there prior to her marriage. She was very active in work with the women and children on the plantation; and during the war she had been, as so many like her, invaluable.

They left before four, after a glass of tea, and drove back in Mrs. Kalen's car. Terry had told Chris that this was her day out. Dinner would be late. He must possess his soul in patience; if his appetite suffered, there was always the icebox.

The white bungalow looked very peaceful, the lawn was green, the hibiscus hedge bloomed brightly. She thought, *I must ask Chris to take me to see the night-blooming cereus when the time comes, I want to see it with him.* Flowers spilled their gold and rose and red into the grass as she went up the path. She knew this house by heart now. The living-room, the screened *lanai*, the big shower and bath, the two bedrooms, the small dining-room, and kitchen. It was a wonderful house. It was furnished with the things from Cordelia's attic, those which had belonged to Chris's parents, and some to Cordelia; simple, sturdy and good; the dining-table was fashioned of koa, the desk had come in a sailing ship, the living-room table was teak.

Chris said lazily, "I thought you'd deserted me."

"No." She pulled off her hat and sailed it across the *lanai*, where he was lying in a big wicker chair. He was thin and brown. He had come in much earlier, showered and changed, and now he sat in a welter of papers and with a long mild drink. She said, "I'll get supper ready in two minutes."

"Sit down. Here." He drew her down

beside him. "There's all the time in the world."

"The Hartley's are coming for bridge at eight."

"There is still all the time in the world."

"The Kalens suggested we go to the beach Sunday for a picnic, that is, if nothing comes up at the hospital. If it does, we can go without him, you, Mrs. Kalen, the kids, and I."

"All right, the beach it is. What have you been doing?"

"Shopping, for some mats and a bathing-suit. I stopped at the bank. I had lunch at the Petersons' with Lilia. She took me to your mother's, and Mrs. Kalen picked me up. And we're having our party Saturday, everyone's coming, including Jack."

"Why ruin a good party?"

"He wants to come."

"You saw him?"

"For a moment," she answered, and he was satisfied. There was nothing unusual about Jack's being home in the middle of the afternoon. And Terry went on. "He's astonished, I think, at the way you've taken hold."

"And how would he know that?"

"Oh," she said, "I told him. But I dare say I'm not the only one."

"Funny," he said, "I can't work up even a

slight sweat over Jack now. I'm tired. It's a good feeling. Yet I minded like hell at first, the getting up before dawn, the interminable hours. I don't now."

Sometimes it seemed to him he had always been here, although this was not a plantation he had known well. But it was like many others allowing for its own difference. Now it had come clear and familiar, he could find his way to this house, among all the houses, blindfold. The offices were known to him, the tall chimneys of the factory, the sweet, heavy smell of sugar. His ears were tuned to the rumble of trucks, the blasting whistle. It was as if he had always seen this particular recreation building, this special hospital, this school, and church, and the big house in which the Langers lived. He knew, by heart, the scent and sound and look of morning, and of evening; the shifting shadows on the colored mountains, the clouds in the pure blue, the sudden slanting of rain. By heart, too, the workers' camps, so-called, tacitly divided by nationality yet not really so, as one nationality merged into the other in the interracial population.

He had become as familiar with his car as with his hand, the heavy boots he drew on each morning were known to him, as were the acres of cane fields, as were the faces he looked for each day and now knew by name.

Terry said, "I'll change now and get supper."

On Saturday night everyone had come, overflowing from living-room to *lanai*. Mrs. Kalen was as efficient in a kitchen as in an operating-room and Kazue, a brown little woman, more precious than gold. They had set up the buffet, of hot rice and chicken, cold crab, salad, raw vegetables, fruit and cheese, and coffee, hot or cold. And Cordelia looked around, remembering her first house, her heart tight with an old sorrow. For she had hated that house on Maui to which Hugo had brought her as a bride. She looked at him now, talking to Kurt Langer, a neglected glass in his hand, his undistinguished face alive with interest, while Langer listened, knowing you can always learn from the men who know. And now Hugo lowered his voice to ask, "How's Chris making out?"

"All right."

It wasn't high praise, but Langer was not given to praise. All right meant just that. He added, "He gets along with his men. They come to him to settle problems, ex officio. Or so I hear. And he does. It's usually something personal — a wayward daughter, a bad-tempered wife, a fight — "

Cordelia could not hear what they said, but she knew that, whatever it was, her husband was pleased. Curious, how fond she had grown of him, she thought. Perhaps inevitable in the circumstances. She knew his faults and his stubbornness, a stubbornness not unlike her own; she recognized his small vanities and his limitations. He was a good man, he had loved her always and been kind and patient, a patience she had tried on more than one occasion.

Beside her, Mrs. Langer was talking about Terry. Everyone liked her, she said. She fitted in. Did Mrs. Russell know Terry had organized a little class of Portuguese women, the older women who spoke so little English? Terry spoke Portuguese as fluently as Spanish. So she taught them English.

Supper was good, conversation relaxed, and no one stayed very late, although Saturday nights they could stay later than other nights. The men abhorred weekday night festivities, always remembering the blast of the whistle in the dark.

Before they left, "I brought you a gift," said Cordelia as Terry followed her into the bedroom.

"But I said no gifts," Terry cried, dismayed. "And Lilia said she wouldn't. Chris and I promised we wouldn't. Not this year."

"But it belongs really to Chris. It was his mother's. I found it among her things in Paris. I suppose he's forgotten it. I kept it, Terry." She smiled. "I don't want it now. Perhaps I haven't wanted it for a long time."

It was a miniature, set in a big locket of gold, seed pearls, and enamel. It opened, and a face looked back at you. Terry held it in her hands and looked at the smiling face that smiled back at her. The man looked like the portrait of Bob grown older, and smiled as Chris did.

"Thank you for giving it to us," she said.

"It's not very good," said Cordelia. She closed the locket and shut it into Terry's hand. "Are you finding it hard here?" she asked.

"Often. I'm not as practical as I thought, and much more ignorant. I don't always want to be silent as I often must be, nor always as polite. I like Mrs. Langer. She's about the most active woman I've ever known, and one of the nicest. I like Mrs. Kalen, too. Some of the others seem trivial to me or uninteresting. They're all ambitious, of course. Some are gossips, some are plain ordinary cats. But most of them work hard for their husbands. We have that much in common. It was more difficult at first, of course, knowing that the gossip had got around and that — " She broke off, then said helplessly, "Sometimes people are nice to you because they're sorry for you and *like* being sorry!"

Cordelia patted her shoulder. She said, "Hand me my wrap, will you?" And then, "You'll make out all right, Terry, you and Chris."

When they had gone Terry was conscious of a letdown, her back ached, and her feet. Also her face, probably from smiling. She emptied ash trays and straightened furniture. Kazue and the little girl, hired for the occasion, had left the kitchen in order. And tomorrow was Sunday.

"Tired?"

"A little. But it was fun. Do you think they liked it?"

"Of course." He put his arm around her. "Oh, you," he said, "you'll do. And you look so pretty."

She wore the yellow dress and the pearls, and said, smiling, "But Lilia's prettier."

"I suppose so, in a way. But I've come to prefer you. It's an acquired taste, like olives."

She released herself and went into the bedroom, and he followed her. She said, "It was sweet of Helen to cable. I wonder if they'd come out this summer? After all, we still have an extra bedroom."

"What do you mean, still?"

"Nothing at the moment. I just thought, in another year, if you're not against the idea, it might be occupied permanently."

"Haven't you enough to do?"

"Has any woman? Look, Chris." She opened the dresser drawer and took out the locket.

He looked at it, open in her hand. "I'd forgotten it. Where in the world did it come from?" he asked.

"Aunt Cordelia had it, and gave it to us tonight. It was like writing finis to a long chapter for her. Does it look like him?"

"Very much. I remember the artist — Father lent him money. I don't know where he picked up the locket. Wait a minute — Yes, I do. In a pawnshop of sorts, in London. That was the year he made quite a little, writing, and we went everywhere, practically. I remember Morocco best."

She said, "Chris, it's incredible, but I don't know your father's given name. Your mother was Olivia. But your father — was he Christopher, too?"

He looked at her in astonishment. "Surely," he said, "you knew that his name was John?"

She took the locket and closed it. "I didn't

know. So Aunt Cordelia gave it to her son, as a middle name. You were called Christopher; and Jack wasn't, although he was older. I've wondered about that."

"I never thought much about it. Terry, are you happy?"

"I've never been so happy."

"Don't think me a reformed character," he warned her. "There are times when I find myself getting that what-the-hell feeling. It doesn't last. But I dare say it will come when things go wrong, when I can't see my way clearly, when I get sore about something, when the whistle blows and I get up and it's raining or there's trouble brewing somewhere or someone steps on a pet corn. But this much I know. I'm going to stick if it kills us both. I've something to work for; someone to work for and with; and something ahead. You'll be fed up lots of times. The difference between the halfhearted job I once did and this is plain enough — I didn't want to like what I was doing then. Now I do." He went back in the living-room and opened the desk drawer. "Come here, Mrs. Russell," he said.

She followed, and he turned, with a little package in his hand. "I broke my promise. I have an anniversary present for you."

"Oh, Chris," she said, distressed, "that's not fair. I kept my promise."

The money for the emerald, banked jointly, for emergencies; it was disaster insurance. They were not to touch it, they had pledged, unless it was vitally necessary. The little house was rent free, they would live on his salary, banking as much as possible of the extra money, his monthly check and hers. For the first time in their lives they would save. And, she had thought, when the time comes there must be money for the future — not her future alone, nor Chris's —

He said, "I didn't tap the bank roll, darling. I squeezed out a little here, a little there, and there's an old Chinese who works reasonably in gold."

"Chris, are you crazy?"

"No. I ordered it after I got the job. It will serve several purposes. As a reminder, as a warning, as a bond." He took her in his arms. "Never take it off, darling, it was once bad luck, but not any more."

He kissed her and then opened the box and took from it a very delicate narrow bracelet, thin and fine. He put it around her wrist, fastened the intricate catch, and she looked at it between tears and laughter. It was a symbol and a promise, the little bracelet, fashioned in the likeness of a golden shoestring.

Better than the emerald, which she sometimes missed, heavy on her hand, better than the pearls, which also could be insurance, coiled about her neck, better than the jewel box glittering with her mother's things and those Cordelia had given her. Better, even, than Chris's rings on her left hand —

He said, "Stop staring at it and come to bed. It's late, and if we're really going on that picnic — "

"It's beautiful, Chris," she said, "I'll never have anything I'll love so much."

"There are times," he said, "when the foresworn extravagance is indicated. Do you think Jack's mentally disturbed? When he left he smote me on the back and said, 'You're doing a good job — all the luck in the world.' Damned if I don't think he meant it. What came over him?"

"Mr. Langer, perhaps. I heard him telling Jack how well you're doing."

"That's no reason, in Jack's book."

She switched out the last light in the room. "Come out on the *lanai* a minute," she said, and when they stood there together, she looked up at the black immensity of the sky, hung with stars, and at the darker shapes of the mountains. She said, "Let the feud die. This is your home, I am your wife, and we have our lives before us."

Someone walked down the street singing, a clear young voice. The flowers dreamed in fragrance, the night was warm and still. Terry's bracelet slid down on her wrist, she could feel its fragile weight. *I shall still wear it,* she thought, *when I am very old.*

She turned to Chris and held fast to him, sorrowing that she must grow old, knowing a wild rebellion that someday she must die, or he before her, yet rejoicing that they were young and loved each other, that in their time they would know struggle and grief, anxiety and fulfillment, and always, the important thing, the sharing of these.

And in that moment she relinquished her last hold on that which was past and turned her eyes toward the veiled and challenging future.

THORNDIKE-MAGNA hopes you have enjoyed this Large Print book. All our Large Print titles are designed for easy reading, and all our books are made to last. Other Thorndike Press or Magna Print books are available at your library, through selected bookstores, or directly from the publishers. For more information about current and upcoming titles, please call or mail your name and address to:

THORNDIKE PRESS
P.O. Box 159
Thorndike, Maine 04986
(800) 223-6121
(207) 948-2962 (in Maine and Canada call collect)

or in the United Kingdom:

MAGNA PRINT BOOKS
Long Preston, Near Skipton
North Yorkshire,
England BD23 4ND
(07294) 225

There is no obligation, of course.